Body
Surfing

Body Surfing

A NOVEL

Anita Shreve

DOUBLEDAY LARGE PRINT HOME LIBRARY EDITION

LITTLE, BROWN AND COMPANY

NEW YORK   BOSTON   LONDON

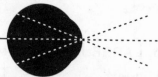

This Large Print Book carries the
Seal of Approval of N.A.V.H.

For

Whitney, Katherine, Alli, Molly, and Chris

2002

Three o'clock, the dead hour. The faint irritation of sand grit between bare foot and floorboards. Wet towels hanging from bedposts and porch railings. A door, caught in a gust, slams, and someone near it emits the expected cry of surprise. A southwest wind, not the norm even in August, sends stifling air into the many rooms of the old summerhouse. The hope is for an east wind off the water, and periodically someone says it.

An east wind now would be a godsend.

The energy of the morning has dissipated itself in fast walks and private lessons, in vigorous reading and lazy tennis. Even in a brief expedition to a showroom in Portsmouth to look at Audi Quattros. Mrs. Edwards, Sydney has been told, will need a new car in the fall.

There are guests in the house who must be attended to. One hopes for visitors with initiative, like a refreshing east wind. They are not Sydney's concern. Her afternoons are free. Her entire life, but for a few hours each day of overpaid tutoring, is disconcertingly free.

She changes into a black tank suit, the elastic sprung in the legs. She is twenty-nine and fit enough. Her hair is no color she has ever been able to describe. She is not a blonde or a brunette, but something in between that washes out in January, comes to life in August. Gold highlights on translucence.

Sydney has been married twice: once divorced and once widowed. Others, hearing this information for the first time, find it surprising, as if this fact might be the most interesting thing about her.

On the porch, red geraniums are artfully arranged against the lime-green of the dune grass, the blue of the water. Not quite primary colors, hues seen only in nature.

Knife blades of grass pierce the wooden slats of the boardwalk. Sweet pea overtakes the thatch. Unwanted fists of thistle push upward from the sand. On the small deck at the end of the boardwalk are two white Adirondack chairs, difficult to get out of, and a faded umbrella lying behind them. Two rusted and immensely heavy iron bases for the umbrella sit in a corner, neither of which, Sydney guesses, will ever leave the deck.

Wooden steps with no railing lead to a crescent-shaped beach to the left, a rocky coastline to the right. Sydney runs across the hot sand to the edge of the water. The surf is a series of sinuous rolls, and when she closes her eyes, she can hear the spray. She prepares herself for the cold. Better than electroshock therapy, Mr. Edwards always says, for clearing the head.

A seizure of frigid water, a roiling of white bubbles. The sting of salt in the sinuses as she surfaces. She stands and stumbles and stands again and shakes herself like a dog. She hugs her hands to her chest and relaxes only when her feet begin to numb. She dives once more, and when she comes up for air she turns onto her back, letting the waves, stronger and taller than they appear from shore, carry her up and over the crest and down again into the trough. She is buoyant flotsam, shocked into sensibility.

She body surfs in the ocean, getting sand down the neckline of her suit. As a child, when she took off her bathing suit, she would find handfuls of sand in the crotch. She lowers herself into the ocean to wash away the mottled clumps against her stomach, but then she sees a good wave coming. She stands and turns her back to it and springs onto the crest. The trick always is to catch the crest. Hands pointed, eyes shut, she is a bullet through the white surge. She scrapes her naked hip and thigh against the bottom.

She crawls onto the sand, the undertow carving hollows beneath her shins. A wave she hasn't braced for hits her back and neck. She wipes the tangle of hair from her face, the water from her eyes. She sees a shape on the beach that wasn't there before. A tanned chest, a splotch of red. A man in bathing trunks is holding a pink cloth, wide and lurid, before her.

"I've been sent with a towel. You're Sydney, right?"

How extraordinary if she weren't. Not another body in the water for a thousand yards.

—∞—

Inside the house, the furniture is white, a good idea in theory, not in practice. The slipcovers on the two sofas are marked with faint smudges and worried stains, navy lint from a woolen sweater. Fine grains of sand have repeatedly scratched the surface of the maple floor as if it had been lightly scoured.

On the stairs down to the basement sits a basket of old newspapers, a wicker catchall for objects that are not part of the neutral decor but might prove useful. A sparkling purple leash. A neon pink pad of Post-it

Notes. A Day-Glo orange life vest. Practicality and sports rife with unnatural color.

Although Mrs. Edwards gives the impression of having inhabited the cottage for decades, perhaps even generations (already there are family rituals, oft-repeated memories, old canning jars full of sea glass used as doorstops), they have owned the house only since 1997. Before then, Mr. Edwards confided, they simply rented other cottages nearby. In contrast to his wife, he seems a man incapable of deceit.

Sydney shares a bathroom with the guests, a couple from New York who have come in search of antiques. In the mornings, there are aqua spills of toothpaste in the sink, pink spots of makeup on the mirror. Used tissues are tucked behind the spigots. Sydney routinely washes out the sink with a hand towel before she uses it. She stuffs the towel into the hamper in the hallway on her way back to her room.

It was obvious immediately to Sydney that the Edwardses' eighteen-year-old daughter, Julie, was slow, that no amount of tutoring would adequately prepare her for the stellar senior year of high school Mrs. Edwards hopes for, a year that is almost certain, in Sydney's opinion, to defeat the girl. Mrs. Edwards speaks knowledgeably of Mount Holyoke and Swarthmore. Skidmore as a safety. Sydney can only blink with wonder. Julie is pliant, eager to please, and extraordinarily beautiful, her skin clear and pink, her eyes a sea-glass blue. Sydney can see that the girl, who seems willing to study all the hours of the day, will disappoint her mother and break her father's heart, the latter not because she won't get into the colleges Mrs. Edwards seems so knowledgeable about, but because she will try so hard and fail.

Salt encrusts the windows of the house on the diagonal, as if water had been thrown against the glass. The windows out to the porch have to be washed twice a week to provide any appreciation of the view, which is spectacular.

Sydney sometimes senses that her presence has upset the family equilibrium. She tries to be available when needed, present but silent when not.

*   *   *

The brothers will sleep in a room called the "boys' dorm." Julie has a room on the ocean side of the house. Mr. and Mrs. Edwards's bedroom looks out over the marshes. The guests, like Sydney, have been relegated to a room with twin beds.

Mr. and Mrs. Edwards have invited Sydney to call them by their first names. When she tries to say *Anna* or *Mark,* however, the words stick in her throat. She finds other ways to refer to the couple, such as *your husband* and *he* and *your dad.*

Sydney's first husband was an air racer. He flew through trees at 250 miles an hour and performed aerobatic stunts over a one-mile course. If he were to graze a gate or become momentarily disoriented by the Gs, he would hurtle to the ground and crash. When she could, Sydney went with Andrew to these races—to Scotland and Vienna and San Francisco—and watched him twist his plane in the air at 420 degrees per second. At air shows, Andrew was a star and signed autographs. He wore fireproof clothing and a crash helmet and was equipped with a parachute—not that a parachute would have been at all helpful thirty feet off the ground. For a year, Sydney found the air races exotic and thrilling. During the second year, she began to be afraid. Contemplating a third year and the possibility of a child, she pictured Andrew's fiery death and said, *Enough.* Her aviator, who seemed genuinely sad to see the marriage end, could not, however, be expected to give up flying.

Sydney met her second husband when she was twenty-six. Her right front tire blew on the Massachusetts Turnpike, and she pulled to the side of the road. A minute later, her Honda Civic was hit from behind. Because she had been standing at the front of the car and looking down at the tire, she was hit and briefly dragged along the pavement. Daniel Feldman, who had to cut the clothes off her body in the emergency room of New-ton-Wellesley Hospital, chided her for pulling to a stop on a bridge. A week later, he took her to Biba in Boston.

Eight months into their marriage, and during his residency at Beth Israel, Daniel suffered a burst aneurysm in his brain. Receiving the news by telephone, Sydney was stunned, bewildered, wide-eyed with shock.

Most people, mindful of the sensitivities, do not point out to Sydney the irony of having divorced a man she was afraid would die only to marry a man who perished in the very place he ought to have been saved. But she can tell that Mr. Edwards is eager to discuss the situation. Despite his kindness and his affability, he cannot help but flirt with the details.

"Is the aviator still flying?" he asks one night as they are washing dishes. "Did you say your husband interned at the B.I.?"

Mrs. Edwards, by contrast, is not afraid of the blunt question.

"Are you Jewish?" she asked as she was showing Sydney to her room.

It wasn't clear to Sydney which answer Mrs. Edwards would have preferred: Jewish being more interesting; not Jewish being more acceptable.

The doctor was Jewish. The aviator was not.

*   *   *

Sydney is both, having a Jewish father and his cheekbones but a Unitarian mother, from whom she has inherited her blue eyes. Even Sydney's hair seems equal parts father and mother—the wayward curl, the nearly colorless blond. Sydney became Bat Mitzvah before her parents separated but then was strenuously raised to be a WASP during her teenage years. She thinks of both phases of her life as episodes of childhood having little to do with the world as she now encounters it, neither religion at all helpful during the divorce and death.

Not unlike a parachute at thirty feet.

For a week last summer, Sydney went to stay with Daniel's parents in Truro. The experiment was a noble one. Mrs. Feldman, whom she had briefly called *Mom,* had had the idea that Sydney's presence would be comforting. In fact the opposite was true, the sight of Sydney sending Mrs. Feldman into contagious fits of weeping.

For days following Daniel's death, Sydney's own mother refused to believe in the simple fact of the event, causing Sydney to have to say, over and over again, that Daniel had died of a brain aneurysm.

"But how?" her mother repeatedly asked.

Sydney's father came up from New York by train for the funeral. He wore a taupe trench coat, put on a yarmulke for the service, and, astonishingly, he wept. Afterwards, at dinner, he tried to reassure her.

"I think of you as resilient," he said over steak and baked potato.

The double blow of the divorce and death left Sydney in a state of emotional paralysis, during which she was unable to finish her thesis in developmental psychology and had to withdraw from her graduate program at Brandeis. Since then, she has taken odd jobs created by friends and family, jobs for which she has been almost ludicrously overqualified or completely out of her depth: a secretary in the microbiology department at Harvard Medical School (overqualified); a dealer's assistant at an art gallery on Newbury Street (out of her depth). She has been grateful for these jobs, for the opportunity to drift and heal, but recently she has begun to

wonder if this strange and unproductive period of her life might be coming to an end.

"You must be the tutor."
  "And you are?"
  "Ben. That's Jeff on the porch."
  "Thank you for the towel."
  "You're quite the body surfer."

Sydney discovers that she minds the loss of
her mourning. When she grieved, she felt
herself to be intimately connected to Daniel.
But with each passing day, he floats away
from her. When she thinks about him now, it
is more as a lost possibility than as a man.
She has forgotten his breath, his muscula-
ture.

"So you answered the ad?"
  "I did."
  Sydney wraps herself in the bubble-gum-
pink towel. In the distance, she can see an-
other man rising from a chair on the porch.
He puts his hands on the railing.
  "Are you a teacher?"
  "No. I'm not much of anything at the mo-
ment."
  "Really."

Sydney cannot read the *really*. Dismissive? Disappointed? Intrigued?

Sydney has an impression of lighter hair, a slighter body. The man who is Jeff shuffles down the first set of stairs from the porch to the boardwalk, and, for a few seconds, he is out of sight. When he emerges onto the deck, she can see that he has on bathing trunks and a navy polo shirt.

Jeff waits for them at the head of the stairs. Sydney greets his feet first (in weathered boat shoes), his legs next (lightly tanned with golden hairs), and, finally, the faded bathing trunks (grayish with purple blotches; she guesses navy originally, an unfortunate wash with bleach). He steps back to make way for the two of them, and there's an awkward introduction in a small space. Sydney's nose begins to run with salt water. She shakes Jeff's hand. Hers, she knows, must feel icy.

"We've heard a lot about you," Jeff says.
Sydney is dismayed. She expected more.

Jeff's face is loose and open, the green eyes guileless. Sydney thinks it is probably not possible to be his age and guileless, but there it is. The family dog, Tullus (short for Catullus?), trots down the boardwalk and plants himself directly below Jeff's hands. This confirms her impression. Animals can always tell.

"Hey," Jeff says, bending to the golden retriever and ruffling him affectionately.

Mr. and Mrs. Edwards and Julie come out onto the porch, a nucleus intact. Ben wraps his arms around Julie and rocks his sister from side to side. Six glasses of iced tea have been set upon a teak table. Jeff picks up a glass and hands it to Sydney, smiling as he does so. She notices that he, like his brother and sister, has remarkably even teeth, and she imagines many thousands in orthodontia. Sydney, whose mother could barely remember to schedule regular checkups, has an imperfect smile, a slightly misaligned eyetooth its distinctive feature.

Ben has brown eyes like his mother. Jeff, Sydney can see, takes after his father.

Sydney leans against the railing and tugs the towel tighter. Her hair, she guesses, must be a horror of Gorgonlike dreads from the salt water.

Mrs. Edwards, who has previously seemed cold, is animated with her sons. On the porch, she is possessive, never still, touching them often, making it easy for them to touch her. She wants to be seen as the perfect mother. No, Sydney decides, she wants Sydney to understand that her sons love their mother best.

Sydney knows these facts about the brothers. Ben, who is thirty-five, works in corporate real estate in Boston. Jeff, thirty-one, is a professor of political science at MIT. Sydney half expects this information to be repeated on the porch, but Mrs. Edwards exercises unusual restraint in front of her sons.

Mrs. Edwards wears khaki culottes and a white polo shirt that reveals an intractable swell between her midriff and her waist. Sydney would advise tailored white shirts left untucked over longer pants—but it is not for her to say. Mr. Edwards dresses like a man who never thinks about his clothes: baggy khakis and even looser golf shirts that droop from his shoulders. Sometimes he puts his hands flat against the stomach that hangs like an adjunct on his tall frame as he lightly bemoans the doughnut he had at breakfast or the piece of coconut pie he gave into at dinner. One senses, however, that he enjoyed these treats, that he is not a man to forgo a fleeting pleasure in favor of vanity. Unlike Mrs. Edwards, who counts her carbs religiously and seems to be hastening herself to an early death with the eggs and meats and cheeses she eats in quantity. Even the low-carb ice-cream bars she snacks on at night seem, with their slick, viscous shine, to be depositing cholesterol molecules directly into her bloodstream.

Mrs. Edwards wears her blond hair below her chin line and often pulls it back in a banana clip that ought to be pretty but instead accentuates the square shape of her head and the half inch of gray roots at the scalp. Sydney would advise a haircut in the same way she might mention the tailored white shirts, but then again, it is not within her job description.

* * *

Jeff leans against the porch railing a few feet from Sydney. His slighter frame and its concavities suggest exposure, whereas Ben's body, comfortably on display, seems fully covered.

There is talk about the backup at the Hampton tolls, idle joking about resorting to civil disobedience to get the state to adopt an E-ZPass system: of finding seven guys to drive into the tollbooths, park their cars, and walk away. Ben releases Julie and picks up a glass of iced tea. He drains it in one go, the ice cubes slamming against his upper lip. His engine operates at higher revolutions than his brother's: he seems anxious to be on the move. He laces his fingers behind his neck and flexes his elbows. He asks his father about his golf game.

"Worse and worser," Mr. Edwards replies, though no one believes the man. One expects self-deprecation from the gentle patriarch.

Mrs. Edwards is queried about the guests, who have gone off to Portsmouth in search of antiques. A fourth for golf is promised for the morning.

*   *   *

The brothers mention dinner. Sydney guesses lobster, steamers, triple-berry pie. This is the first visit Jeff and Ben have made to the cottage since she arrived in early July. It is, in fact, their first visit since mid-June, work and other commitments having kept them from the summerhouse—a situation that will soon be rectified, Ben promises. When they come next, it will be for a week. Mrs. Edwards's eyes focus and unfocus. One can see her planning dinners, counting linens.

Jeff laughs easily, but Sydney notices that he stands with his arms crossed over his chest. She wonders what he thinks about when he is not actively listening. Cost-benefit analyses of regime changes in Sudan? Complex algorithms involving terrorists and the relative price of oil?

Sydney can easily picture Ben at his job. In his shirtsleeves and tie, he would make a stolid, handsome presence, the dark eyes suggesting gravity, the smile a light touch. Perhaps he makes the same gestures at work as he does at home: lacing the fingers behind his neck, flexing the elbows.

The nucleus drinks its tea, clinking the ice cubes. The Stewarts and a couple named Morrison are mentioned. There is talk about a sail to Gloucester and back. Sydney has a sense of trying to put together an accurate history of the family with half the relevant sentences in the text blacked out, the accessible sentences referring to a chapter she hasn't yet read. A woman named Victoria is coming Saturday. There are to be, Sydney gradually comes to understand, a number of people present for the weekend.

A strange couple approach the house from the beach and point. Perhaps they have walked from the public parking lot at the crescent's other end. Sydney knows precisely what they are saying. *Remember the Vision crash? The one in Ireland?*

Sydney wonders if Mr. and Mrs. Edwards mind the mild celebrity of having bought the house from the culpable pilot's widow. She wonders if they got it for a song.

*   *   *

Ben rubs his hands together. "Have you had the grand tour?" he asks.

Sydney is confused. "Of?"

"We'll leave the harbor, swing around the point. I'm told you haven't been on the boat yet."

"No, I haven't."

Ben addresses his sister, who is standing close to her father. "Julie, want to come with us?"

But no one is surprised when the girl says *no*. It is a well-known fact that she is afraid of the water.

"Julie's going to help me with the roses," Mr. Edwards says.

A sweatshirt and a fresh towel are produced. Sydney finds her sneakers by the back door. The two brothers and she climb up into Ben's Land Rover. Sydney sits in front. Jeff asks her questions, easy enough to answer.

"What were you studying at Brandeis?"

"The emotional and sexual development of adolescent girls."

"Not a moment too soon," Ben says and chuckles to himself.

Neither brother, surely briefed, mentions the aviator or the doctor.

* * *

Ben drives along a sandy road to the center of the beach community, too small to be called a village. There's a lobster pound and a general store. Carrying life preservers, the three make their way down a gravel drive to the end of a wooden pier. Jeff speaks to a young man in shorts and T-shirt who shakes his hand and smiles. Sydney, the brothers, and the young man ride in a small boat through the harbor. They are deposited at a Boston Whaler.

Once inside the Whaler, Sydney sits on a small bait box. Ben takes the wheel, while Jeff stands near Sydney, one hand on the console railing. There is a low-throated rumble of an engine and an instant breeze. She puts on the sweatshirt, which covers her tank suit but leaves her legs bare. She feels more naked than she did with just the suit on.

The Whaler fights the incoming tide, and for a time the boat seems to stand motionless in the water. Ben says they've timed it exactly wrong. But Sydney likes the sensation of suspension: the motor straining, the water insistent. She thinks of gulls just outside her window. Of the aviator in a deliberate stall.

Close quarters in the boat produce a kind of intimacy. For moments, Sydney's face is inches from Jeff's bare thigh. Were they lovers, she would lean forward and kiss it. It would be expected.

This is simply an observation Sydney makes and not a desire. But it occurs to her that it is an observation she might not have made a month ago.

As they cross the harbor, Ben obligingly points out the massive cottages along the shore and tells an anecdote with each. The Whaler rounds the point and runs parallel to the long beach. Jeff indicates the family cottage at its end. Sydney contemplates the drive in the car, the walk to the dock, the ferry out to the boat, the struggle against the tide, the rounding of the point, and the motoring along the beach. She thinks it a long way to go a short distance.

"Whose girlfriend is coming for the weekend?" she asks as they idle in the gentle swells.

"Mine," Jeff says.

That night, they are eight at dinner, Mr. and Mrs. Edwards anchoring a walnut table Mr. Edwards made, the oval surface polished to a high gloss, the beveled lip uneven, as if the router had occasionally got away from him. Sydney makes a point of sitting near Julie, a point that wasn't as necessary when there were only four or five of them in the dining room. But with the brothers and the guests who have returned from Portsmouth triumphant—not to mention all the paraphernalia and detritus that accompany a lobster dinner, bibs and all—Julie seems, as the guests near their seats, a bit lost and unsure of herself.

"I did the math," Julie confides.

Forget the math, Sydney wants to say.

"Good," she says instead in what she has come to understand is her encouraging teacher voice. "Very good, Julie."

"I won't have to do any homework to-night," the girl says and then pauses. "Well, I mean, I could . . ."

"No," Sydney says. "Not tonight. Tonight is special."

"It is?"

"Your brothers are home."

Julie smiles, looking first at Ben and then at Jeff. She beams, but not possessively.

When Sydney arrived at the house, she in-tuited immediately that she might be ex-pected (for all that money) to spend more time with Julie than was strictly necessary for tutoring. Sydney doesn't mind. She and Julie walk the beach together, the girl col-lecting sea glass and sand dollars, her eyes remarkably sharp, more so than Sydney's, who often doesn't spot the piece until Julie has bent to pick it up. Earlier in the day, Julie found a thick amethyst chunk on which Sydney could see two faint circles, and, at the apex of the inner circle, a glass blower's mark.

*   *   *

The guests, Wendy and Art, are over-dressed for lobster, and already Sydney can see small squiggles of white flesh on Art's pink oxford cuff.

Ben attacks his lobster with relish. Jeff breaks the soft-shell claws with his fingers and eats the sweet meat without butter. Mrs. Edwards drenches even the smallest shreds in the yellow liquid. No carbs in butter.

Neither Wendy nor Art addresses Sydney during dinner, having ascertained when they arrived the day before that she was there for Julie, much like an upper servant might have been a century earlier. Wendy has on a chocolate-brown Armani sweater wrapped casually around her shoulders, the tied arms dangerously in the way. Sydney knows it's Armani because the label, flipped up and visible behind her neck, says so.

Through the open door, the surf hammers the shore, oddly boisterous on such a hot night. The dining room is airless, even with all the windows open. Sydney wants to be out on the beach. She wants to be in the water, swimming.

Three or four times in her life, Sydney has truly relished a lobster dinner, regarding it as a celebration rather than just a meal. Tonight, however, she eats perfunctorily, breaking the claws, drawing the meat out with a pick. The heat has stolen her appetite.

Sydney notes, throughout the dinner, that Ben is always present, while Jeff seems elsewhere. Ben is clearly a gourmand; Jeff appears to be indifferent to his meal. Ben has perfect manners vis à vis the guests who are going on at exhaustive length about a lamp made from an antique car horn they got for a steal in Portsmouth. Jeff leans into his father for a private conversation. Sydney hears the words *shutters* and *help you with that.*

"We just loved Portsmouth," Wendy says. "All those coffeehouses and little boutiques."

"Crowded," Art says.

"The city turned itself around in the eighties," Mr. Edwards says. "It used to be a rough place with the shipyard."

"We ate on the water," Wendy says. "Art had the chowder, and I had the fried calamari."

"Couldn't find anywhere to park," Art says.

"Then we were walking along that main street there, and I saw the lamp in a window."

"You should bring it in and show it to us," Mr. Edwards says.

"It's all wrapped up," Art says.

"You can take a ferry from Portsmouth out to the Isles of Shoals," Ben offers.

"Maybe we'll do that tomorrow?" Wendy asks in her husband's direction.

"So what are you up to, Jeff?" Art asks as he wipes his mouth with a foot of paper towel.

Jeff, startled, raises a pale eyebrow. "Teaching," he says amiably. "In the fall. Research now."

"Like what? What courses?"

"Postcolonial East Africa," Jeff says. "Genocide in the Twentieth Century."

"Nothing about the Middle East? The War on Terror?"

Art is bald on top but hirsute elsewhere, curly tufts emerging from the open V of his dress shirt. Sydney searches for a connection between the man and Mr. Edwards but can't find one. She reasons that the true friends are Mrs. Edwards and Wendy, both of whom seem nearly giddy at the prospect of a visit to Emporia, a local flea market, in the morning.

"I've found all my etched glass there," Mrs. Edwards says, raising her long-stemmed wineglass. "I never pay more than two dollars for one."

Sydney raises hers as well and admires the delicate workmanship. She wonders how old the glasses are, to whom they once belonged.

"He'll ruin us all," Mr. Edwards says with feeling. From prior conversations, Sydney knows he is referring to the president of the United States.

Shortly after her arrival, Sydney learned that Mr. Edwards switched his political allegiance, the conversion taking place during the contested presidential election. Mrs.

Edwards appears to invent and groom her political opinions in anticipation of her sons' visits.

"He's set us back a century," Mr. Edwards adds with surprising vehemence. "Two centuries."

That would be, Sydney calculates, 1802. Her command of history is poor. Was the country in bad shape then?

"You think he can get reelected?" Art asks.

With his lobster pick, Mr. Edwards stabs the air in the direction of the waxy container in which the already-cooked lobsters arrived from the lobster pound. "I'd vote for that [stab] paper [stab] bag over there if I thought it would get rid of the guy," he says.

Displays of anger from Mr. Edwards are rare. Respect is paid in silence. A silence that appears to annoy Mrs. Edwards, who drops her metal lobster cracker into her deep tin lobster plate, making quite a racket.

"Bread?" Sydney offers, picking up a basket.

Mrs. Edwards stares. Mrs. Edwards does not eat bread.

*   *   *

In the distance, there's a distinct but low rumble.

"Fireworks!" Julie says.

"Big storm coming later tonight," Art informs the gathering.

"Good," Mrs. Edwards says. "Clear the air out."

As if it smelled, Sydney thinks.

(For Sydney, the sudden smell of Troy. Sydney is eight or nine. Onions from her grandmother upstairs. Diesel fumes from the delivery trucks. Cigarette smoke woven into the old upholstery. Her father smokes Marlboros, her mother Virginia Slims. Sometimes, coming home from school, Sydney finds lit cigarettes in ashtrays in the bathroom, near the kitchen sink, and in her parents' bedroom, where her mother sits at her sewing machine making purses out of silk and cotton, the colors too bright, never seen in nature. Hot pink and shiny aqua, slicker-yellow, neon orange. Her mother reaching for the cigarette as she says hello to Sydney, her upper lip puckering into lines that will soon become permanent. "What do you think?" her mother asks, holding aloft a design of a purple convertible, the women in it with royal blue head scarves and red arms flying. This is meant to suggest, Sydney guesses, freedom.

Outside the front windows, color enough. None of it in nature, either. The fat pink of the *Troy Pork* sign. Magenta curtains on a brass rod in an apartment across the street. Yellowed Venetian blinds at the office of J. F. Riley, DDS. *Kodak, Molson, Kent* in the window of the candy store on the corner. The apartment a railroad flat in a row house, theirs identical to all the others on the street, in the city for that matter. Two windows in front, two in back looking out to the covered deck. The only sun through the front two, a couple hours in late morning. If you missed it, you were out of luck.

"They look happy, don't you think?" her mother, who never looks happy, asks. The purses are the life that is leaking out of her.

"Wild," Sydney says.)

Sydney learns that Art is in the paper business—sheets of paper, rolls of it—and that Wendy, retired now, was once a magazine editor in New York (or an assistant editor, or possibly even an assistant to an assistant—

this isn't quite clear). One child, a daughter, is completing graduate work at the University of Vermont, while a son has recently graduated from Williams. Wendy mentions Williams twice more in passing the way others use Harvard as currency. Sons are in ascendancy tonight, Sydney thinks, and immediately has sympathy for the girl at UVM, who, for all Sydney knows, might be her father's favorite.

A petal falls from a bouquet picked earlier in the day by Julie and her father. Sydney touches it and rubs the velvet between her index finger and her thumb. A perfume is released. When she looks up, both Ben and Jeff are watching her.

"What are these called?" she asks Mr. Edwards.

"Cabbage," he says. "Those are Damask. Pride of nineteenth-century gardeners. They're drought resistant, which makes them good for the shore."

"This one's my favorite," Julie says, fingering a heavy beige blossom.

Sydney waits, hoping for more from the girl, who usually offers only a sentence or

two at the table. But Julie immediately
bends to her meal.

"What happened to the woman, the
widow?" Sydney asks after a long silence,
Sydney having an affinity for both widows
and pilots, culpable or not.

Beside her, she can feel Mrs. Edwards
stiffen. Perhaps the guests have not been
told they are sleeping in the house of a
mildly notorious celebrity.

"She and her daughter moved in with her
mother here in town," Jeff answers. "Then I
think the widow went to live in London."

Jeff gives these facts in a polite but businesslike way, as though to signal the end
of the conversation. The sons, Sydney can
see, defer when necessary to their mother's
emotional weather. Perhaps they have heard
rumbles in the distance and fear a storm.

Julie's face is flushed pink with heat and
happiness, the girl seemingly not at all at-
tuned to her mother's mood. Her thick blond
hair has been tied into a careless knot,
unfortunately emphasizing her mother's
sprayed banana clip. The girl's lashes are
blond as well, long and beautifully shaped.
Julie appears not to worry about her weight,

and, as a result, there is an appealing volup-
tuousness about the girl. The brothers must
be watchful, Sydney thinks. Someone needs
to be watchful.

"Victoria will be here in the morning," Mrs.
Edwards announces, and it is clear that the
guests have been briefed, for both glance
over at Jeff, who is sipping a Rolling Rock.

"Lovely girl," Mr. Edwards says, his political vitriol a dozen comments back and
seemingly forgotten.

Ben looks pointedly at Jeff. "She certainly
is," he says.

Apart from a possible blush, Jeff gives no
indication that he's heard a word. The blush
might mean anything. Unhappiness at being
singled out? A mention of the very thing
dearest to his heart? A history of prior teas-
ing?

"I'm looking for a new condo," Ben says,
abruptly changing the subject.

"You're the man to go to," Jeff says.

"I'm tired of the South End. Like to give
the waterfront a try."

"They say never live on the water year-round," Mr. Edwards says. "Depressing as hell."

"Some terrific luxury condos going up," Ben says.

Mr. Edwards plants an elbow on the table and points his hand toward Ben. "It will be your generation who will suffer," the older man says, his anger apparently not having been forgotten after all. "You'll be decades extricating yourself from this mess. Monstrous debt. Terrorists. Abysmal foreign policy."

The table ponders the future, which does indeed look grim. Mrs. Edwards sets her jaw (one imagines a sharp dressing-down later in the privacy of the marital bedroom). "You'll scare the children, Mark," she says. "And you're ruining a perfectly lovely dinner."

Mr. Edwards studies his wife from the length of the walnut table. "Why would our children not want to know what the future holds?" he asks ingenuously. "Besides, I'm not saying anything Ben and Jeff don't already know. Jeff, I imagine, could tell us all a thing or two."

One imagines Jeff could tell them a thing

or two or three, though he seems disinclined to do so.

"Sox playing tonight?" Ben asks.

"Oh, ho, we're in Sox territory here!" Art
says with mock fright, grabbing playfully at
his wife's wrist. "Who's pitching?"

—————ww—————

Mr. Edwards and Sydney stand to collect
the dishes, as they do each night. Mr. Edwards says, *Wait a minute,* and returns from
the kitchen with a large black garbage bag.
He holds it open and makes the rounds, the
diners sliding the remains of the meal—
shells, bodies, green tomalley, red roe—into
the plastic sack, trying not to splash any of
the lobster liquor onto their clothing. Sydney collects the deep tin plates, on which
the red crustaceans have been enameled
(another Emporia find) and backs through
the swinging door to the kitchen. Each time
she emerges again into the dining room,
fewer people are sitting at the table. First
Julie leaves. Then Ben and Jeff. Finally only
Mrs. Edwards and her guests remain.

*   *   *

Mr. Edwards and Sydney have perfected a routine in the kitchen. Mr. Edwards soaks the silverware in a wide-mouth ceramic vase kept on the counter for the purpose. He rinses each plate and sets it in the sink. Sydney wonders if he's still pondering the paper bag he would vote for in order to unseat an incumbent president. Sydney's task, at which she is very good, is to stack the dishwasher as efficiently as possible so that only one load is necessary.

She sets the glasses in an upper plastic-coated wire trough, flips down the rack, and puts the ramekins on top. When she is finished, not another item could be squeezed into the appliance. She turns the dials and shuts the dishwasher with her hip. She listens for the quiet hum of the water draining. In the two years since Daniel died, she has had to learn all over again the satisfying pleasure of household tasks completed: a grocery list checked off, two errands accomplished in a single afternoon, dishwasher-loading as performance art.

"I'll do the tablecloth," she says, looking for further occupation.

"I'll warm the pies."

Sydney can see spots of lobster juice on

Mr. Edwards's pale green polo shirt, other discolorations from previous washes. She senses a reluctance on his part to greet his guests on the porch, where pie and coffee will be served. Perhaps he isn't wild about Art.

Sydney scrubs the bright-blue-and-red oil-cloth while it is still on the table. Then she rinses and scrubs it again. When she took the cloth, used only for lobster dinners, out of the drawer earlier in the evening, an un-pleasant smell of old dinners rose to her nostrils. Rotted fish. Congealed butter.

Sydney is on her second rinse when Ben enters the room. He takes the dry dish towel dangling from her left hand and polishes the tablecloth in her wake.

"Thank you," she says as their fingers meet on the first round of stretch-and-fold, the heavy oilcloth dangling below them.

"No, thank *you*," Ben insists. He takes the cloth from her and expertly stretches it again and makes a perfect second fold. He folds and folds until it is the size of a flag given to a widow.

"Want to go night surfing?" he asks.

Sydney is confused. Does he mean surf casting? Surfing on boards?

"Sure," she says.

"Wear your suit under your clothes. My mother hates it when we do this."

Sydney heads upstairs to her room, a small chamber papered in pale azure with miniature cream roses, the woodwork and the narrow beds painted white. In the daytime, through the sole window, Sydney can see the ocean. If she sits on one of the beds to read, which she often does in the late afternoon (allowing the Edwardses to think that she is napping), she has an ocean-liner view. On the middle ledge of the window is a tall cobalt-blue bottle with a gull's feather in its opening. To one side is an enameled red chair, and near it two shallow closets. Sydney is puzzled by the two closets side by side and has come up with no satisfactory explanation. One for suits; one for casual wear? One for dresses; one for nightgowns? One for her; one for him?

Sydney likes her room and thinks it perfect for the time being. It reminds her of old photographs of hospital rooms with women in starched wimples and aprons tending to patients on beds with sheets tightly drawn.

She shakes the sand from her black tank suit into the wastebasket. She puts it on and covers it with the shirt and shorts she wore at dinner. She sticks her feet into her flip-flops and descends the stairs, announcing her arrival with her sandals. Everyone has gathered on the porch, most with plates in hand. Forks are in motion. Jeff and Ben are leaning against the railing, having refused dessert.

"We thought we'd take Sydney for a walk," Ben says.

Mrs. Edwards turns and looks at Sydney, perhaps sensing something illicit in Ben's announcement, however innocently delivered. She opens her mouth and closes it again. Maybe she was going to ask Sydney if she had finished the dishes.

"Take a flashlight," Mr. Edwards says.

Ben holds aloft a Maglite heavy enough to kill a man.

Ben switches on the light for the walk along the boardwalk and the descent of the stairs, but then he switches it off.

"Best to let your eyes adjust," he says. "Leave your shoes here."

Sydney steps out of the flip-flops and sets them on the bottom step. As if by prior arrangement, she walks between the two brothers. The something illicit begins to molt, unleashing in Sydney a sensation close to giddiness. It seems that any minute now, one of the brothers will take off running, challenging the other to a race.

They head down the beach, the sand cool underfoot. The voices on the porch recede at once, muffled by the white noise of the surf. Sydney watches her legs, out of sync with the brothers' longer strides. There's a half-moon in the sky, some lights from the cottages along the beach.

"You'll be able to see the surf once your eyes adjust," Jeff says.

"You guys do this often?" she asks.

"It's kind of a first-night ritual," Ben answers.

"Even if it's raining?" Sydney asks. "Even if it's cold?"

"The trick is to keep your feet planted when you stand," Jeff says. "That way, you can feel the direction of the undertow."

"You'll be amazed at how well you'll be able to see," Ben adds.

Sydney has no choice but to take his word for it. Already, she has stepped on something sharp she might have avoided in the daylight. Perhaps he is right, though, for she can see a ruffle of white along the shoreline.

"We'll leave our clothes here," Ben says, stopping suddenly. "The tide's coming in."

"How do you find your clothes afterwards?" Sydney asks.

Beside her, she can just make out the shape of a man drawing his shirt over his head. She steps out of her shorts and begins to unbutton her blouse. Only by height can she tell the brothers apart, Ben having an inch, two inches, on Jeff.

"Are you afraid?" Jeff asks.

"No," Sydney says, her answer pure bravado. And then she wonders if perhaps she has disappointed the brothers, fear being half the fun.

The water, when it hits Sydney's feet, is a vise around her ankles. She lets out an involuntary yelp.

"If you get into trouble," Ben says, "just

stand up and holler. One of us will hear
you."

He touches her lightly on the shoulder.
She turns and tries to see his face, but she
can't. Not really.

"But you won't get into trouble," he reas-
sures her, letting his hand fall to his side.

Sydney watches as he runs forward to
meet the ocean, high-stepping over the surf.
"First one in . . . ," he calls and instantly
both brothers are gone, swallowed up
by the waves. No wonder Mrs. Edwards
doesn't like this, Sydney thinks.

Sydney feels shells and small pebbles being
sucked beneath her feet. She lets her calves
go numb and then her thighs. She hears
a hoot, one brother calling to another. She
sees the white curling edges of a wave coming and dives into it, letting its force wash
over her. When she stands, the ocean seems
to empty out at her knees. She shakes her
head, wiping the salt from her eyes.

"You catch one yet?" someone calls.

"No," Sydney answers.

"Go for it."

There is nothing but cold and surf, shifting
sand beneath her feet. She is hit suddenly

from the side and understands that already she is disoriented. She searches for the line of lights from the cottages in the distance. A wave hits her from behind and pushes her down into the water. She scrapes her shoulder hard. She hears another hoot from one brother to the other.

Simple tasks seem monumental, distances extreme, like learning to walk after a long illness. When the water level is just below her waist, she listens for a coming swell. She lets one pass and then another. She plants her feet and watches as a wave advances, showing its white teeth. With years of body memory, Sydney leaps onto the crest, her timing perfect.

A roar in her ears, the utter black of the water. She has no power, none at all, and couldn't release herself from the wave even if she wanted to. The surge seems a living thing that has no purpose but to carry her along at tremendous speed. She has never felt so frightened, so exhilarated.

She flails, arches her back, and takes a breath. She is beached, the sand giving way beneath her. She tries to stand.

"My god," she says, wiping the water from her eyes.

"You okay?" Ben asks, apparently beached as well.

"That was unbelievable."

And then Ben is gone, eager for another ride. Sydney searches for Jeff but cannot see him. It occurs to her that drowning here would be easier than anyone has let on. A certain death with no hope of rescue.

Sydney learns the night topography of the ocean as a hunter might the night woods. She rides a second wave and a third and then too many to count. Occasionally, she calls out and receives a reassuring response.

"I'm staggering," Sydney cries after a time. Her legs barely keep her upright. She wants to sink to her knees and let the waves wash over her. Crawl out onto dry land and sleep there.

"One more," someone yells.

Sydney faces the ocean. A sense of mild competition, perhaps of pride, pushes her forward. She will not be the first to quit. She shivers in a sudden east wind (*now* the east wind) and hugs her arms. She propels herself forward. She swings her legs and body from side to side, trying to make headway. Again, she waits for what she thinks will be a good wave. In the distance, she can see it coming, the white lace. She points her arms and stands poised. When it is just upon her, she sails onto its crest.

Again, the blackness all around her, the sense of speed. She feels a shape, flesh, beneath her. The flesh slithers the length of her body, touching her, feeling her. She tries to force herself out of the surge, but she can't. She would scream if she could.

She fights to get up onto her knees. There is water in her mouth and nose. She rises, then stumbles. She has to crawl out of the water.

Was it a fish? she wonders, her heart pumping hard. A shark?

She replays the touch in her mind. She remembers the slither along her right breast, her stomach, her pubic bone, her thigh. The touch fleeting, and yet deliberate. She is certain now that it was a hand. She plays the memory again. The touch would have been difficult to accomplish and was thus intentional.

She stands on the beach, unwilling to call out. Her arms are gooseflesh, the feathers recently plucked. She doesn't know where her clothes are, how far the swells have pushed the three of them along the beach. There are lighted windows to her left and right as far as she can see. She could walk up to the seawall and hug it to the Edwardses' cottage. But then she would have to step onto the porch without her clothes, her suit and hair wet, her feet sandy.

It might have been a fish, she thinks.

"Hey," a voice calls. "Sydney?"

"I'm here," she answers, and then clears her throat. "I'm here," she calls again.

She waits until she sees a shape walking toward her.

She could ask: *Was it you?*

The touch, she is certain now, a stolen one. Not meant to be identified.

She waits for the shape to announce itself. Ben is staggering, too.

"Wow," he says. "That was fantastic."

"Where's Jeff?" Sydney asks.

Ben calls for his brother, waits an interval, and calls again. Jeff returns the call, but faintly, his ship beached quite a bit farther along the shore than Sydney's.

"You're cold," Ben says, reaching out an arm.

"No, I'm fine," Sydney says, slipping out from under him.

Ben, then, Sydney guesses. Jeff is simply too far away.

The next morning, the fog imprisons. Vigorous wisps rush through posts in the railing, sentries surrounding the house. The mist drips off the screen in rivulets, the air itself turning liquid. An asthmatic could be forgiven for thinking he might drown. In less than ten minutes the shoreline disappears. The entire Atlantic Ocean disappears. Sydney can hear the surf but not see it. A visitor coming to the house would have to take the view on faith.

Sydney feels sorry for the family that lives just a quarter mile down the road on the beach. She has seen the tent erected, the sign in the driveway announcing *The Christopher/Rapp Wedding*. She imagines an outdoor wedding planned and wonders if the guests will be able to see the bride at the makeshift altar. Expensive coiffures will be undone in seconds.

The brothers go for a run together. Sydney avoids them in the hallway. She has generally been expert in her timing, managing to arrive in the kitchen after the Edwardses have breakfasted but before the guests have come down. When Sydney enters the kitchen, there are crumbs next to the toaster, an uncovered butter dish on the counter, plates with the residue of sliced pears in the sink. A coffee cup, the rings already drawn, sits at the edge of the island, suggesting Ben stood to drink his breakfast. How does Sydney know that it is Ben, of all of them, who might stand to drink his breakfast?

The small gravel driveway just beyond the back door is thick with cars: Mrs. Edwards's maroon Volvo; Mr. Edwards's Subaru Outback; Sydney's gray Civic; Ben's black Land Rover. Sydney wonders what the girlfriend drives and spends quite a lot of time thinking about it. Possibly a Passat, but more likely a Lexus. Sydney hopes for the Lexus. She imagines the girlfriend to be cool and blond, but actually she cannot picture Jeff with a girlfriend. It is not that she thinks he does not deserve one or that he is not attractive enough. It is simply that she cannot picture it.

Sydney walks out to the porch with her tea and commandeers the teak chaise with the white cushion. She can hear the faint annoyed tone of a lost-key crisis from inside the house.

I know I had it in my pocket. Did you do a wash?

(Years ago in Troy, and her father has lost a key, or her mother has. To the apartment? To the car? To what else would her parents have had keys? A simmering tension igniting on that sweltering Memorial Day, as if in celebration. Sydney—maybe eleven—sitting out on the front cement steps, a stoop identical to all the others on the street, hearing through the open windows her father's low accusations, her mother's near hysteria, the fight not about a key but about failed expectations. Did Sydney really hear the word *Jew* hurled from the room? When her father met her mother at a concert at Russell Sage, he was living in Troy and working for an alternative paper. Sydney's mother thought her father a writer. He thought her an artist. Her father, unusually laconic—now driven to shouting; did he really say her mother's purses were *cheap and tawdry?*—lived in his mother's apartment house, an acceptable arrangement for a couple with a baby on the way and artistic fantasies to fulfill. Sydney's mother's family in Connecticut refused to come to the wedding of their pregnant daughter to a Jew in Troy, the dead-end city at least as unacceptable as the religion. One couldn't help being a Jew, the thinking went, but one could certainly be expected to do better than Troy.

When the alternative paper failed, her father took a job with the *Troy Record,* a tabloid filled with ads, local sports, and obits. Her mother made silk purses and bristled if anyone said the word *crafts* within her hearing. Each was fatally disappointed in the other, feeling swindled, feeling duped. Perhaps her father less so, for he seemed congenitally used to failure. His own father, a tailor two blocks over, had had to sell his shop to a butcher when the neighborhood had gone Italian. Sydney's grandmother, in a shrewd move, had saved enough money to buy the row house. She lived on the top floor and rented out the two below her.

Sydney's father coming out onto the stoop, mindful that his daughter is sitting alone, waiting to go on the family picnic. The Olds, parked in front of the house, locked.

"Ice cream?" her father asks.)

With biblical drama, the fog lifts. The water scintillates, a sequined surface. Even the dune grass is shiny, giving off more light than green. The air seems freshly laundered. Sydney thinks of good drying weather. It occurs to her that she hasn't seen a wash on the line in years.

"What a day," Ben says through a small opening in the screen door, having already returned from his run. He takes a swig of orange juice straight from the carton, an oddly boorish gesture that renders the juice unfit for anyone else to drink. Sydney doesn't say a word. "There might not be another like it all summer," Ben adds, looking pointedly in her direction.

*   *   *

When the screen door opens again, Tullus leaps out, as if having been imprisoned for years. He gives Sydney's bare leg a sniff with his cold nose, and then sprints the length of the boardwalk. At the deck, he waits, panting.

"Want to come?" Jeff asks. In his hand is the purple leash. The invitation is a casual one, made more so by Jeff's nimble descent of the front steps as he speaks.

"Sure," Sydney says, setting down her coffee cup. She is not expected to work on weekends.

Sydney follows Jeff out to the deck, where Tullus is running in a tight circle.

"Stay," Jeff says, struggling to snag the collar so that he can fasten the clip. But Tullus, in his excitement, won't be still.

"You have to wonder how smart he is," Jeff says. "He knows we can't go for the walk until I get the leash on. He wants to go for the walk more than anything in the world. But he won't let me put it on him."

"Does he need a leash?" she asks.

"He'd chase a gull, and we wouldn't see him again for hours. Worse, he'd eat it."

Tullus demands a brisk pace, and Sydney digs her toes into the cool sand. She is surprised to see that Jeff has on the same shirt and bathing trunks he wore the day before. When Sydney catches up to him, he gives off the unwashed scent of a man who hasn't had his shower yet.

"What a day," Jeff says, unwittingly echoing his brother.

For a time, Sydney and Jeff walk in silence. The brilliance of the water is almost too painful to look at, but something about its visual fizz contributes directly to Sydney's sense of well-being.

Along the seawall, people emerge from cottages. A woman in a white bathrobe and sunglasses scans the horizon. A man sits on a bench and rigs a fly rod. A couple stand on the steps with coffee cups in hand. It would be impossible, Sydney thinks, to greet this day and not remark upon its clarity.

"Where do you live?" Jeff asks after a time.

"Waltham."

"I'm sorry about your husband."

"Thank you."

"What will you do in the fall?"

Tullus noses a clump of seaweed. Jeff and Sydney pause beside him.

"I'm not sure," Sydney says. "I should go back to school and finish my degree. But I don't know that I want to return to Brandeis."

"Why is that?"

"I'd rather be in the city. I'm an old enough student as it is."

"I've got one student who's forty-two."

Jeff pauses while Tullus attends to his business. Sydney turns discreetly away and studies the horizon.

"What drew you to academia?" Sydney asks.

"I'm not sure exactly. Sometimes I think it's not so much being drawn to academia as never getting off the bus."

She tries to picture Jeff in a classroom, a piece of chalk in hand, culled words on a blackboard, dust on the cuffs of his sweater. The image is appealing.

"I really like Julie," she says. "It's interesting that there are so many years between you."

Jeff is silent a moment, and Sydney wonders if she has made too personal a comment.

"We were always encouraged to believe that Julie was not an accident," Jeff says finally, burying the pile with a toy shovel he's had in his pocket. He digs the shovel into clean sand, scouring it. "It's part of the family mythology."

Sydney wants to ask what happened to Julie to make her slow but can think of no good way to phrase the question.

"My father says you're terrific with her," Jeff offers, letting Tullus reestablish the pace.

"She's easy to be with."

"My mother was forty-one when she had Julie. My dad was fifty."

Is this an explanation? A dedicated breeze makes Sydney's hair fly in wings above her ears. "What does Julie love to do?" she asks suddenly. "I ask because it might not be possible for her to go to the kind of school your parents want for her."

"Love?" Jeff turns, surprised by the question. His skin is lightly freckled. He has the coloring of a northern man. "Gardening," he answers after a minute. "Walking Tullus."

He pauses. "Anyway, it's my mother with the hopes. I think my father pretty much gets the picture."

"I notice that Julie's often in the rose garden."

"She'll find a man," Jeff announces. "She'll be all right."

Sydney is taken aback. Though, possibly, in Julie's case, an independent life is not a reasonable expectation.

"I think the man will find *her*," Sydney corrects.

"Not too soon, I hope."

Sydney smiles. "No, not too soon."

Sydney notes that the topography of the beach is vastly different in the daylight. The night before, while she stood at the water's edge, the houses seemed far away. This morning, they are so close as to be intrusive.

"What do *you* love?" Jeff asks.

"What do I love?"

Unprepared for the volley and return, Sydney cannot think. She puts a hand to her temple. She could say with ease what she used to love, but Daniel is gone now.

"I like this," she says, gesturing.

"The beach?"

"Walking on it. Looking at it." She feels heat in her face. Her response is lame at best, uninspired. "I like being with Julie and your father. I like kayaking . . ."

About to say *body surfing,* Sydney stops herself, not wanting to be reminded of the night before, that slithering touch. She is aware that she has not listed Ben or Mrs. Edwards as among the people or things she likes. If she had, she doubts Jeff would have believed her. After an evening and a night spent in the house, Jeff cannot fail to be aware of a certain dismissive tone in Mrs. Edwards's voice when speaking to Sydney, a certain disingenuousness in Sydney's when replying.

Sydney decides not to ask Jeff what he loves. She wonders if he would say Victoria.

"Presumably you liked school," Jeff says after a time.

"I did."

"Will you go back?"

"Not sure. I did like the idea that my life was based on asking questions. And finding answers to those questions. I suppose I believe that being wise is more important in the long run than having a lot of money." Sydney laughs. "Which is good because I'm never going to have any."

Jeff smiles.

"I suppose I could have achieved that goal in any field if I'd worked hard enough," she continues. "Biology or chemistry, say. So it's probably more that I'm fascinated by what makes humans tick." She shrugs her shoulders. "Or maybe it's simply that I had a grandiose idea of adding in my small way to the collective sum of human knowledge."

"I know all about grandiose fantasies," Jeff says.

Sydney tries to match her stride to Jeff's. "What does your dad do?" she asks.

Remarkably, no one has told her. She hasn't wanted to inquire in case Mr. Edwards is unemployed—too well-off to have to work, recently downsized from a hefty corporate job, or simply retired.

"He's an architect."

Sydney stops, reined in by surprise. She does a quick mental tour of the house. No architectural models, no framed drawings—

at least none that she has noticed. "I'd never have guessed that," she says.

"He has his own practice in Boston. Or did. He works from home most of the time now."

"I'd love to see something he's done."

"It's possible he has some work with him in his room. You'd have to go to Needham, though, to see the models and the drawings. They're very beautiful."

"I'm not sure I've ever met a man capable of going weeks without once mentioning his profession."

"You could know my father two years and he wouldn't tell you if you didn't ask."

"Unusual these days, when a man is often measured by what he does, by how successful he is."

"Not Dad. He couldn't care less."

"And you?"

"Me? Oh, you'd know within the week."

"And Ben?"

"Before the day was over."

Sydney and Jeff reach the far end of the beach, at which there seems to be a lot of seaweed. When they turn around, Tullus is panting hard, the leash less taut, their pace slower.

"I was just wondering," Jeff says. "Can you really quantify emotional development?"

"Can you make politics scientific?" Sydney asks.

Jeff bends down and lets Tullus go. The dog, unleashed, heads for the water, chasing a gull. When he comes out, he shakes himself, spraying droplets everywhere.

"Thing I love about dogs," Jeff says, "they're so predictable."

As they near the house, Sydney notices that families have begun to spread out along the beach. They pass a woman reading in a low plastic chair. Three small children are digging a hole at her feet.

"When is Victoria coming?" Sydney asks.

"Vicki," Jeff says. "I'm picking her up at eleven-fifteen at the bus station."

Sydney makes a slight adjustment to her mental portrait of Victoria. Someone willing to take a bus.

"Have you known her long?" Sydney asks.

"All my life. Her family has been coming

here for years. I think I first became aware of her in sailing class when I was six or seven. We used to rent cottages then."

"And you've been together all that time?" Sydney asks, astonished.

"No," Jeff says, laughing. "We met again last year at a fund-raiser in Boston. She works for the Jimmy Fund. It's a cancer foundation."

"I know what the Jimmy Fund is," Sydney says, and even she can hear the slight churlishness in her voice. She feels distracted by the constantly shifting portrait of Victoria—who rides a bus, who is really called Vicki, who took sailing lessons at six, who works for a nonprofit organization—as if a crime artist kept adjusting a computer image based on a witness's testimony.

"I'll bet she gets great seats at Fenway," Sydney offers, consciously lightening her tone.

"Best part of her job," Jeff says.

Jeff calls to Tullus, who joins them at the foot of the wooden steps.

"Now he'll want a treat," Jeff explains. "He thinks he's just taken *us* for a walk."

Sydney climbs the steps with sandy feet, aware of Jeff just inches behind her.

———

The announcement of Victoria's arrival can be heard throughout the house. Raised voices. A call. A greeting. Sydney is contentedly hulling strawberries in the kitchen. Mr. Edwards is reading the directions for a new panini maker recently delivered by Federal Express. Sydney likes the small frown of concentration between his eyes. Mr. Edwards sets the pamphlet on the counter; Sydney abandons the strawberries in the colander. They walk into the hallway to see what the commotion is all about, even though they both know perfectly well what the commotion is all about.

Victoria, with long, dark, wavy hair, stands just inside the front door. Over her shoulder is a white canvas bag with leather trim. She has on a pale summer skirt, cut on the bias, the material thin. A tiny aqua sweater with pearl buttons is casually draped over a tank top. At the ends of her long, tanned legs are white flip-flops with a jewel at each big toe.

Her nose is aquiline, almost masculine, her mouth bare. It is apparent immediately that Victoria is possessed of both gravity and beauty, a winning combination. Sydney wonders where the woman is sleeping.

Victoria embraces Mrs. Edwards. An elaborate and gushing introduction is made to Wendy and Art, who seem to have caught a kind of contagious beaming from Mrs. Edwards. Victoria extends one long, straight bare arm, the wrist slightly bent, seemingly drawing the other person toward her. It is a marvelous gesture, one Sydney admires.

Sydney waits, arms crossed against her chest. Mrs. Edwards says, "You remember Julie." Victoria gives the girl a quick hug and in doing so catches Sydney's eye. Sydney smiles and steps forward, her own hand extended.

"I'm Sydney Sklar," she says.

"Sydney's here for Julie," Mrs. Edwards says quickly, an extraordinary lapse in manners that Mr. Edwards immediately seeks to redress.

"I hope for all of us," he says.

Mrs. Edwards appears not to have heard.

A moment of awkward silence is blessedly broken by Ben. "I'll take that up," he says, gesturing toward Victoria's bag.

Up where? Sydney wonders again.

With mumbled excuses, Victoria slips away from the gathering. Though willing to travel by bus, the woman was apparently unable to use that vehicle's facilities.

It is impossible not to hear, from the front-hall bathroom, the sounds of tinkling, an un-mistakable sigh of relief, and the wobbling of the loose toilet-paper roll. To cover the noise, Mr. Edwards clears his throat and then blows his nose into a white handker-chief he keeps in his back pocket.

"You made good time," he says to Jeff.

Having discovered the unfortunate acous-tics early in her stay with the Edwardses, Sydney has contrived never to have to use the front-hall bathroom.

When Victoria emerges, she gives a shy smile and walks directly through the house to the porch door. Jeff joins her.

"My god," she says of a view she must have seen a thousand times.

*   *   *

From the front hallway, Wendy and Art and Mrs. Edwards study Victoria's narrow back.

"She's lovely," Wendy says.

"A looker," Art agrees.

"Mark and I are hoping either this weekend or the next . . . ," Mrs. Edwards confides.

"An announcement?" Art inquires.

"Really?" Julie asks, surprised.

Mrs. Edwards glances with some alarm at her daughter, whom she has apparently forgotten. The mother mimes "sealed lips" in Julie's direction.

Sydney, too, gazes at the lovely woman in the porch doorway. What is there not to like about Victoria? *Vicki,* actually, who does not resemble in the slightest the computer image of earlier, even with its many alterations. The crime artist will have to be fired.

Mr. Edwards announces that lunch will be served on the porch. He retreats to the kitchen, and Sydney willingly follows. Mr. Edwards appears to like the challenge of cooking, a skill he learned only later in life. In Troy, her father never went near the kitchen.

Sydney offers, when she has finished hulling the strawberries, to set the table, a task that requires carrying armloads of dishes and glasses and silverware out to the round teak table in the corner of the porch. A tricky screen door that wants to catch the back of her ankle has to be negotiated. Napkins have to be anchored in the stiff breeze.

When she makes her last trip, Sydney discovers that Ben and Victoria and Jeff are sitting in the heavy teak chairs around the table.

"Can I help?" Victoria asks.

"Thanks, but I'm all done," Sydney says.

"Join us, then," Ben says.

Jeff catches Sydney's eye. An invitation or a warning? The moment passes before it has fully registered.

Sydney sits, not liking the rudimentary math. Jeff and Victoria. Ben and Sydney. She wishes for the emergence of one other person, even Mrs. Edwards (perhaps especially Mrs. Edwards, with her knack for rendering Sydney invisible) to change the sum.

Ever since Victoria arrived, Sydney has been aware of shifting configurations. Mrs. Edwards, hands clasped together at her breast, her posture slightly tilted back, presenting Victoria as if the young woman might have distant royal blood. Mr. Edwards, casually draping an arm around Julie. Jeff discreet, not needing to hover over or touch his girlfriend; perhaps they already kissed passionately in the Land Rover on the way back from the bus station. Ben, Diet Coke in hand, perched on the landing of the stairs, surveying the scene from on high.

Because of the bright sunshine, dark glasses are de rigueur on the porch at lunch. An entire family incognito. The sandwiches that Mr. Edwards delivers are sublime—confections of mozzarella, tomato, basil, and olive oil between slices of crusty bread. Mrs. Edwards stares at the panini her husband sets in front of her as if to ask, *What am I supposed to do with this?* Doubtless she would like to pry apart the slices of bread and scrape out only the cheese, but she cannot do so in polite company. Certainly not in Victoria's presence.

Victoria is asked about numbers, and she names a fabulous sum. She speaks with confidence about baseball, acute myeloid leukemia, and a restaurant failure on St. Botolph Street. Ben perks up noticeably at the mention of possible real estate for sale.

Sydney observes Julie from across the table. The girl seems subdued. Perhaps Julie sees in Victoria a woman she will never be. Maybe she minds an outsider's claim on her brother. Or is it simply that she already hears the sounds of everyone leaving her for activities to which she will not be invited? Sydney makes a mental note to ask the girl for a walk after lunch.

Sydney is seldom told directly of future household events. Rather, she is meant to deduce them as the day progresses—from bits of conversation, from extra bags of produce on the granite counter, or, more subtly, from Mrs. Edwards's second shower at three o'clock so that her hair will be fresh for the evening's festivities.

Today, at lunch, a reference is made to needing two more bottles of Shiraz for dinner. A debate is held regarding the strength of the breeze and whether or not having drinks on the porch is even feasible. But it is this sequence of sentences—*Ferris doesn't drink; Marissa likes Pellegrino; Claire said Will can come after all*—that leads Sydney to arrive at the sum of thirteen for dinner long before she passes the dining room, elaborately set three hours ahead of time with etched glasses, mismatched antique china, and damask linens (all Emporia finds) for precisely that number.

Victoria delicately wipes her mouth and praises the lunch. She and Jeff and Ben are going to play tennis. Jeff extends an invitation to Sydney, but she begs off, declaring that she's a terrible player, which is, more or less, an accurate statement. But once again, the rudimentary math is troublesome.

"I'll play," Mr. Edwards, ever accommodating, offers.

Talents are weighed and measured. Ben and Mr. Edwards will take on Vicki and Jeff. From this, Sydney concludes that Ben is the best player of the four.

Sydney does not do the dishes more than once a day. It is a private rule she never breaks, even under dire circumstances, such as on the first Friday night of her stay, when

an impromptu cocktail party required up-
wards of thirty glasses and hors d'oeuvres
plates, not to mention four cheese-encrusted
cookie sheets on which Mr. Edwards had
hastily baked crostini. Sydney had already
emptied and reloaded the dishwasher earlier in the day and so simply retreated to her
room to listen to the Sox on WEEI. Today,
she effects a similar retreat, knowing that
much will be required of her after the evening meal. She is happy to help out, but she
has her limits.

Sydney enters her room and is immediately
overwhelmed by grief for Daniel. By simply
shutting the door, she has been hurtled
back to an understanding of precisely what
it is that she has lost. The expectation of
a normal life. A buffer against the dead
hour, fast approaching. A respite from the
necessity to remake a future, to enter the
peculiarly *other* universes of strangers. She
presses a hand to her stomach, which
seems to have taken the worst of the blow.
    She remembers their particular fit, her
pale leg slipping between his two when they
lay together after making love, as if their
limbs had been deliberately fashioned for

this purpose. The way Daniel would never cross a room without glancing at her face. The way he'd come home from his shift, drained, searching for her, room to room, only the sight of her allowing him access to a normal life.

The sensation fades, leaving in its wake a desire not to be left alone. Sydney walks to the dresser with its mirror. She has had two weddings, one in a church and one in a temple. One at which her mother wept with happiness; one at which her father seemed privately pleased. Surely, Sydney thinks, that is any woman's quota. Another wedding would be greedy, faintly ridiculous. She couldn't wear white, expect gifts, have a reception. Is she done, then? Is it all over? And if so, what will she do with herself? Become a doctor? Could she do well enough on the MCATs? Could she learn to fly?

A puzzle has been dumped upon a table in a corner of the living room. Julie is bent over a thousand pieces. Privately, Sydney hates puzzles—the frustration, the headachy sense of having nothing better to do, the disappointment at the end when the final image is not a Bonnard or a Matisse after all, but instead a saccharine landscape reminiscent of Thomas Kinkade. (The stupefying boredom of summers on the cement front stoops of Troy, the games of hopscotch and marbles and jump rope exhausted, the change from the errand to the corner store already spent. Midafternoon, the dead hour, her friend Kelly whining about the heat, her mother napping upstairs. The public pool was slimy underfoot; Kelly wouldn't go there. One afternoon Sydney walked to the end of the street, looking for shade. She crossed to the next street and then to the next and then to the next until she found herself in a vacant lot with a chain-link fence. A boy tried to sell her cigarettes and then asked her to pull her shorts down. Just like that. He would give her a dollar. A dollar would buy an ice-cream cone. Sydney walked slowly away, hunching her shoulders for a blow from behind, moving toward a corner of the fence where there was an opening through which a slender girl could slip. When she reached the corner, she saw, to her horror, that the gap had been repaired. She turned. The boy had his own pants down and was touching himself frantically. Sydney, panic rising, scooted around him and ran as if for her life, and it wasn't until she was married to Andrew that she could even say the word *penis*.)

"I'm finding all the border pieces," Julie announces.

"Can I join you?"

"You can help."

Sydney sits opposite the girl and studies the cover of the box. A house is perched on rocks overlooking the Atlantic, the painting bearing enough of a resemblance to the one they are in to suggest the motives of the purchaser.

"I'll do the house," Sydney says. "I'll find all the white ones and put them together."

Sydney feels dull-witted and slow. Too many decisions, she discovers, have to be made. Is this part of the house or part of a seagull? Is that a bit of a whitecap or a cloud?

Sydney glances up and notices the speed with which Julie spots a piece and flicks it to one side. Within minutes, it seems, Julie has assembled all the straight edges. She begins to work them into a plausible frame.

Sydney watches in amazement as Julie's nimble fingers build a border.

"Julie," Sydney says. "I want you to try something."

Julie looks up at her, her frown of concentration flattening out.

"I want you to switch seats with me and find all the pieces of the house."

Julie tilts her head. She doesn't understand.

"I love doing the border," Sydney lies. "It's my favorite part."

"Oh," Julie says with some reluctance. "Sure."

After each is seated in the other's chair, Sydney makes a half-hearted attempt to connect part of the border. Surreptitiously, she observes Julie. With a sharp eye and a deft touch, Julie accurately spots the relevant shards of white and within minutes has a house in bits. She begins maneuvering them into place. Whenever she has two that match, she snaps them together.

"You're very good at this," Sydney remarks.

In her room, Sydney finds a packet of photos she recently picked up at the drugstore in Portsmouth. Most are pictures of the beach, of the village, of the exterior of the house. She takes them down into the living room and makes a neat stack on the coffee table.

"Julie, I just want to try something else," she says to the girl. "If you could come over here?"

Julie turns and stares at Sydney, as if gradually bringing her into focus. "Sure," she says. She joins Sydney on the couch.

"These are pictures I took with my camera," Sydney explains. "I was thinking of getting a frame and making a collage. You know what a collage is, right?"

Julie nods.

"I wondered if you would lay them out on the table for me so that they'd make a nice composition."

Sydney sits back on the sofa, ceding the table to Julie. The girl, who is used to following Sydney's instructions, flicks through the packet of photos and begins to sort them. Beachscapes. Pictures of the house. Photographs of the lobster pound and the grocery store in the center of town. After a time, Julie begins to place them on the coffee table. Sydney watches with growing excitement.

Selecting nine photographs from the pile, some vertical, some horizontal, Julie sets each down in relationship to the one before. She does not hesitate and she does not pick up a photograph once she has put it down. When she has finished, she sits back, squints at the collage, then pulls the photographs apart from one another by a quarter inch. Then she puts her hands in her lap. Done.

Sydney leans forward to examine the assemblage. A sole picture of the house in shadow, the darkest photo of the lot, sits just below and to the right of center and acts as an anchor. The other photos bleed out from that central picture in color and tone and in actual geographic proximity to the house. More surprising is the selection of just the nine pictures, four to one side, five to the other, the extra photograph on the left balancing the weight of the central dark image. The girl knew instinctively not to use all of the photos. The end result is visually pleasing. More than pleasing. Accomplished. Julie, who cannot understand eighth-grade math and is incapable of mastering basic punctuation, is clearly gifted at the art of composition.

"You've got quite an eye," Sydney says.

But the girl seems disturbed.

"What's wrong?" Sydney asks.

"There aren't any people in your pictures," Julie notes.

—⚬⚬⚬—

"How about a walk?" Sydney asks after a time.

Julie examines Sydney as if through a film Sydney has come to think of as milky. "All right," Julie says, ever compliant in the way of a girl who finds most of life pleasurable.

"We'll go through town. Stop by and watch them playing tennis." Sydney bends forward, collecting the photographs, wishing she didn't have to destroy Julie's effortless composition. "We'll do this again," she says.

The village center on a Saturday afternoon is crowded with packed SUVs and two sets of renters: the first group wistful, reluctant to leave after their two-week stay; the other buoyant, fetching provisions in anticipation of a long-awaited vacation. Julie and Sydney skirt the lobster pound and the general store and head along a tree-shaded lane. Even the meanest asbestos-shingled cottage and the weediest lawn seem inviting in the hard sunshine.

Sydney can hear the thwack of the ball before she can see the players. A thwack and a grunt. She tries to identify the source of the exertion. Male or female? Young or old?
When Julie and Sydney reach the court, they stop, by unspoken agreement, just short of revealing themselves. Sydney is intrigued and wonders at Julie's motives. Not wanting to be seen wanting? She wonders something else: Are her own motives the same?

In the distance, she can make out Victoria in tennis pinks and what looks to be a pair of new running shoes. Jeff, beside her, about to serve, has large sweat stains under his armpits, rivulets of perspiration trickling down the sides of his face. He brings his racquet down in a ferocious display of pure power. The ball hits just inside the line and seemingly out of the reach of Ben, who nevertheless makes a nifty return. Having had a smattering of tennis lessons during her strenuously WASP period, Sydney can follow the game. Beside her, Julie has her fingers pressed to her mouth.

"What?" Sydney asks, smiling.

"Dad."

Julie's father has on an abbreviated pair of tennis shorts he might have bought forty years ago—pale gray from many washings and so worn as to be comically revealing. His white legs are shocking; he looks a different race than his partner and his opponents. He sometimes flails at the ball, but he has a surprisingly accurate serve, a fact that appears to please him, even though he answers *pure luck* to Ben's *nice serve.* To Ben's serves, Jeff responds with speed, his backhand almost faster than the eye can register, trying to erase the carefully placed shots.

"Julie," Jeff says, noticing his sister. He has his hands on his hips, and he is panting hard.

"Hey, guys," Julie says, stepping forward.

"Want to play?" Ben asks.

Julie lifts a shoulder to her cheek.

"Just taking a walk," Sydney explains, moving away from the shadow of the trees as well. "Who's winning?"

"We are," Jeff answers quickly, revealing a certain investment in the game.

"Great," Sydney says, although she feels confused. She cannot think of any reason she would root for Ben over Jeff, though it would give her great satisfaction to see Mr. Edwards come home with a victory.

"We'll watch for a minute," Sydney says. "Don't mind us."

But the players do appear to mind Julie and Sydney, or at least to pay them mind. Sydney registers a self-consciousness that wasn't there before: in Victoria's exaggerated moue of disappointment when she misses a shot; in a dramatic lifting backhand from Ben; even in a spectacular net smash by Jeff from which he walks away with unnatural indifference. For a moment, Sydney longs to be on the court with them, paired with Jeff, lost in the competition, the easy laughs, the sweat.

"Do you play?" Sydney asks Julie.

"I've had lessons."

"Would you like to play later?"

But each of them knows that to play later would be to invite a sense of afterthought. The only game that matters is the one happening now, and they are not a part of it.

"Had enough?" Sydney asks after a time.

"I guess so."

"Want to go out to the rocks?"

"Maybe."

They turn away from the court. Sydney notices two boys, perhaps seventeen or eighteen years old, walking in their direction. Deep in conversation, they carry golf bags on their shoulders. The taller of the two glances up. "Julie," he says with some surprise.

"Joe," Julie answers, dipping her head as she does so. She crosses her arms over her chest.

"I didn't know you were here," Joe says, hoisting his bag further up his shoulder. Dressed in a white golf shirt and a pair of khakis, the boy has thick brown hair that invites fingers, maternal or otherwise. "You know Nick, right?"

"I think so," Julie says. "This is Sydney," the girl adds, remembering her manners.

"Hello," Sydney says, nodding to the boys.

There is an awkward pause, during which no one speaks.

"Well," Joe says finally. "Maybe we'll see you around?"

"Maybe," Julie repeats, clearly at a loss for words.

Through the trees, Sydney hears a shout from Jeff.

"So . . . ," Joe says, apparently reluctant to move on.

"Good luck with the golf!" Sydney offers with some finality.

With a small wave, the boys pass by. Sydney doesn't have to turn around to know that Joe, the one with the lovely brown hair, has stopped to look at Julie from behind. After a minute, she lets Julie get a step ahead of her. Sydney studies the girl through the eyes of an eighteen-year-old boy.

Luscious is a word that comes to mind.

Ripe for the picking.

On the rocks, Sydney leads the way, though she is less sure of foot than Julie, who is more afraid than incapable.

"We'll sit on that one," Sydney says, pointing to a flat rock far enough out from shore for them to feel that they've accomplished something, but not so far as to feel the spray of the ocean.

Julie hesitates, and Sydney takes her hand. Together, they negotiate the jagged surfaces of the granite boulders, their feet sometimes slipping on bits of seaweed.

"There," Sydney says when they are settled.

The sky is aqua with fast-moving fair-weather clouds. A spray, majestic and rhythmic, beats against the least sheltered of the boulders. To the left is an abandoned lighthouse, the red roof of its keeper's cottage picturesque in the bold light. Sydney cannot imagine the isolation of such a life, the need to perform a single task over and over, its responsibilities grave. The desolation would drive her mad.

Offshore, a lobsterman, late to his traps, trawls near a set of rocks that will become more visible as the tide recedes. The smell of the sea and the clean air is potent, and Sydney inhales a lungful. Not far from them, a Sunday painter has set up shop with an easel. The tableau gives her an idea for Julie that she files away for Monday.

"Why are you so afraid of the water?" Sydney asks.

"I once almost drowned."

Sydney knows this fact but wants more. "How did that happen?"

Julie seems hesitant.

"I don't want to dredge up bad memories," Sydney says.

"No, that's okay." Julie takes a breath for courage. "My dad was fishing on the beach one day after a bad storm. The waves were huge." Julie, who has a habit of speaking with her hands, uses them to indicate the height of the waves. "My cousin, Samantha, had a boogie board, but she put it down because she was scared of the waves. I thought she had just left it for a minute and that I could grab it and use it."

"How old were you?"

"Seven. Samantha was nine, I think. I floated for a minute and then I could feel myself being pulled out to sea." Beside Sydney, Julie stiffens with the memory. "I tried to swim in, but I couldn't. I yelled for Dad. He looked over and saw me and dropped his fishing pole and dove in after me. When he got to the boogie board, he told me to hold on tight. But then he realized he couldn't get us back in—the riptide was too powerful for him—so he started yelling to Samantha, who was jumping up and down on the sand and screaming, to go get the lifeguard."

Sydney puts her arm around the girl. "You must have been really frightened," she says.

"I was. After a while, the lifeguard came with his surfboard and put me on top of it and told Dad to hang on to a rope he had off the back. He paddled us in."

"I'm sorry that happened to you."

Julie is silent.

"They say that in a riptide, you should swim parallel to shore so that you can break out of the rip."

"It doesn't matter," Julie says. "I'm never going in again anyway."

"When we get back to the house," Sydney says, "we'll put on our suits and go in up to our ankles. Just our ankles."

Julie, who has her arms wrapped around her knees, shakes her head. "I don't know," she says.

"That's all we'll do," Sydney insists, knowing that she is being pushy. But she has a plan. "Just our ankles. Unless you want to go out to your knees. I'll let you go to your knees, but no more than that."

"I don't think so. No offense."

"No offense," Sydney says.

———ɯɯ———

The breeze dies down, leaving the water docile. Sydney's tank suit is still damp from having been left on the floor of her closet. Last night, she couldn't get it off fast enough. Now she wishes she had thought to wash it. It seems to Sydney to reek of stealth. Of cunning.

Sydney has seen Julie in her aqua bikini several times on the deck. The suit, though skimpy, appeared appropriate there, full attire, Julie's bare skin glistening with a sunblock with a low SPF. Now at the water's edge, the bathing suit seems but pitiful armor against the Atlantic Ocean.

"Just the ankles," Sydney says.

*   *   *

Julie instinctively reaches for Sydney's hand. Sydney can feel the tug and pull of the girl's weight as Julie, even in the shallow water, adjusts to the undertow. She looks clumsy in her fear, though Sydney suspects she is a natural athlete—something in the ratio of the size of her feet to the length of her legs, in the strength of her shoulders.

"It's freezing," Julie says.

"You'll get used to it."

In the water, which today has taken on a slightly greenish tinge, there are bits of sea-weed that sometimes brush against the legs. Also in the water, Sydney knows, are striped bass, schools of bluefish, baby seals, and even benign sharks—a fact she thinks she will neglect to mention to the girl beside her.

Two young boys skim-board along the shoreline. They leap onto flat boards at the water's edge and ride them, sometimes for surprisingly long stretches. Sydney knows, from personal experience and the memory of a long, painful bruise, that it's not as easy as it looks.

"Want to go to the knees?" Sydney asks.

She expects Julie to demur, but the girl, in a moment of bravery, lets go of Sydney's hand and ventures farther out on her own. In a few steps, the knees are reached. When a wave comes, the water touches the tops of her thighs. Sydney watches Julie go rigid, and then relax as it recedes.

"How do you feel?" she asks when she is at Julie's side.

"GOOD!" Julie shouts, as if Sydney were a hundred feet away. "I'M OKAY."

"GREAT!"

"SHOULD WE GO OUT FURTHER?" Julie asks.

"NO. THIS IS FINE."

Julie and Sydney stand in the water, looking out to sea. Julie dips once into a wave and shoots up like a rocket, the water sloughing off her like booster debris. An ultralight passes overhead. Sydney cannot see the pilot, even though the machine is low to the ground. There was a time, not so long ago, when she'd have said to herself, *What a kick,* but those days are gone now. She has a momentary thought of her aviator. The sight of any flying machine, large or small, brings on thoughts of Andrew. (The day she met him at the Boston Marathon, which on a whim she had decided to enter. She stopped just at the point where he had veered off the track. He was bent at the waist, panting for breath. Sydney offered him her water bottle, and he staged a physical comeback right before her eyes, as if his sudden life's goal was to impress her.) Sydney suspects it will be this way all her life. She wonders what could possibly trigger reciprocal memories on Andrew's part. A psychology textbook? Hair that is no color anyone can describe?

Sydney's legs are so numb she's lost communication with her feet. "So, what do you think?" she asks Julie, whose attention is on a young woman in a wet suit surfing fifty feet away from them.

"She's good," Julie says.

"No, I mean about heading back."

"Oh," Julie says. "Sure." She watches the woman catch a wave. She puts her hands to her mouth like a megaphone. "GOOD ONE!" she shouts.

When Julie and Sydney turn to head for shore, which appears in the interval to have come to greet them, Sydney sees Jeff, still in tennis whites, standing at the water's edge. In his hand is an empty bottle of Poland Spring, which he waves in greeting.

Sydney remembers with dismay her sagging tank suit with its sprung legs, more visible now in the bright sunshine than it was the night before. Julie leaps out of the water to tell her brother her good news—a lifelong fear conquered. Well, almost conquered. Sydney watches as Jeff hugs his sister, allowing her to soak his shirtfront.

"Who won?" Sydney asks when she emerges from the water.

"They did," Jeff says. "Ben is something else."

"I hope it was fun."

Jeff's hair is darker now, pasted to his head with sweat. "Vicki's changing into her suit. We thought we'd go for a swim. How's the water?"

"Ice," Sydney says, wiping her hair from her forehead.

"Sounds good."

"I'll get some towels," Julie offers, running ahead. Sydney decides, watching her, *A child in a woman's body.*

*   *   *

"That's a great thing you just did," Jeff says. "No one's been able to get her to go near the water in years."

Sydney thinks to herself: *You can't have been trying very hard.*

"Were you there?" Sydney asks. "The day of the riptide?"

"It was awful." Jeff flips the empty plastic bottle between the second and third fingers of his right hand. "Did Julie tell you what she said to my father?"

"No."

"When my father reached her, Julie was holding on to the boogie board. She looked right at him and said—amazingly calmly, given the situation—*We're going to die, aren't we?*"

"Was your father frightened?"

"Yeah, I think he was. He was pretty sure he could get himself back to shore, but he was afraid Julie would let go of the board, and he'd lose her."

"Incredible."

"I remember when Julie and my dad came back to the house we were renting then, Julie walked straight up onto the porch and lay facedown on the floor. No one could get her to say a word. I'm not sure she's ever talked about it before now."

"For a seven-year-old to be convinced she's going to die . . . ," Sydney begins.

But Jeff is glancing up. Sydney follows his eyes. Victoria—polished, bikini-clad, and with perhaps the tiniest frown on her brow— is standing on the deck, gazing down at them.

Drinks on the porch. A lowering sun has turned the water mauve. A candle at the center of the teak table flickers in the breeze. It will almost certainly go out, Sydney thinks.

Sydney has a light beer, as does Mr. Edwards. Mrs. Edwards always drinks red wine, about which she appears to be quite knowledgeable. Jeff looks to be holding a glass of something stronger, a gin and tonic perhaps, while Victoria is fondling the stem of a glass of champagne. Sydney might have predicted the champagne.

Julie has a Coke. Ferris, the recovering alcoholic, a glass of plain water. Marissa, who has come with Ferris, the Pellegrino.

*   *   *

A strong smell of sea wafts from the shore. The tide is dead low, revealing a luxurious stretch of beach. The owners of the beach houses, Sydney decides, must have the sense of possessing more property at low tide than at high.

Sydney notes that Julie is more dressed up than usual, with a tank top under her skimpy sweater, the pale blue silk billowing over her breasts. Her jeans are long and tight. She and Victoria, beautiful women, represent two centers of gravity on the porch, the eyes unable to let them be, much to the visible annoyance of Marissa, a lanky but toned redhead whose investment in her looks is not paying off tonight. Marissa crosses and recrosses her pale legs, then slips off her own tiny sweater to reveal her buff physique. Ben pays attention, but his eyes drift to Victoria, and then, uncomfortably, to Sydney. She is underdressed for the party in a sleeveless white blouse and a pair of navy shorts. Avoiding eye contact with Ben is more difficult than she would have thought, even perched as she is on the stairs, there being an insufficient number of chairs for the thirteen celebrants of this spectacular August evening.

Sitting near a couple who have introduced themselves as Claire and Will, Sydney is asked expected questions. Where do you live? Do you tutor all year? What were you studying? She answers as best she can, but there are gaps in her history—years for which she doesn't want to answer just now—that gradually make the couple turn away. Will stands and offers to refill Sydney's glass. When she declines, Claire excuses herself and joins a gathering that consists of Mr. Edwards, Jeff, and Art. Sydney can hear the words *morning* and *fishfinder.*

Sydney is mildly confused by the lack of physicality between Jeff and Victoria. Have they known each other for so long they no longer need to touch in public? Or is Jeff self-conscious in the company of his parents and his parents' friends, a trait that Victoria—*Vicki*—might find just the tiniest bit unattractive? Certainly, they do not look like a couple about to announce an engagement, which must be something of a disappointment to Mrs. Edwards, who is unaccountably clad, given her fifty-nine-year-old upper arms, in a fuchsia chiffon tank top and black palazzo pants.

With a sense of foreboding, Sydney watches Ben stand and make the rounds with a bottle of red in one hand, a bottle of white in the other.

"You're drinking a beer," he says when he reaches her.

"I am," she answers, also stating the obvious.

"Ready for another?"

Sydney would like another drink but is reluctant to be beholden to Ben, even for something as innocuous as a glass of beer. "I'm fine," she says.

Ben sets the wine bottles on the teak table and takes a seat opposite Sydney on the step. He leans against the railing. Sydney is immediately aware of her bare legs, one crooked under the other, in a way she wasn't before.

She is aware, too, that Ben is studying her, and she minds the scrutiny. He has a fashionable stubble on his cheeks and chin, simply the result, Sydney guesses, of two days without a razor. At work, he would be clean-shaven.

"I'll bet you play a mean game of tennis," he says, eyeing her.

"Not as mean as yours," she says, staring at the top of her beer.

"I hear you got Julie in the water."

"I think she got herself in the water."

"You're too modest."

"Not really," she says, taking a sip.

"It must be hard to be at a party where you don't know anyone."

"I know Julie. I know your father," she says, and then immediately regrets her defensive tone.

"And that's enough?"

"For the time being."

"Two more weeks of the grind, and then freedom," Ben says.

Sydney wonders how she will negotiate Ben's vacation. "You don't have a girlfriend yourself?" she asks.

"No," he says, as if he understands exactly Sydney's wariness. "Not anymore."

*   *   *

Sydney is quite sure that if Ben and Jeff were presented in a lineup, seven out of ten women would prefer Ben to his brother. He has the stronger face, certainly the stronger body, dark eyes, and long lashes. A sense of confidence that teeters on arrogance but doesn't quite cross the line. There is, too, about Ben, a bit of mystery, an unreadable face, a quality many women would find intriguing.

"You play golf?" Ben asks.

"No."

"So what do you do on your days off?"

Is the question intended to remind Sydney that she is hired help? "Depends on the weather," she says.

"More of the same tomorrow," Ben predicts, gesturing to indicate the sky and the Atlantic and, possibly, the entire universe.

"Read," Sydney says. "Walk."

"We might all go into Portsmouth," Ben says casually.

"Sounds like fun," Sydney says, though she is hard-pressed to think of what can be happening in Portsmouth on a Sunday.

"Want to come with us?"

"Thanks, but I have to go in on Monday anyway. No point going in twice in a row."

Ben smiles at her. Sydney remembers her father saying, years ago, *Somebody's always got your number.*

Sydney stands.

"Where are you going?" Ben asks.

"To get another beer," she announces, desperate to get away.

In the kitchen, she presses her head to the stainless steel door of the Sub-Zero.

"Are you okay?"

The question is not an entirely sympathetic one, suggesting that this is not an opportune moment to be indisposed. Mrs. Edwards sets an empty plate on the granite island.

"I'm fine," Sydney says, turning.

"Would you mind giving me a hand?" Mrs. Edwards asks.

"I'd be glad to," she answers.

—⁓—

Sydney is seated at a part of the oval table that can only be described as nonexistent.

She has a chair, in which she is trapped, and space enough for a plate, but not enough for silverware, which has been set near her water glass. She eats with her arms pressed to her sides so as not to bother Mrs. Edwards to her right or Ferris to her left. There might as well have been a children's table, Sydney thinks, and then wonders if, possibly, she is not meant to be at the dinner. No, she decides, Mr. Edwards would never allow her absence.

"Washington and Tehran have crucial interests in common," Jeff is saying, "but for historical and ideological reasons, neither wants to be seen dealing with the other."

"Bush has made no secret of his intention to help liberate the Iraqis from Saddam," Art offers.

"An objective that was part of the late Ayatollah Khomeini's primary agenda," Jeff points out.

Mr. and Mrs. Edwards once again anchor the table. Claire and Will, generationally cast adrift (they are not as old as Mrs. Edwards; not as young as Ben), present a united front, even managing to pull their chairs together, upsetting Mrs. Edwards's seating plan, which almost immediately has to be abandoned. Marissa, imagined slights forgotten, seems mesmerized by Wendy's inside scoop of the New York magazine world. Sydney sees a fast friendship beginning, though it is not clear yet what Marissa has to offer Wendy apart from riveted attention. Marissa's husband, Ferris, has the studied reticence of a recovering alcoholic surrounded by alcohol. Victoria is speaking somewhat louder than necessary and is having trouble with the word *decision*. Before her sits a nearly empty champagne bottle from which only she has been drinking, Mr. Edwards—ever the genial host—pouring liberally. Sydney is fascinated by the way alcohol blurs the features as well as the consonants. Victoria's mouth has relaxed considerably, and the whites of her eyes have grown pinkish. Even the skin *under* her eyes has loosened. In a subtle though somewhat devastating transformation, Victoria can no longer be said to be the most beautiful woman at the table.

"You've heard about Princeton and Yale," Ben is saying.

"Princeton's scandal, really," Jeff says.

"No, what?" Art asks.

"Princeton was caught breaking into Yale's admissions files," Ben announces with some glee.

Perhaps the man did not get into Princeton, Sydney thinks.

"I thought they said they didn't use the information," Mr. Edwards says.

"Dad, they broke into the Yale computer fourteen times over a three-day period."

"Heads will roll," Art pronounces.

The dinner party cannot be said to be entirely successful. The lamb is underdone. Wendy and Art bicker publicly, Wendy annoyed at being drawn away from her conversation with Marissa by Art's constant queries. *When is that screening we're going to? I already told you, the twentieth. Honey? What?* Ben is quiet, and Jeff casts worried glances in Victoria's direction. Mrs. Edwards, her attention on the dessert, does not ask where Julie is going or when she will be home when the girl rises with a quick good-bye—a lapse of parental attention Sydney finds unnerving. It is all she can do to stop herself from jumping up and following Julie into the kitchen. And jumping up is what she'd have to do, because Julie is almost instantly out the door. The girl doesn't drive. Is she walking? Or is a car waiting for her on the road by prearrangement? And when exactly was this getaway prearranged? After Julie's jubilant foray into the water? By phone? Initiated by the boy with the lovely brown hair or by Julie herself?

Sydney feels the responsibility of a parent. Mr. Edwards, locked in at the far end of the table, appears not even to have seen Julie's departure.

Eleven o'clock, Sydney decides. She will not start worrying until eleven o'clock.

—⁊⁊⁊—

"The Acela's been shut down," Ferris ventures in one of his few contributions to the dinner conversation. Perhaps he has been saving it up all evening.

"You're kidding," Art says.

"Cracks in the shock absorbers."

This has the makings of a major crisis. How will Art and Wendy get home? Even Sydney knows that the plan is for them to

take the bus to Boston on Monday morning,
the Acela, the high-speed train, to Manhattan later that afternoon. Mrs. Edwards looks
momentarily stricken.

The dirty dishes are monstrous. Jeff comes
in to help, and no one shoos him away.
"Dad, I'll take over," he says, putting a hand
on his father's shoulder. Mr. Edwards appears exhausted, a sail collapsing in a dearth
of wind.

   Jeff rolls the sleeves of his blue oxford
shirt. For a moment, Sydney studies his
wrists.

The dishes are dotted with pink globules
of fat, reminding Sydney of Mrs. Edwards's
hardening arteries. Plates of cake reveal
varying appetites for a confection she knows
was a trick, a cake mix doctored with Miracle Whip, instant vanilla pudding, and orange juice to make it look and taste homemade. Sydney has seen the recipes in Mrs.
Edwards's cookbook, the bizarre ingre-
dients listed there: lemon Jell-O, chopped
Snickers bars, condensed tomato soup. It is
Sydney's considered opinion, having had
four bites of her piece of cake, that neither

the Miracle Whip nor the instant pudding successfully masked the store-bought chemical aftertaste.

Sydney develops an inconvenient revulsion to the leavings of the guests. Is this dirty fork one that Will had in his mouth? Is this Victoria's lipstick? Jeff works as if he's done considerable time in a restaurant kitchen. His organizational skills rival Sydney's, or perhaps she is a little drunk herself and it only seems that way. Dozens of glasses are smeared with lip and fingerprints, a forensic fantasy if only a crime had been committed.

"Where's Vicki?" Sydney asks.

"Upstairs. Lying down."

"Is she okay?"

"Works hard, plays hard."

"Good plan," Sydney says, slightly embarrassed for having called attention to Victoria's altered state. For having even mentioned Vicki's name.

"You don't like her, do you?" Jeff says.

Sydney is startled by the abruptness of the question. Also by its accuracy.

"I *do*," she protests.

But the *do* is damning, suggesting an un-negotiable flaw.

The space between the sink and the island is narrow, and a kind of dance needs to be choreographed so that no part of Sydney's body touches Jeff's. She is not aware of needing to perform such a dance when Mr. Edwards does the dishes.

Claire and Will linger an unconscionable amount of time after dinner is over, a puzzle given that the couple seem to want only to be together. To do what? Sydney wonders. Talk? Unwind? Have sex? Watch *Sports-Center*? The fact that they have so little to say to others fascinates Sydney, their offerings distinctly minimalist.

"Lunch counter gone this year."
"Noticed that."
"You kayak?"
"No, you?"

Ben and Jeff and Sydney sit on the porch with the Edwardses, both of whom need their bed. Mrs. Edwards tosses subtle hints into the ocean air.

"Mark, you'll have to get up early for the paper. They go fast on Sundays."

Sydney's contributions to the conversation are nonexistent, her mind preoccupied with Julie. Only Jeff seems visibly to share her worry, occasionally glancing at his watch and once leaning over to her. "Did Julie say where she was going?" he asks.

"No," Sydney says, "she didn't."

At twenty minutes to eleven, Claire puts a hand on Will's knee, a sign everyone chooses to interpret as a wife's signal to her husband that it's time to leave. All present stand in unison, Mr. Edwards already unleashing a salvo of hearty good-byes. *So glad you could come.* Mutual boating trips are promised but without the requisite dates and times, all but guaranteeing the imagined journeys will not actually take place.

"They weren't *my* idea," Mrs. Edwards says in the kitchen, snapping off her clip earrings and setting them hard on the granite counter.

"He seemed a nice enough fellow," Mr.

Edwards says, fetching a glass of water to take upstairs.

"Nice enough where? On the golf course?"

"He had quite a lot to say about old maps."

Mrs. Edwards unfastens her banana clip. Sydney notes that not a single hair falls to her neck.

Mr. and Mrs. Edwards climb the stairs, Mr. Edwards hanging on to the banister as he does so. It is understood that the remainder of the dishes—the after-dinner glasses, the coffee cups with the dark rings—will be left until the morning, when the first one up will empty the dishwasher and dispatch the detritus of the party. Sydney wanders to the kitchen window and looks out.

"You're worried about Julie," Jeff says behind her.

Sydney turns, smoothing her hair behind her ears. "I am. What time is it now?"

"Ten of eleven." He answers quickly, a man who has recently consulted his watch.

"I so wish I'd asked her where she was going."

"You want to take a ride with me?" Jeff asks, tension in his eyes, on his brow.

"Sure," Sydney says with some relief. "It's better than waiting here."

"I'll just tell Ben we're going. He can call us if she comes in."

A fair-weather mist, so fine as to be barely detectable, surrounds Sydney's face. In the distance, there are fireworks. There are always fireworks, Sydney has noticed, each township possessive about its displays. Sometimes at night, observing from an upper-story bedroom, Sydney can see small explosions, like bursts of artillery fire, all along the horizon.

The Land Rover bumps along the beach road to the village. The streetlights provide only small cones of visibility. Houses loom in the darkness, one or two still with lighted windows. Sydney turns away from the houses and looks at Jeff behind the wheel of the Land Rover.

"Where are we going?" Sydney asks.

"I know some places," Jeff says, his answer hinting at years of clandestine sex and drinking as a teenager. It must have been, Sydney decides, a glorious adolescence.

*   *   *

Jeff parks at the end of a lane similar to the one on which the tennis court was located. He leads Sydney to a small beach she did not know existed. She has a sense of trespassing. Away from the sea breezes, the mosquitoes are ferocious. Jeff calls his sister's name softly, as if not wishing to disturb any lovers who might also be on the beach. He does not receive a reply. The beach is only fifty feet across, and once Sydney's eyes adjust, she can see that there is nothing on it but clumps of dried seaweed.

The car travels slowly down another quiet street. Sydney can hear a fan from an open window. Jeff, both hands on the wheel, is bent slightly forward. Sydney has her arms crossed over her chest.

"There doesn't seem to be much happening here," she says. "What are we looking for?"

"A party," Jeff says tightly.

Sydney's mild fear seems to have morphed into something like full-blown panic in Jeff, the way a virus will jump to a new host and mutate into a stronger and more lethal strain.

*   *   *

Sydney peers into the lighted windows of the cottages, hoping for a glimpse of Julie, and is intrigued to see how people live their lives on vacation on the coast of New Hampshire. The lack of blue flickering TV screens is heartening, as are the surprising number of round tables with playing cards on them.

"Are you sure she didn't mention any plans?" Jeff says.

"Earlier, we met two boys. Joe and Nick. They were headed to play golf and stopped to say hello to Julie. One of the boys, Joe, seemed interested in her and even mentioned getting together sometime."

"Why didn't you tell me this earlier?" Jeff asks.

Sydney feels the slight sting of having been scolded. "Do the names mean anything to you?" she asks.

Jeff narrows his eyes. "No. Did you catch a last name?"

Sydney shakes her head. "She could be at a friend's house. A girlfriend."

"Are you aware of any friends Julie has?"

"No."

Another car approaches them, and both Sydney and Jeff stare at the passengers.

"She's such a sweet girl," Sydney says.

"That's what's worrying me."

"I'm not sure she's been out at night by herself the whole time I've been here," Sydney points out.

"We haven't had to deal with this much. I don't know if she's even had the curfew discussion yet. Or the cell-phone discussion."

Sydney wonders, but does not ask, about the never-have-unprotected-sex discussion.

"I'm sure she's fine," she says instead.

They drive to a spot near a lighthouse that Jeff knows about. They do not speak much, in the way of people who are preoccupied. They drive along an uneven road that leads to acres of scrub brush. They stop at a parking lot in the middle of the long crescent beach on which the Edwardses' house is located. They walk a few hundred yards along the sand in opposite directions. They meet back at the car.

"This is stupid," Jeff says. He checks his cell phone again to make sure he didn't receive a call.

"Julie and I went somewhere this afternoon that she might have returned to," Sydney says, thinking.

"Where?"

"The rocks at the end of the beach."

"You're kidding," he says, putting the cell phone in his pocket.

Sydney is silent.

"Jesus, Sydney." The gravel lot is dark, and she can't make out his face.

"But no one would go there at night," Sydney adds quickly.

Yet each of them knows that Julie might be pleased to suggest to a boy a destination of her own making. And each of them understands as well that, having been invited, few would decline to follow her.

"Watch your footing," Jeff advises. He holds the flashlight straight down so that Sydney can see where his feet are and put hers in his footsteps. Though she cannot see the surf, she can hear it.

Jeff yells, *Julie!* again and again, but each time, the name is blown back at him. The rocks are slippery underfoot. Sydney resists the impulse to lower herself to a crouch.

*   *   *

Sydney thinks about the way Julie tugged at her hand earlier in the day. "I don't believe she's here," she says to Jeff.

She loses her footing on a slippery bit of seaweed. Jeff reaches out a quick hand, and Sydney grabs it.

"Watch it," he says.

"Thanks."

"This is nuts. We should head back."

But for a number of seconds, perhaps even seven or eight, Jeff continues to hold Sydney's hand. Neither of them turns to the other. Neither of them moves.

His fingers barely clasp hers.

The touch is not a promise, and it is certainly not a pass. It is—indeed, if it is anything at all—the merest suggestion of a possibility.

Jeff's fingers are distinctly palpable. Insistently *there.*

A computerized tune erupts from Jeff's pocket. He lets go of Sydney's hand and opens his cell phone. The voice on the other end is so loud that even she can hear it.

"You'd better get back here," Ben is saying.

Julie sits on one of the two white sofas, her hand poised on its arm, her body pointed in the direction of the bathroom, which, it would appear, she has already visited, to judge from the spill of what can only be vomit on her tank top. But it is not that detail that briefly causes Sydney to shut her eyes with a mixture of heartache and dread. She wonders if anyone else has noticed the small tear at the place where the pale blue strap meets the neckline. Three, four, five tiny stitches have been ripped apart.

Ben, hands in pockets, is pacing. "Someone dropped her off, and she came in like this."

"Who dropped her off?" Jeff wants to know.

"She won't say. She *can't* say."

*   *   *

Sydney sits down beside Julie, but something in the motion upsets Julie's fragile physical equilibrium. The girl puts a hand to her mouth and concentrates.

"Julie," Sydney says softly, bending toward the girl.

Julie shakes her head once quickly, and Sydney withdraws.

"She can't drink," Ben says. "She just can't."

"Has this ever happened before?" Jeff asks.

"I don't know, but look at her."

"We're sure this is alcohol?"

Ben rolls his eyes. Sydney can smell the drink. She nods in Jeff's direction.

He puts a hand to his head. "I'll kill the son of a bitch."

"We don't even know who the son of a bitch is," Ben points out.

Sydney does not mention, and may not ever mention, the tiny stitches that have come apart.

"Julie," she says, "let me take you up."

For a moment, Julie ponders this idea.

Sydney helps her to her feet. But that simple motion trips the wire, and Julie sprints for the hallway bathroom, the one with the remarkable acoustics.

In the living room, Sydney and the brothers listen and say nothing. Ben stands in front of a window, looking out to an ocean he cannot see. His brow is tense with concentration, as if he could, by vigorous thinking, conjure up a name. Jeff, perched at the edge of a chair, is bent forward, hands clasped behind his neck. His head snaps up.

"Ben, the name Joe or Nick mean anything to you? Boys Julie's age?"

Ben turns. His eyes dart from side to side as he thinks first of one boy and then of another to whom he may have given sailing lessons, young men he may have seen on the golf course. "There was a guy—Jared something, Jared . . . but he'd be in his midtwenties now."

Julie emerges from the bathroom. Sydney stands and touches her on her bare arm. Her skin is cold and moist. Sydney hopes Julie has rid herself of most of the alcohol. She is still unsteady on her feet, and Sydney has to link arms. Julie breathes through her mouth. Her hair is matted against her scalp.

"I'm taking her up," Sydney tells the brothers.

Julie and Sydney negotiate first the stairs and then the landing. Sydney has the distinct sense that Julie doesn't know where she is, that if Sydney were to let go of her arm, Julie would simply crumple to the floor.

The girl is worse off than Sydney thought. Perhaps putting Julie to bed is not the best idea. Sydney has read the stories in the newspapers of frat boys dying in their sleep, having overdosed on shots and beer. Letting a friend "sleep it off" now akin to negligent homicide.

Julie, boneless, flops onto the bed. She lands in an awkward position, and Sydney straightens her limbs. There's no need to remove any of her clothing.

"Julie," Sydney says, not so gently now.

Julie opens her eyes.

"Where did you go?"

Her eyes swim. "A parry," she says with great effort.

"Whose party? Who took you there?"

But Sydney has asked one question too many. Julie shakes her head.

"Do you know where the party was?" Sydney asks.

Julie makes a motion that is almost a shrug.

"Did you walk to the party?"

Sydney can see the girl searching her memory, as if Sydney had asked her what she wore for Halloween when she was ten.

"Whose car did you go in?"

Julie shakes her head again.

"Nick? Joe?" Sydney asks, but Julie closes her eyes.

Sydney slides the thin coverlet out from under the girl's nearly dead weight and lays it over her. She smooths her brow. Julie's skin is cold and clammy. Though Sydney herself has been drunk enough on occasion to be unable to keep the room from spinning, she has never been in this position before—neither as the caretaker nor as the person passed out.

The only light is from the hallway. In one murky corner of Julie's room is a short shelf of stuffed animals, all without color in the dark. On an old-fashioned dressing table covered with a lace cloth are bits of jewelry, a bottle of contact lens solution, a hairbrush, a CD case, and several hair ties. On the floor are two pieces of cloth Sydney knows to be the aqua bikini. The sight of the discarded bathing suit, worn with such pride earlier in the day, causes a clench in Sydney's chest.

Through an open window, Sydney can hear the ocean. Two houses down from the Edwardses is a renovated cottage. The woman who owns it demanded that the builders install triple-paned glass so that she wouldn't have to listen to the surf.

Why come to the shore if not for the crashing of the waves?

Beside her, Julie stirs.

"Julie?" Sydney calls.

But the girl only murmurs and then sinks again into sleep.

After she has roused Julie several times, it becomes apparent to Sydney that she will need a cup of coffee if she is to maintain her vigil. When she is satisfied that Julie can be woken a fifth time, she leaves the room and descends the stairs. Ben is nowhere to be seen, but, surprisingly, Jeff is still sitting in the living room.

"How is she?" he asks when Sydney has reached the bottom step. He looks pale and tired.

"Asleep, but I'm waking her every half hour just in case."

No need to say why. Jeff, too, reads the papers.

"Where's Ben?"

"He's dozing. He said to wake him when we need a break."

"Actually, I think I'd like some coffee," Sydney says.

"You sit. I'll make it."

Sydney settles herself on the bottom step and watches Jeff fill the pot with water and pour it into the coffee machine. When he has finished the task, he leans against the counter, hands in pockets. In the background is the unmistakable swish and gurgle of coffee being brewed.

"She tell you anything?" he asks.

"She went to a party. She either doesn't

know or isn't saying the name of the person who took her. It's hard to tell what she knows and doesn't know."

"Not Nick or Joe?"

"Apparently not."

"You'll keep an eye on her?" Jeff asks. "I have to leave tomorrow. Maybe I should have a talk with my mother."

This strikes Sydney as a bad idea. "I think Julie is the one you should be talking to," she suggests.

"She's so innocent," he says, shaking his head slowly.

"Yes, she is."

Very few eighteen-year-olds, Sydney believes, can be considered *innocent,* but Julie comes as close to that description as anyone Sydney can remember meeting or reading about. Sydney briefly wonders at the correlation between intelligence and guilt.

The coffee machine makes its unique hiss and rumble, signaling the end of the brewing process. Jeff fills a mug and hands it to Sydney.

"Thank you."

"I'll come up in half an hour and spell you.

Let you get some sleep. If we need him, I'll wake Ben." He pauses. "Listen," he says, "I was wrong before."

The surface of Sydney's skin is instantly hot. She is certain Jeff is about to mention the incident on the rocks.

"I shouldn't have asked you to keep an eye on her," he says. "Julie's not your responsibility."

Sydney is a beat late in responding. "Well, yes, she is."

"You're certainly not her keeper."

He means, Sydney thinks, *You are not family.*

"And I don't know if my mother or father said this to you," he adds, "but you should feel free to invite anyone here you'd like. A friend."

The word trails off and lingers in the room. Sydney wants to explain to Jeff what happens to women who are once divorced and once widowed. The friends Sydney had with the aviator belonged more or less to the aviator, and when the marriage dissolved, they tended to stay with him, like spoils that had been divided. The friends Sydney had with Daniel contact her from time to time, but their calls and visits are invariably sad and quiet, and she believes none of them is eager to repeat the experience. Sydney has friends from school—Becky, who lives in New York City now, and Emily in Boston—but she cannot imagine either of them driving to New Hampshire to share her small room with the narrow beds, eating dinners with the Edwardses.

"Maybe I'll do that," Sydney says.

Jeff holds her eyes a second longer than necessary—or perhaps it is Sydney who holds his eyes a second longer than necessary; or possibly this second is entirely necessary to communicate the fact that though Sydney is not family, she is not to think of herself as separate—but there is no mention of the touch of fingers on the rocks. It occurs to Sydney that not having been with a man in over two years, she may have forgotten the relevant signs.

———⟨⟨⟨———

In the morning, Julie seems no more knowledgeable about the geography of the evening before than when she was drunk. After a long sleep, she makes an appearance in the kitchen, but only for Advil. Julie's headache is so ferocious, Sydney begins to think she has one herself.

Excuses are made. "Julie isn't feeling well. She came down and then went back up." This Sydney says to Mr. Edwards, minding a lie to a man who probably would not lie to her. Indeed, she wants to confide in Julie's father, ask his advice, but this is not the plan Jeff and Ben and she decided upon at six a.m. over oatmeal, a plan that is not Sydney's to dismantle.

It was an odd threesome, each of them exhausted, each of them wondering if perhaps they had made more of the incident than was warranted; or if the reverse was true: they hadn't taken it seriously enough by not alerting either of the parents. Sydney felt like a junior officer who had been on deck all night. The oatmeal tasted like paste, but then again, she thought, it often tasted like paste. There seemed to be among the three of them an unspoken agreement that if Julie had survived the night, she was in the clear. Someone later in the day would have to take Julie aside and have the curfew discussion, the cell-phone talk, and the speech about surrendering names and places. The perils of drink might be discussed, a prohibition issued. Perhaps someone should mention what can happen to girls who drink too much in the presence of boys, how boys can take advantage of girls in ways that can be emotionally and physically dangerous. Perhaps that someone will be Sydney.

After Mr. Edwards leaves the house in search of the Sunday papers, Victoria, pink and healthy, appears in the kitchen. Sydney wonders what brilliant tonic the woman takes to produce a glow that seems to have erased the night before, even to call into question one's perception of it.

Victoria is wearing a yellow sundress, and for a moment Sydney imagines she has rallied in order to attend church. Instead, Victoria rummages through the fridge and the cabinets and puts together an appetizing breakfast of fruit-filled French toast made

with brioche left over from the morning before. She sets the table as for an event, with
the ivory china and etched glass. She pours
syrup into an antique pitcher and uses a
linen napkin. Sydney has the sense that Victoria is trying to re-create the feel of a bed-
and-breakfast meal.

Sydney takes her coffee to the round
kitchen table. "That looks good," she says.
　"Want some?"
　"No, I just ate."
　Victoria's eyebrows have been plucked
nearly straight across. She wears topaz earrings that match her eyes. Her hair is wet
from the shower, drying into soft waves as
she eats. She is a naturally wealthy woman,
someone upon whom nature has bestowed
a great many gifts: the clear skin, the luxurious hair, the perfect teeth (though one
imagines she has had some help with
those), the slender body, the utterly charming smile.
　"I'd wait for Jeff," Victoria says, making a
small apology, "but he's beat. He says he
was up half the night talking to Ben. I'm so
glad, because even though they both live in
Boston—well, technically Cambridge and

Boston—they hardly ever see each other. This place is gorgeous," she adds with what appears to be true reverence for the Atlantic, demonstrating its best today through the open doors. "I've been coming here for years, but I always think it."

"You've been lucky with the weather this weekend," Sydney says. But Sydney is not thinking about the weather. Instead, she is mulling over the astonishing fact that Jeff did not tell his girlfriend about the search for Julie, the vigil during the night. Sydney wonders why he felt the omission necessary.

"You'll be here for how long?" Victoria asks. "I'm not sure anybody's said."

"Till the end of the month. Possibly I'll stay after Labor Day. I'm supposed to be preparing Julie for her SATs in October, so I suppose I might have to visit her at home when she goes back to school."

Sydney is making this up as she goes along. In fact, no one has yet discussed how long Sydney is to stay, whether or not she is to travel to Needham.

"The family never stays after Labor Day," Victoria says knowingly. "Never."

*   *   *

Sydney lets the advisory sink in.

"Jeff works so hard, he needs his rest," Victoria says in an apparent non sequitur. Or perhaps it is not. Possibly Victoria thinks about Jeff all the time, even when she seems not to be. "I'll let him sleep until eleven, and then I'll wake him. I think we're going to Portsmouth for lunch." Victoria glances sideways at Sydney, not sure if she ought to have mentioned an excursion to someone who might not have been invited. "Anna's jogging," Victoria says in what is or is not another non sequitur.

Sydney thinks about the prospect of Anna Edwards jogging.

"Your job must be very satisfying," Sydney says, cupping her hands around her mug. She is, in Victoria's presence, acutely aware that she has not showered or brushed her teeth, a fact that, curiously, did not bother her at breakfast with Ben and Jeff. She watches as Victoria cuts her French toast with her fork, scraping it against the ivory plate. A spill of warm berries emerges from the brioche, and Sydney wishes she had accepted Victoria's offer.

"Well," Victoria says, "it's like anything else. There are frustrations and successes. I'm better at it than I used to be."

"What do you do exactly?"

"I coordinate fund-raisers."

Yes, Sydney can see this—Victoria organizing black-tie events at the .406 Club at Fenway, all in aid of children with leukemia. She is, Sydney decides, despite her suspect beauty, entirely worthy of Jeff. Victoria lets him sleep, she is not extravagant, she does good works, she can cook.

"I never know who will be here," Victoria says, spearing a strawberry. Sydney wonders if she should take this as a small affront.

"What's in Portsmouth on a Sunday?" Sydney asks.

Victoria blinks but makes a near-perfect recovery. "A wonderful clam bar," she says. "I think you'll love it."

———∿∿∿———

Sydney wants only to sleep. She doesn't want to interact with Jeff or Ben or Mrs. Edwards or even Julie. She senses a certain degree of seepage—of overinvolvement on her part, of the family getting under her skin—that makes her uncomfortable. She wishes herself away, alone.

She sleeps until four o'clock. She lies in bed for a few moments longer, listening to the farewells in the front hallway. Ben and Jeff and Victoria are leaving for Boston. There are instructions about what to bring when they come in two weeks, mention of up-coming social events (presumably adjust-ments in wardrobes may be necessary), promises to hurry back. Sydney hears the screen door slap shut after them.

Immediately, the house deflates, Mr. and Mrs. Edwards retreating without a word to different rooms. Wendy and Art will find a cool reception when they return from wher-ever they have gone—Appledore? Ports-mouth?—and perhaps not even a meal waiting for them. Exhaustion coupled with a sense of having discharged all social obliga-tions may make for a prickly evening with the hosts. Do these hosts, Sydney wonders, have any idea yet about what may or may not have happened to their only daughter the evening before?

Sydney descends the stairs warily, not wishing to encounter anyone more evolved than Tullus. Too much has happened in too short a time: Julie's drunken episode; searching for the girl with Jeff; having to negotiate her way around both Ben and Victoria. Hungry, Sydney needs a piece of cheese, a handful of nuts, but making a meal seems unnecessarily formal, an insistence upon ritual when clearly ritual should be dispensed with.

The light through the kitchen window is sharp and orange and beckons her outside. She thinks about how to get from the kitchen, at the back of the house, to the beach, at the front, without running into anyone from the Edwards family. She chooses the bold move, walking barefoot straight through the house, ready with a greeting on the fly if needed. But Sydney is in luck. No one is in the hallway or the living room or even on the porch on this fine evening. She imagines Anna Edwards flat on her back in bed, a cold washcloth on her forehead. She pictures Mark Edwards on his knees in his rose garden, pulling out the weeds that have dared to attempt a coup while he was otherwise engaged. She imagines Julie, curled into a fetal position on her bed, alternately dozing and then waking, bewildered when she does, trying to make sense of the images, few of them welcome, that float across her vision.

Having executed a decorous escape, Sydney walks briskly away from the house. The light on the ocean has turned the water aqua, and Sydney feels an urge she often has to capture it. She knows from past experience that a photograph will not do. It may later trigger a recollection, but the reality of the moment—the feel of the breeze on the skin under her ears, the blue dust on the horizon—will last only seconds and then disappear.

Sydney walks fast, trying to put considerable distance between herself and the house at the end of the beach. The exercise is good, and her calf muscles tingle. She breaks into a jog. She is not a runner by nature, preferring the brisk stroll with its opportunity to observe to the run, which focuses attention on the body, but the urge to run is unexpectedly overwhelming.

She reaches the end of the beach, a distance of two miles, and slows down. She collapses into a cross-legged sitting position on the sand. The sun is setting noticeably earlier than it did in July, and already there is a suggestion of dusk. Below these observations, Sydney is aware of half-thoughts of Jeff. Despite her unusual marital history, she has never been unfaithful to any man, nor has she ever been in a relationship in which a man was unfaithful to his wife or his girlfriend. She cannot claim any great virtue in this; it is, she believes, simply a matter of circumstances. But to have inklings of desire for a man who is all but engaged to a woman Sydney has met is surely reason enough to have run from the house at the other end of the beach as if it were a burning building.

The concavities of bones. The tanned calf. Sydney remembers, at the dinner table, Jeff's sense of being elsewhere, a place she wanted to visit. She thinks about the panic that connected them as they ran through the streets of the village in search of Julie, who may have been in trouble—a sister he loves, a girl Sydney finds winning. And she remembers that actual connection, a brief but distinct touch of fingers, a gesture so seemingly casual as to be nearly nonexistent. Nonexistent, but incendiary. Sydney stands, knowing she must return to the house she has so recently fled—she has no flashlight; she needs water—wondering if Jeff is at this moment thinking of her. She decides that he is not. Sitting in the backseat of the Land Rover, with Victoria just a bit forward and to his right in the passenger seat, Jeff will be studying her profile as she talks to Ben.

This traffic is terrible, Victoria will be saying. *I have to get up at five.*

—⚏—

When Sydney returns to the house, she walks directly to the garden. Mr. Edwards is bent over, deadheading the roses. So intent is he on his task, he doesn't notice her presence until she speaks.

"Hey," she says.

Startled, he snaps up too quickly, putting a hand to his back. He has on an old flannel shirt, a pair of khakis stained at the knees. "Hi there," he says.

The roses are magnificent. They are rust-colored and lavender and mauve and ivory. No common scarlet or boisterous yellow. Though she has often seen both Julie and Mr. Edwards working in the garden, she has never been this close to it. At its center is a stone bench.

"These are beautiful," Sydney says, bending to inhale the perfume of a faintly salmon bloom.

"Thank you. They get away from me sometimes."

"I've seen Julie working out here, too."

"She seems to enjoy it."

Sydney can see that Mr. Edwards knows she has come to talk, that she is not merely passing by on her way into the house. He waits patiently, clippers in hand.

"Actually," she says, fingering another bloom, "I'm a little worried about Julie."

"How so?" he asks, his face immediately serious.

"Could we talk a minute?"

"Sure," Mr. Edwards says, gesturing to the stone bench.

Sydney sits at one end. Mr. Edwards takes the other. His hands are dirty, his fingernails caked with mud.

"I'd like to speak freely without getting anyone in trouble."

Mr. Edwards nods slowly, watching her face.

"You may not know this, but Julie went out last night. She slipped away from the table before any of us could ask her where she was going. Around ten-forty-five, Jeff and I went to look for her. We couldn't find her, but she came home on her own close to midnight." Sydney pauses. "She was drunk. Very drunk." She pauses again. "Dangerously drunk, I would have to say."

Mr. Edwards closes his eyes.

"She wouldn't—or couldn't—say where she had been," Sydney adds. "She was sick to her stomach, and I think got rid of most of the alcohol. But she was in bad shape. Jeff and Ben and I took turns staying up with her."

Mr. Edwards lets out a long sigh.

"I'm not telling you this so that Julie will

get into trouble. I don't want that at all. But I think someone needs to talk to her about letting us . . . *you* . . . know where she is going."

"Yes."

"I know that she's . . ."

"Yes, you had every right to be very worried. All summer she's more or less kept to herself. I felt your coming here was a gift, really. I've liked it very much that she had someone to be with. It's clear she adores you."

"Well, I, too . . ."

"But she's had very little experience with the way the world works. I honestly didn't think we were going to have to worry about this yet, but I've been an idiot. She's eighteen. You only have to look at her."

Sydney opens her palms. "I worry because she seems like someone who might be taken advantage of," she says slowly.

"I'll talk to her," he says.

Sydney notes that he does not say, *I'll have Anna talk to her.*

"She may not remember anything," Sydney says. "Or much of anything."

"She's a good girl," says Mr. Edwards, a

man suddenly struggling to control his emotions.

"Oh, she is," Sydney says quickly.

There is a long silence, during which neither of them looks at the other. Sydney puts her hands in her lap and studies the roses. Mr. Edwards appears to be examining the scrub brush that borders the property. To stand up and leave this man seems wrong. Sitting with him, however, is excruciating.

"The roses are really beautiful," Sydney says after a time, her voice sounding thin.

"Do you think so?"

"I do, yes."

"The thing about roses," Mr. Edwards begins but then seems to forget what he was going to say. "The thing about roses . . ."

"Actually," Sydney says, "I was thinking of taking Julie into Portsmouth with me tomorrow to get some art supplies."

Mr. Edwards glances at Sydney, a question in his eyes.

She clears her throat. "I have an idea for her. She's very gifted at . . . for lack of a better word . . . composition. I thought I might get her some drawing pencils, maybe some paints. I won't let it interfere with the tutoring. I'll just—"

But Mr. Edwards waves his hand, as if to suggest that she not worry about the tutoring.

"I think she may have some talent in this direction," Sydney adds. "From what I hear, I guess she comes by it naturally."

Mr. Edwards nods once and smiles, but his eyes, Sydney can see, are elsewhere. He is thinking still about what he will have to say to his daughter. She does not envy him this task.

"We have no idea where she was?" he asks.

"No. She went to a party. That's all I could get out of her."

Mr. Edwards inhales a long breath. He looks noticeably older than he did the night before, and it is not simply the work clothes, the hunched spine, the dirty hands.

"I'm sure she'll be fine," Sydney adds, unable to refrain from delivering this platitude. She wants suddenly for this man not to have to worry about his daughter.

Sydney stands. While they have been talking, dusk has turned into evening. A mosquito bites her ankle. She hears tree frogs, the constant surf. In the house, a light goes on. "Well," she says, "I'd better be getting in."

Mr. Edwards stands as well, making a conscious effort to straighten his spine. "Thank you, Sydney," he says. "I appreciate your coming to me."

His formality is disturbing.

Sydney turns away. When she enters the house and glances back, she sees that Mr. Edwards has not moved away from the bench.

—⚬⚬⚬—

Mrs. Edwards, in her bathrobe, is stretched along one of the white sofas. She smiles perfunctorily when she sees Sydney. Sydney can hear Wendy and Art in the kitchen, rummaging through the cupboards and the refrigerator, looking for something to eat. She can't hear their words, but the tone is clearly one of bickering. She imagines they are miffed at not having come back to a meal. Mrs. Edwards seems blissfully unconcerned about her guests, however, as she turns the pages of the novel she is reading.

"Where's Julie?" Sydney asks.

"She was down earlier for some toast," she answers without looking up from her page. "She's got a bug."

"She's okay?" Sydney asks, noticing that the soles of Mrs. Edwards's feet are decidedly not clean.

"Oh, she'll be fine."

Sydney nods. She is hungry as well, but she makes the decision to go up to her room and wait for the squall to pass. As she puts her bare foot on the bottom step, the phone rings. Mrs. Edwards, recumbent, springs into action, even though no one else is making the slightest attempt to get to the phone before she does.

Her smile is instantaneous. Her eyes peer inward, seeing only the person at the other end of the line. She laughs, asks a question, seems reluctant to say good-bye. She is, Sydney discovers, remarkably gifted at extending a conversation. Sydney pretends to be examining a callus on her foot. *See you soon,* she hears the matriarch croon. Mrs. Edwards waits a second longer in case the person at the other end has something more to say. Finally, she hangs up the phone and tightens the sash about her robe. She looks in Sydney's direction.

"That was Jeff," she says with immense satisfaction. "Got home fine."

In the back lot of the row house in Troy, old vegetation. Lilac and hosta and walnut. Violets and mulberry and hydrangea. Everything wild and unkempt, nothing trimmed or neat. Sydney's mother set out milk bottles with the first roses of the season on the sill in the kitchen—ancient pink rugosa, flat-petaled and treacherously thorned.

Red plaid wallpaper over the sink. Yellow curtains at the windows. Where did that ocher Bakelite clock go, the one with the frayed cord? Sydney remembers the brown Norge fridge; the day her mother had the washer and dryer installed. The cellar floor was still dirt. A week later, her mother was carrying a basket of laundry to the washer and saw a rat as big as a small dog. Sydney's mother cornered it and beat it to death while Sydney watched. An act of frenzy and violence that left Sydney speechless for hours.

Sydney remembers crumbling plaster walls. The narrow floorboards, unvarnished and nearly black, that ran the length of the long hallway. Linoleum in the kitchen. There were two bedrooms, a living room, and a bathroom, and, at the end of the hallway, the kitchen. In Sydney's room, she had a bed, a desk, and a wall of cupboards. She had shimmering purple curtains and a pink duvet. She had a plastic bedside table with drawers in which she put her nail polish, her diary, scribbled notes from friends, and recent birthday cards. As she climbed up the cement stoop each day after school and made her way to her bedroom, it seemed to her that she had swum briefly through the past and emerged safely into the present.

When Sydney was thirteen, she came home from school one afternoon to find the apartment unusually tidy. Her mother was sitting at the kitchen table, waiting for her. She asked Sydney to sit down.

"Did you clean up?" Sydney asked, glancing at the bare shelves.

"Sort of," her mother answered.

Her mother announced that Sydney and she were leaving, that they were going to live in a real house in Massachusetts. Her mother made it sound like fun. Sydney would have two homes to live in, two sets of friends, two rooms of her own. She would go back and forth from Massachusetts to New York.

What her mother didn't say was that she was fed up with the brown Norge and the cement stoop, with having to wait for her husband to fulfill his artistic promise. She didn't say that she had met another man. She didn't say that she hadn't told Sydney's father yet.

That night, after Sydney and her mother moved into the Massachusetts house with its dishwasher and microwave and spiffy new laundry room, the telephone rang. Sydney picked it up and listened. Her father was crying.

This is how Sydney thinks of her parents now: a border runs up from Manhattan; the topography is clear but for two stick figures, one on the left side, one on the right.

—ɱ—

Sydney makes the trip into Portsmouth on Monday morning and returns with an easel, a sketch pad, canvases, drawing pencils, oil paints, and two books, one on how to draw, one on how to paint. Mr. Edwards tries to give her money to pay for these supplies, but Sydney explains to him that this is her experiment.

Later that evening, Sydney sees Mr. Edwards enter Julie's room. When he emerges, pink-eyed, he fumbles for his handkerchief in his pocket. Sydney notes that he visited Julie while Mrs. Edwards was at a cocktail party. Mr. Edwards was invited as well, but he begged off, using the excuse of a stomachache.

The week passes. A storm rolls in from the northeast. Pellets of rain hit the windows. To walk outside to the car is to be blown forward with such force that one trips and stumbles. The rain lasts for days, and Sydney forgets what the beach looked like in the sunshine. It seems that it has always been raining, that this is what she signed up for.

Sydney spends hours in Julie's room. Sometimes she teaches the girl math, but mostly she watches Julie arrange objects and draw them. Sydney is slightly amazed that neither of the parents realized their daughter's innate gift. Perhaps they thought that because there seemed to be a deficit, there was little point in probing. But were there not childhood drawings? Paintings Julie brought home from grade school?

Julie is drawn to pears. Sydney attributes this to something more than just the coincidence of having a bowl of pears on the granite counter when she gave Julie the supplies. Sydney herself is intrigued by the shape of the fruit, the bulbous heavy bottom, the way it sits off-balance, the flat planes of the skin, which she has never noticed before.

Julie sets the pears in relation to one another on the dressing table that used to hold her hair ties and jewelry. She attacks the

drawing assignments with the same inten-
sity she brings to thousand-piece puzzles.

Occasionally, Sydney catches herself wondering what Jeff is doing. She pictures him
in an airless office in a nondescript building
at MIT. She tries to guess what he wears to
work. A dress shirt and khaki pants? Shorts
when there are no formal classes? Does he
leave his desk to go to lunch? Does he walk
through the rainy streets of Cambridge to
his apartment, a worn canvas backpack
slung over his shoulder? And what does he
do when he gets home? Sprawl in a chair,
watch the Red Sox, and drink a Rolling
Rock? Does the phone ring, Victoria on the
other end? Will Vicki have plans for the
evening?

Toward the end of the first week, Sydney
breaks out the paints. While Julie has been
drawing, Sydney has been reading art books.
She has had to go back to Portsmouth for
supplies she didn't know would be needed.
Turpentine. Linseed oil. Tracing paper. Sydney explains to Julie as best she can the
concept of an oil painting—gessoing the

canvas, painting the background first, the need for patience while the paint dries. Sydney parrots the text.

Julie draws three pears on the canvas. Pear shapes are entirely sexual, Sydney discovers, a fact to which she has never given much thought. Sydney cannot say what part of the anatomy, male or female, they resemble, but there is no mistaking their suggestiveness. She wonders if this is the appeal of the pear for Julie. She wonders, too, if Julie is aware of this.

Julie is tentative with the paint, and the results are rudimentary. Patience, however, will not be a problem. Julie has the patience of a monk illuminating a manuscript. Sydney watches her apply ocher paint over a green background, then leaves the room to have her lunch. She steps outside for a walk in the rain. When she returns to the house and enters Julie's room three hours later, the girl is still working on the same area of canvas as when Sydney left her.

Julie appears not to be aware of Sydney. She doesn't eat unless Sydney puts a sandwich beside her and nudges her elbow. Julie is lost in a place Sydney has never been. Perhaps, Sydney thinks, Julie has done poorly at school because too much was thrown at her at one time. Possibly she needed to do only one activity for weeks. This strikes Sydney, as she watches Julie, as sound educational policy.

Mrs. Edwards is disapproving.

"All very well, the painting, but what about the SATs? I specifically said Julie was to do two hours a day of math."

Sydney later hears Mrs. Edwards in discussion with her husband, the words unclear but the tone distinct. Mr. Edwards takes the blame. He cannot be fired.

Sydney makes a mental note never to begin a sentence with the words *I specifically said.*

The days pass. The two weeks seem endless. The household learns, via the *Boston Globe,* that the weather is expected to remain abysmal. Another storm system is making its way up the coast.

"Oh, for god's sake," Mrs. Edwards says.

*   *   *

One evening, mother, father, and daughter are invited to dinner with friends. Sydney is invited, too, but begs off, citing the stomach bug that is "going around." Mr. Edwards looks at Sydney oddly.

"Well, if you get hungry," Mrs. Edwards says, "there's shrimp in the fridge."

"Oh, don't even *mention* food," Sydney says, putting a hand to her stomach.

When they are gone, Sydney takes herself on a leisurely tour of the house. She enters rooms into which she has not been invited. It seems a necessary activity if she is to understand the family she is living with. Or perhaps it is only that she is curious.

On the second floor, there is a long hallway with many bedrooms. Sydney enters the boys' dorm first. Three twin beds have been arranged, two on one side of a window, one on the other. The bedding is a green plaid fabric from an era Sydney doesn't believe she ever lived through. On the floor is a sheet of wrapping paper, a roll of Scotch tape. Slung from the bedposts are various baseball caps, most from the Red Sox, one from a private school west of Boston. Sydney imagines Jeff and Victoria and Ben sleeping in the three identical beds like children. She wonders which bed is Jeff's.

Guest rooms lie dormant, waiting to be filled. Samples of crewel embroidery hang on the walls. Someone has tried to update the rooms with white bedding and quilts, but occasionally previous incarnations show through. A maple dresser with a mirror. A candlewick lampshade. A teal-and-red crocheted afghan tossed over a ladder-back chair.

Sydney knows Julie's room nearly as well as her own, but she has never been inside the Edwardses' bedroom at the end of the hall. Respect for Mr. Edwards makes Sydney hesitate before the slightly opened door. With the back of her hand, Sydney nudges it a bit further. Committed, she enters.

Sydney is surprised at the marital bed: it is barely queen-size. The Edwardses strike Sydney as being large people. It would be impossible, Sydney thinks, for them not to touch on such a small mattress.

The corner room has several windows. Under one is a desk covered with what Sydney takes to be masculine apparatus: a spill of bills; a ceramic mug of mismatched pens; a metal tape measure; a bulky brown radio that might be older than Sydney. She walks closer to the desk and peers down at a photograph. It is of a slender young woman with long blond hair in a white halter-top bathing suit. A man, lanky and curly-haired, has wrapped his arms around her from behind and is nuzzling her shoulder and smiling. The woman is stunningly beautiful and deeply tanned, her eyes turned toward the man who is kissing her shoulder. If Sydney had any question about why Mr. Edwards married Mrs. Edwards, it has been answered by the look that passes between the man and the woman in the photograph.

Against a wall is a bureau that can only belong to Mrs. Edwards. On it is a Plexiglas organizer in which the woman has placed her makeup: moisturizer, expensive jars of foundation, long tubes of glossy lipstick. Sydney recognizes the brands. Banana clips and bright blue rollers are scattered upon a mahogany surface. An empty bottle of Poland Spring is on its side.

Sydney notes other objects in the room— a treadmill on which Mr. Edwards has hung a shirt, a plastic bin of unfolded laundry, a picture of the three children posed with the ocean as a backdrop—but it is the marital bed that draws her eye again and again. It cannot be a queen, Sydney decides—it is only a full—yet the bedroom is big enough to have taken a king. That the Edwardses have chosen to sleep on such a small bed together confounds Sydney, rattling her preconceptions.

—⟪⟫—

Jeff arrives early on the Friday afternoon of the weekend the brothers are to begin their vacation, startling his mother, who lets out a yelp. Sydney, who has been reading in the living room, stands to see what is happening. She watches Jeff shake off the weather at the end of the dark hallway. He sets down a duffel bag and hangs his windbreaker on a hook by the door. His hair is wild with sea air and wind, as if he had walked from the bus station. He gives no indication he has seen Sydney but instead enters the kitchen.

Sydney adjusts her position slightly so that she can witness, through an open doorway, the tableau in the kitchen of mother, father, and son. Mrs. Edwards puts a hand to her mouth and then turns away to the sink. Mr. Edwards, hands in pockets, slowly nods. Sydney wonders at the news. Has a friend died? Has Jeff been fired? Has he been caught plagiarizing?

After a time, Jeff emerges from the kitchen. He shoulders his duffel bag, and when he turns, he sees Sydney standing in the hallway. Without greeting, he walks in her direction. His shirt collar is soaked, and he has not shaved. The fact that he hasn't spoken unnerves her.

"Hey," she says finally.

"Hey."

Sydney searches for a question. She uses a name she knows Jeff is fond of.

"Where's Vicki?" she asks.

He pauses a moment. She is aware of his eyes but cannot look directly at them.

"I wouldn't know," Jeff says finally.

Sydney sits on the teak deck chair on the porch. The rain falls in sheets beyond the overhang. The ocean is pockmarked and gray. On the beach, not far from the house, a man is fishing. Is this a good time to be fishing? Sydney wonders. What would be worth the misery of standing in such a hard rain? A sea bass? A bluefish?

Sydney wraps her arms tightly around herself, trying to keep warm. A parka wouldn't be out of the question.

A few minutes earlier, Mrs. Edwards came to the screen door, looked out, and then disappeared. Julie will be upstairs painting pears. Does Ben know anything? He must, as the two brothers were supposed to come with Vicki. Sydney is pretty sure that was the plan.

Sydney hears the screen door open and then slap against its wooden frame. Zipping up his windbreaker, Jeff takes a seat on a chair close to Sydney's.

He has showered and shaved.

"So, how are you?" he asks.

"I'm good," Sydney says.

Jeff looks away and back again. "You asked about Vicki," he says.

She waits.

"We are, to use the common phrase, taking a break."

Sydney wraps her slicker more tightly around herself. "How long a break?"

"Long."

His face is pale in the gray light.

"Was this mutual?" Sydney asks.

"Not exactly," Jeff says.

He leans forward in his chair, puts his elbows on his knees, and studies Sydney's face, as if, having put down a hefty deposit on a fine piece of jewelry, he wants to get a better look at it. "You can't possibly *not* know what this is all about," he says quietly.

Sydney cannot say the obvious. To have a thought, a desire, become reality seems an astonishing act of physics. Like lightning on the water. Or flight.

Jeff trails his finger from her knee to the hem of her shorts, his first deliberate touch. The hairline touch saying everything that needs to be said, in case she wasn't listening.

She did not imagine this so fast, nor Jeff so certain. Instinctively, she moves her leg away.

"Maybe you're still in mourning," Jeff says.

"I'm losing that."

"Then . . . what?" he asks.

"When did you know?"

He thinks a minute. "That day on the porch," he says, but immediately he amends his statement. "No, when you were body surfing and came out of the water. You were having fun. You seemed entirely unself-conscious."

Are such things possible? Sydney wonders. To see a person and to know? To scratch through all the defensive layers and know?

"It's hard to believe in that," she says. She tries to smile, to make it light.

"In retrospect, I can see it. I can't say I knew it that instant."

"You were about to become engaged," Sydney says.

Jeff leans back in his chair. "I knew when I didn't tell her about Julie. It seemed natural not to, that I'd somehow, in the hours you and I were searching for Julie in the village, passed from one life into another. If I'd had doubts before, I had none then."

"So, when you got back to Boston you told her?" Sydney asks.

"Something like that."

"Was she upset? Sad?"

Jeff glances over the railing. "Piqued, I'd say. Annoyed I'd done it first. She said as much when we argued. That she'd had doubts, too. Offers I hadn't known about. Though, of course, she would have remained loyal. She made a point of that."

"You didn't mention . . . ?"

"You? No. She wouldn't have believed me."

The thought stings. Vicki wouldn't have believed Jeff because Sydney is so much less attractive than Vicki? Or does he mean only that no one would believe in so much based on so little? As, indeed, Sydney can hardly do.

"I didn't want you part of it," he explains. "I didn't want to say your name, though I've been saying it over and over since then. Even, sometimes, out loud." He chuckles, as if at a memory of himself.

Sydney tries to picture this. Jeff in an apartment she has to invent, saying her name as he cooks his eggs. Jeff in a traffic jam in Central Square, saying her name to the windshield.

He is—already—so far ahead of her.

He smooths a bit of hair off her forehead. "Ben will be furious," he says. He bends to kiss her.

The kiss takes Sydney by surprise, and he catches the side of her mouth. When he pulls away, she feels overwhelmed and cannot look at him.

A sudden break in the overcast sky brightens the day. The rain has stopped without Sydney's having noticed. The porch feels less intimate, subject to invasion.

"How is Julie?" Jeff asks, leaning back in his chair.

"Julie."

Sydney misses a beat, still trembling from the surprise of the kiss.

"Julie's great."

"Really?"

Sydney is distracted. Didn't Jeff just tell her that he broke it off with Victoria to be with her? "She's painting," she says.

"Painting as in paintings?"

"Yeah."

"How did that happen?" Jeff seems remarkably calm. Shouldn't he be shaking a little, too?

"I'm substituting art for math." With a long breath, Sydney eases herself back in the deck chair. She clutches her hands together. "She has an uncanny ability to focus on one task at a time."

"She must get it from Dad," Jeff says, nodding to himself.

"I know nothing about art," Sydney says. "I was hired to help her with English and math."

"Doesn't matter," Jeff says.

"I told your father."

Now it is Jeff who misses a beat. "About that Saturday night?"

"I felt he should know. I told him alone. Your mother wasn't there. He seemed sad."

Jeff whistles. "I'll bet he was sad."

"I think he talked to Julie. I saw him coming out of her room the next night. He looked upset."

"Julie's said nothing?"

"Not to me."

Jeff looks away into the distance as if trying to picture the scene with Julie and his father.

"Is it someone's birthday?" Sydney asks.

"My father's."

Sydney lets her hands go slack in her lap. "When?"

"Tomorrow. But we're celebrating it to-night."

"I wish someone had told me," Sydney says.

Jeff tilts his head. "You aren't expected to give a gift."

"But I want to. I like him so much."

Jeff smiles. "I know you do," he says.

He puts his hands on his knees. "I think I'll get the kayaks out," he says. "Want to come?"

She tries to answer him, but can't.

"I've upset you," he says.

"I'm . . ."

He waits. "You're . . . ?"

She studies Jeff, a man she hardly knows. He leans forward and kisses her again, and this time his aim is perfect. Sydney feels herself growing lighter and lighter, so light that it seems she might fly.

—⁓—

Sydney remains in the deck chair gazing out to sea. Jeff, in life vest and then in kayak,

crosses her field of vision. She doesn't follow him with her eyes. She thinks there will
be time, a luxury of time.

She replays the touch along her thigh. The
first kiss. And then the second. A small sensation—a tiny flip inside her abdomen, familiar and not entirely forgotten—makes her
smile.

Occasional rents in the cloud cover, blue
silk, cannot promise a fine weekend. The
meteorologists have spoken. It will rain until
Monday.

Sydney wonders if Julie knows yet about
Victoria. Sydney doubts the girl will be sad.
Mr. Edwards, Sydney guesses, has retreated
to his garden, not because he has taken the
news of Jeff's breakup so hard, but because
his wife has. If Mr. Edwards remains in the
house, he will have to bear the brunt of her
dismay.

A slant of sunlight falls on a diagonal across
the water. Sydney can see, in the slice, par-
ticles and bits, the stuff of atmosphere. For
a brief moment, the sea has vibrant color.

A gull, giddy and soaring, takes on a coral hue. Sydney sits up straight—anyone would—marveling at this trick of light. She longs for it to linger, knows that it won't. She wishes Jeff would slip into the band of color. He will not. He is long gone, already behind the distant rocks.

——⚎——

Rain against an upstairs window. Sydney pens her name to a birthday card and tucks it into a small brown paper bag she has used to wrap Mr. Edwards's birthday present: several packages of red Gummy Lobsters, a candy so sweet it hurts her teeth, but one she knows the man to be immensely fond of. It is a small gift, but it is something.

With her thumbnail, she traces the precise line Jeff made on her thigh with his finger.

She will have a bath, and she will do her nails. She will wear a long voile skirt and a black silk blouse she's been saving for a special occasion—clothes fit for a birthday celebration.

But Jeff will know why she has dressed

with care. Ben will know. Mrs. Edwards will know.

—⁓—

Footsteps on the porch can be felt throughout the house. Metal on metal as a sauté pan hits a burner. Sydney cannot tell if there is anger in the sound or not. Mrs. Edwards is cooking blackened scallops tonight, her husband's favorite. Tomorrow there was to be another dinner party, not for the patriarch, but to celebrate a son and his girlfriend. What will happen to that party now?

As Sydney descends the stairs, she hears voices at the front door, strangers' voices, for which she is glad. Other people are buffers. First there is Ben's greeting (when did he arrive?) and then the genuine welcome of the host. *You shouldn't have.* From the kitchen, the decidedly aggressive whir of the mixer. Mrs. Edwards is concocting a cake out of Kahlúa liqueur and semisweet chocolate chips.

Sydney divests herself of the brown paper bag, setting it beside a chair. She adjusts her posture. Jeff opens the screen door and passes through the living room on his way upstairs to the shower. He is late, moving briskly. He looks like a man who has just had a vigorous encounter with the weather—his cheeks reddened, his hair matted, his feet still wet. He stops when he encounters Sydney and says, in a normal voice, as if he were merely a son of the household complimenting a friend, "You look nice." He skirts Sydney's body as he takes the stairs two at a time.

There will be no rules, Sydney realizes. No rules and possibly many surprises.

Mrs. Edwards's mouth is a straight line that barely moves. She is still wearing her apron, a startling clue to her emotional state. The guests, old friends, must sense that something is amiss, but they appear to be only mildly bothered by the frost. Perhaps, within the circle of the Edwardses' friends, spouses often do not speak at parties.

Because drinks cannot be had on the porch in the weather, the guests and the Edwardses arrange themselves on the white sofas. The couches are designed for two sitting positions—sinking back or perching forward. Tonight, everyone is perched forward, even Ben, who usually makes a show of achieving comfort. Sydney sits at the edge of a wooden chair, not entitled, this particular evening, to any comfort whatsoever. She cannot remember the guests' names. Julie is sitting on a hassock, knees up, drinking a Diet Coke. At odd moments, she smiles, then glances shyly at Sydney.

An artist in rapture, Sydney thinks. A kind of ecstasy.

When Jeff comes down, he is wearing a striped navy polo shirt and khaki shorts. He makes himself a gin and tonic and sits beside his mother, a conscious appeasement.

Ben, eyeing Sydney over the rim of his drink, appears to have noticed Sydney's deliberate glancing away from Jeff. But who can tell what Ben notices or does not? His look might simply be one of admiration, for Sydney has taken more care than usual tonight. The skirt. The blouse. Her hair pulled back into a loose knot.

*   *   *

Julie cries, "Open your presents!"

"Oh, you shouldn't have," Mr. Edwards says again.

Sydney is glad for the distraction and takes her first full breath of the evening. She has a long sip of her drink, startled to realize she is drinking gin as well. Who handed her this drink? She cannot remember. Has she picked up someone else's glass?

Mr. Edwards, either nervous or eager, accidentally tears the cover of an oversized book about maritime painters as he rips the wrapping off. He says, *Oooof,* and apologizes profusely. The book is a gift from his wife, who stares at the ceiling. Mr. Edwards smooths the edges of the torn cover together and says he can tape it from the back. No, he can do better than that, he can graft it so that no one will ever notice. He adds that this is a book *he's had his eye on for some time* and gives his wife a quick peck on the cheek. She smiles for the sake of the company.

Julie, not surprisingly, gives her father a drawing of pears. He either truly admires it or pretends convincingly to. "I'll have it framed," he says.

Julie stands and embraces her father. She holds on tightly, and for a moment Mr. Edwards shuts his eyes, clearly moved.

Ben and Jeff have together given their father an updated navigational device for the Whaler. Ben offers to refill the empty glasses. Mrs. Edwards notices her apron and slides it from her waist. She cranes her neck to look at the clock. Julie lurches forward from her hassock to dip a shrimp into the cocktail sauce. The configuration of the room is such that the appetizers can be close to one sofa only. Sydney, unaccountably, is ravenous, but she doesn't trust her legs.

"This is just a little something," she says, handing the paper bag to Mr. Edwards.

Mrs. Edwards makes a quick frown with her eyebrows, a commentary either on the packaging or on Sydney's presuming to give a gift. Mr. Edwards holds aloft the lobster Gummys.

"Oh, she knows my weakness," he says with a grin.

—〰—

Ben announces at dinner that he has made a big sale: a block of six condos to a large insurance company that will use them for visiting executives. Ben declares his good fortune the same way Sydney imagines the boy announcing that he made the varsity football team. Sydney wonders if Jeff ever made similar pronouncements. An A in pre-calc? Elected president of the debate club?

Life for the Edwardses, Sydney has come to understand, centers around the dinner table. It is where triumphs are praised, politics aired, lies told, the truth occasionally released.

Sydney glances over at Jeff, and perhaps noticing the quick movement of her head, he looks up at her. He smiles, producing in Sydney a sensation close to panic. Did anyone see his smile? Mrs. Edwards? Ben?

"We had hoped Victoria Beacon would be joining us for dinner," Mrs. Edwards says.

Jeff's fork pauses on its way to his mouth. He waits for more. Sydney waits for more.

Ben, ever helpful, explains to the guests

that Jeff and Vicki Beacon were once together and now aren't. There is something
in his tone—not exactly sarcasm—that momentarily piques Sydney's interest.

"We know Vicki," the female guest says,
and Sydney recalls that Victoria has been
coming to the beach community for years.
"Such a sweet girl," the woman adds.

Ben nods and smiles. Sydney wonders if
he's contemplating giving Vicki a call.

Once the matter of Victoria Beacon has
been dispensed with, Mrs. Edwards tries to
rise to the occasion. She teases her husband about his age and tells him she has
made his favorite dessert. Mr. Edwards
flushes with anticipatory pleasure.

Sydney thinks of capitalizing on Mrs. Edwards's rare moment of cheer and suggesting that she one day accompany the woman
on one of her forays to the much-touted
Emporia. But Mrs. Edwards is no fool. She
will see the transparent gesture precisely for
what it is.

The cake, when Mrs. Edwards emerges with
it, is lopsided, suggesting an oven with a tilt.
An effort has been made to cover the gap

with solidified ganache. Mr. Edwards shuts his eyes, a child making a wish. Everyone claps when he blows out the candles in one go. The smoke from sixty-eight wicks wafts across the table. Sydney wonders what Mr. Edwards wished for. Good health for all of his family? A safe berth for Julie? A relaxed year of marital goodwill?

The dessert is unexpectedly delicious, the texture moist, the ganache tasting of expensive dark chocolate. Sydney compliments Mrs. Edwards and devours her piece. When seconds are offered, Sydney holds out her plate. Jeff, across the table, smiles.

"A girl with an appetite," he says admiringly.

——————

After Sydney has washed the dishes with Mr. Edwards and Ben (Ben, who never offers to do the dishes), she lifts her navy slicker from a hook. She takes a flashlight with her.

She walks fast along the beach, her wet skirt sticking to her legs. The hood of the slicker, too big for her, shields her face from the rain. She sees that the cottages are up to their old tricks again, having moved away from the shore as they seem to do each night.

Water on one side, seawall on the other. She reminds herself that she cannot get lost.

On the horizon, there is a light. A barge? A cruise ship? Was that thunder she just heard? Sydney has always been afraid of lightning, for no particular reason other than that her mother was. (Sitting in the exact center of the apartment hallway with her mother during a storm, the woman insisting Sydney remain with her. *Safest place in the house,* her mother would say, smoking two, three cigarettes before Sydney was allowed to leave.

Her father would be out on the stoop, watching the show.)

Jeff is upon her without a sound. When she turns, gasping, he puts his hands inside her hood. His own hair is wet and matted. He has been running.

"This might be a mistake," she says.

He kisses her, his mouth wet with rain.

She manages his name.

He finds the clasp of the zipper under her chin and lowers it. His hands are cold, and she shivers.

Jeff is decisive. Sensations Sydney hasn't experienced in over two years surprise and then astonish her. Both memory and desire are triggered, each competing with the other, so that it seems a kind of grief for Daniel reaches a crescendo even as her body responds to Jeff. And then Jeff is inside her, and the sexual feelings overwhelm the past. There is some relief in this: Sydney aware of leaving Daniel behind; Jeff becoming all there is. Becoming everything.

They find shelter on the floor of an abandoned gazebo and lie in its direct center to avoid the spitting rain. Minutes pass. Hours. Intermittently, Sydney is aware of the sea just beyond them.

"What time is it?" she asks.

Jeff peers at his watch but cannot read the dial. Sydney finds the flashlight and switches it on so that he can see the face. "Four-forty-five," he says.

"No one will be up yet. I could make you eggs."

Sydney imagines herself and Jeff in the kitchen, Jeff sitting at the table, Sydney with a spatula and frying pan. One small light will be on, and there will be shadows. In better weather, if it ever comes again, they will go out onto the porch. They will take walks and watch the sun rise. In the afternoons, when everyone is elsewhere, they will nap in her bed.

A hot bath, she thinks, would be divine.

For warmth, they have left most of their clothes on. Her black silk blouse has ridden over her breasts. Jeff, with his free hand, adjusts it.

"Losing your husband must have been brutal," he says in a gentle voice.

"It was."

He smooths the hair out of her face. "I'm sorry," he says.

"It's better now."

"Time?"

"Yes," Sydney says.

"What was he like?" Jeff asks.

She is surprised by the question. "He was smart and funny. And patient. I think he would have made a good teacher. You know, at the hospital."

Jeff glances to one side. "Good-looking?" he asks after a moment.

"Yes," Sydney answers honestly.

Jeff seems to ponder her reply. "Do you have a picture?" he asks.

"I do. In my room. Do you want to see it?"

Jeff thinks. "I don't know," he says. "Maybe not."

He runs his finger along Sydney's arm.

"Your mother doesn't like me," she says.

"I know."

"She'll believe I'm responsible for you and Victoria."

"You are." Jeff lays his hand on her waist and kisses her.

"She's never liked it that I'm half Jewish. Now that I'm involved with her son, she'll hate it."

Jeff is silent.

"That doesn't bother you?" Sydney asks.

He kisses her shoulder, and Sydney thinks of the photograph in the Edwardses' bedroom.

"It bothers me, but more in the abstract than in reality. I'd like to think my mother wasn't like that, but there's not a lot I can do about it. Years ago, she and I had all the arguments a boy and his mother can have. I realized after a while that I'd never change her."

"I should probably leave the house."

"If you go, I'll follow you. And where will we be then? In my squalid apartment in Cambridge?" He puts his arm around her and pulls her to him.

"I'll love your squalid apartment in Cambridge."

"Don't be so sure about that."

Afterwards, Jeff helps her to her feet. Away from his skin and his warmth, she feels the cold penetrating. He brings the zipper of her slicker to her chin. He takes her hand and leads her onto the sand. In bare feet, carrying their shoes, they head in the direction of the house.

Sydney is surprised to see, as they draw closer, a light still on. As she climbs the porch steps, her mouth feels frozen. She cannot make it work properly. There is something she wants to say to Jeff, something that will convey to him the significance of what they have just done on the beach, but her thoughts are nearly as rigid as her mouth.

*   *   *

Once inside the front door, Jeff hesitates. The light is from the kitchen. Around Jeff and through the passageway, Sydney can see Ben sitting at the table. He has moved from gin to bourbon, a bottle of Maker's Mark half empty beside him.

Jeff and Sydney enter the kitchen, even the one light making them squint. There is a sense of having been caught and called to task. Of impending interrogation. Ben is silent, staring at them both. Sydney can see that he is very drunk. It's in his face, the loosening of the features.

"Julie's gone," he says.

Julie has left, in an upright rounded hand, a note. Ben, seething with frustration, his handsome features corrupted, pushes the torn piece of notebook paper across the table to Jeff, who has to wipe the salty rain from his brow and eyes to read it.

Sorry but I'm fine. ~~I've~~ I'm ~~gone~~ going on a little trip with ~~some~~ someone ~~who you don't who you haven't~~. It's just a little ~~trip~~ vacation for a couple of days. I'll call you soon. Don't worry and ~~I'm fine okay~~ I'M OK. (Thankyou Sidney.)

"She left? She's gone?"
   Jeff, pale under the best of circumstances, seems drained of all life force, earlier in great abundance.

"Apparently."

"Where's Dad? Where's Mom?"

"The police station."

"Without the note?"

"The police were here already."

Sydney notices two mugs with spoons, a cream pitcher, and the sugar bowl. None of the Edwardses take sugar or cream with their coffee.

"They came, they left," Ben says, gesturing with a flick of his fingers. "Julie's eighteen, apparently went willingly. Frankly, they're not all that interested. They said wait until morning, she'll probably call."

"Did Dad tell them that Julie's . . . ?"

"Slow? Yeah, Jeff, he told them Julie's slow."

Ben's anger will show itself in sarcasm, then, Sydney thinks, making it hard to know what the Edwardses have or have not said to the police.

Jeff flings his windbreaker into the air. It comes to rest in front of the sink, where Tullus, curious, noses it.

"So, where have you guys been?" Ben asks casually.

"This is serious," Jeff says.

"So I gather," says Ben, deliberately misreading his brother.

Sydney sits at the table and draws the note toward her. As she reads, something flits across her brain and then immediately drifts away. She scans the note again, trying to retrieve the thought, the image. She shuts her eyes and tries to think. "Where did she leave this?" she asks.

"On her pillow," Ben answers. "No one noticed it until we went looking for her."

Jeff sticks his fingers into his hair, the gesture of a wild man. "We should be . . ."

"What, Jeff?" Ben asks. "Driving around, looking for her? In which direction should we go? North? South? To Portsmouth? To Boston?"

Jeff lowers his hands. "Dad must be beside himself."

"You think?"

Ben balances on the hind legs of the wooden chair. He holds his drink and appears to be studying the tension of its oily surface. "You know, Jeff, you're good."

Jeff grabs a dish towel from the fridge handle, dries his face and head.

"You told Vicki, what, Tuesday night? Yeah, Tuesday, because she called me at work Wednesday morning. So, let's see . . . this is Friday night, *was* Friday night, and you've already . . . well . . . *nailed,* so to speak, old Sydney here."

(Ben will be furious.)

"Shut up, Ben."

"Works fast," Ben says, turning to Sydney. "Always did. You impressed? You ought to be impressed."

"Julie's missing," she reminds the brothers. Somewhere out there, Sydney thinks, Julie is driving in a car or Julie is eating a hamburger or Julie is laughing.

"Yeah. So. We're fucked," Ben says, sitting forward, slamming the chair legs against the floor. Sydney flinches at both the word and the sound.

Jeff tosses the towel onto the granite counter. "You're drunk, Ben. Go to bed."

"Yeah. We're fucked. This whole family is fucked."

Sydney's skirt feels wet and gritty against her bare legs. She slides the slicker from her arms. When she glances up, Ben is staring at her blouse. Did she misbutton it in the dark?

"I'm *glad* Julie's gone," he says, looking up at Jeff. "What kind of a life did she have here? She was a prisoner. Oh, she *painted.* Big fucking deal. Oh, she worked in the *rose garden.* She was a prisoner in her own house. She was never going to get free."

(I think the man will find her.

Not too soon, I hope.

No, not too soon.)

"Let's just work this through," Sydney says.

"She wants to help now," Ben reports to Jeff.

"That's uncalled for," Jeff says with the odd politeness of an academic.

"Uncalled for? *Uncalled for?*" Ben snaps his glass upon the kitchen table. "Then I say, call for it!" He hitches himself forward in the chair. "Julie takes off, and where is Sydney, her new best friend? Fucking my brother in the sand, that's where."

With one swift motion, Jeff upends the kitchen table onto Ben's lap. Ben scoots back, and the lip of the table hits the floor. The bottle of Maker's Mark breaks at Sydney's feet. Sydney watches as Julie's note flutters onto the puddle of bourbon. She bends over and snatches it away.

As if summoned by the commotion, Mr. Edwards opens the kitchen door. He holds it for his wife. "What . . . ?"

Both parents, Sydney notices, are red-eyed, either from lack of sleep or weeping.

"Is Julie back?" Mr. Edwards asks.

The brothers, full of hate a minute earlier, swiftly become a team. Sydney suspects years of childhood practice.

"What did the police say?" Jeff asks, deflecting a question with a question.

Mr. Edwards steps into the room. "What the hell happened here?"

His wife, shoulders hunched, clutches her purse to her chest.

"I stumbled," Jeff says. "Knocked against the table. Ben, hand me that box over there, will you? I'll get this glass."

Sydney, astonished, watches as the brothers work like janitors to erase the explosion of moments before. At the counter, Sydney gently blots the note with a paper towel.

When Sydney turns, the table is upright.

"I think we should all sit down," Mr. Edwards declares, holding on to the back of a kitchen chair. Already, fear has diminished him.

There aren't enough chairs. Ben, who suddenly seems remarkably sober, leans against the island.

"Sydney," Mr. Edwards says. He is a decade older than he was at his birthday celebration. Did he wish for too much when he blew out the candles? Did he make the gods angry? Cruel fate that they should so soon upend his good fortune.

"I know this is a confusing time," he says, "but just think back. Did Julie leave the house on a regular basis? To meet someone perhaps?"

Sydney is aware of all eyes upon her. She wants, for Julie's sake, for Mr. Edwards's sake, to be as clear and as precise as possible. "I wasn't with her every minute," she begins. "There were times when I would go for a walk or to my room. I suppose it was possible. But not on a regular basis. And I never saw it happen."

"Think!" Mrs. Edwards commands.

"She is," Mr. Edwards says, putting a hand over his wife's fist on the table.

"You should have kept your eye on her," Mrs. Edwards snaps. "It's what we paid you for." Her face appears to have closed in on itself, forming a neat square with squat lines where the eyes and mouth should be.

"Mom," Ben says.

"Every minute?" Jeff asks.

"Well, I find it very difficult to believe that my daughter could have struck up a relationship with someone without Sydney's noticing."

For a moment, the accusation lies on the table—unanswered, undefended—while behind them the wood-and-brass barometer goes on recording atmospheric pressure.

"What I don't get," Mr. Edwards says, "is why Julie didn't say where she was going. Why the secrecy?"

"Because you'd have gone and gotten her," Ben says simply, "and then brought her home."

"Oh, I hate to even say this," Mr. Edwards suggests, putting his head in his hands, "but do you suppose she was forced to write the note?"

Sydney, who has the note in front of her,

reads it again. Most of the letters are blurred and wavy, but knowing what it says makes it possible to decipher it.

"This is Julie," Sydney says. "I don't just mean her handwriting. This is how she would write. What she would say. Even the mis-spelling of my name."

"So, you knew her well enough to know how she wrote," Mrs. Edwards accuses, all but Frisbee-ing the words across the table, "but you didn't know her well enough to know she was about to run away?"

The woman's anger makes her head shake.

Sydney attempts an explanation. "After that first incident, there was no reason to think—"

"What incident?" asks Mrs. Edwards, sharp-eared even in distress.

Too late, Sydney remembers that Mrs. Ed-wards doesn't know of Julie's drunken binge.

"One night, two weeks ago," Jeff offers quickly, "Julie came home late and she'd been drinking."

"Drinking what?"

"We're not sure."

"She was drunk, you mean?"

"Yes."

"Why wasn't I told?"

No one answers the woman.

"You all knew?" Mrs. Edwards asks, her voice rising. "Mark, you knew?"

With reluctance, Mr. Edwards looks his wife in the eye. Sydney can see how much the effort costs him. "Yes, I did," he says. "Sydney came to tell me one night when you were out." (Not quite the truth, Sydney thinks. Mrs. Edwards was lying on the sofa, reading.)

Mrs. Edwards presses her lips together and then lets out a small explosion of air. "I do not understand why I, her mother, wasn't told. And I don't understand something else. Why"—she snatches the note from Sydney—"why does Julie *thank* Sydney? Thank her for what?"

"I think for the—" Sydney begins, and then she has a thought. "Did the police go into Julie's room?" she asks.

"They did."

But they might not have known what to look for. She rises from the table. "I'll be right back," she says.

She leaves the kitchen and heads up the stairs. The door to Julie's room is open.

Sydney steps inside and scans the contents.

Light-headed, she reaches behind herself for the bed and sits at its edge. For the first time, she feels the full blow of Julie's disappearance. She wraps her arms around her stomach.

Images of Julie laughing in the front seat of a car entangle themselves with recent memories of Jeff laughing on the floor of the gazebo. At the urgency, the absurdity of passion, now fulfilled. A grown man and woman fumbling through wet clothes to make each other naked. She remembers Jeff's cheekbone pressed hard into hers. Something he said into her neck that she couldn't quite hear. The exquisite tenderness with which he covered her. As he pulled her close to him, her slicker released a rivulet of water that ran down her neck and along her collarbone. She shivered. Her feet were cold. She could feel the rain on her bare skin. She brought them up and tucked them between Jeff's thighs. He reached down with his hand and held them there.

"This should have been such a happy night," Jeff says from the doorway.

Sydney tries to smile.

He joins Sydney on the bed, the weight of the two bodies making a deep V in the soft mattress. "It was impetuous what I did," he says. "Even careless. But I felt very certain."

Sydney nods.

"What do you feel now?" he asks, and Sydney can hear the tiny hitch in his breath. Is he nervous about her answer?

She takes his hand so that he will understand that she is still with him. "I feel sad," she says. "Julie's really gone."

"How do you know?"

"She's taken the canvases. She's taken the paints."

Jeff turns his head in the direction of the corner where the easel should be. She can feel his sigh in his shoulders.

She releases his hand and walks to the window. Through the glass, she sees a sunny afternoon, Julie standing in the water. Sydney snags the thing that was in Julie's note, the thing that flitted across her brain.

I'M OK.

A young woman in a wet suit catching a wave.

"What is it?" Jeff asks.

"I think I know who Julie ran off with," Sydney says.

"Who is he?" Jeff asks from the bed.

"It might not be a he," Sydney says, turning.

2003

———✎———

A greenish sheen on the surface. The water thick and jellied. Overhead, yellow clouds trap the heat. Sydney waits through a succession of waves, picking the tallest one. Her timing is off. She cannot get her rhythm.

Tonight and tomorrow, guests will arrive at the beach house. There will be a caterer, a girl named Harriet from the village who does "this sort of thing," though surely there cannot be enough weddings in the village and in the beach houses, Sydney thinks, to keep a caterer in business. Harriet must cook for cocktail parties as well, the ones at which spouses sometimes do not speak to each other.

The weekend weather will be *iffy,* the word batted around like a badminton birdie. Sydney hears it from the upstairs hallway, from the kitchen. Beyond that, no one is willing to say.

If the weather is simply iffy, the wedding will be held on the porch. If worse, the ceremony will take place in the living room, the furniture temporarily removed. It is to be a small affair, family and close friends only. The phrase makes Sydney uncomfortable, reminding her of a funeral.

Sydney's parents will arrive separately. The wedding will be conducted by a minister from Needham who has happily accepted the best guest room upstairs. Sydney's friends Emily and Becky will come tomorrow. Jeff will be better represented by Ivers and Sahir and Peter and Frank, an excess of groomsmen.

Sydney calculates that there will be eleven tonight at dinner. Technically a rehearsal dinner, though the rehearsal itself will take all of ten minutes. The wedding not paid for, as is customary, by Sydney's parents, who, in any case, might not have agreed on a venue. Instead, both the wedding and the rehearsal dinner will be underwritten by Mr. and Mrs. Edwards and organized by Mrs. Edwards, who has made it clear, by a series of clever suggestions and a Rolodex of service personnel, that she can handle all the annoying little details.

Though they have insisted that Sydney call them Mark and Anna now, she cannot think of them as anything but Mr. and Mrs. Edwards.

"There won't be any yarmulkes or anything," Mrs. Edwards announced early on to Jeff, thereby decisively settling the Jewish question. Not acceptable.

"Don't be ridiculous," Jeff said.

Sydney spots an exceptionally tall wave in the distance. She knows she ought to retreat, let the surge catch her on the backs of her knees, push her hard into the sand. Or she could take her chances diving headfirst into its face, aiming low to miss its rolling power. Sydney glances to her left and right.

No one else in the water today, which, in any case, looks unappealing and filthy.

The wave advances. Sydney can hear its anger. She turns her back and waits. The trick always is to catch the crest.

A wild recklessness, perhaps even anger of her own, makes her raise her arms and put her hands together. A fierce undertow nearly buckles her legs. A beach, a cottage, and a seawall are all before her, but she sees nothing. It is as though she hears with her eyes.

She cannot hesitate. Her timing has to be perfect.

The wave upon her, Sydney leaps. Too late, she understands that she has miscalculated. The wave hits her square in the back, and the water slams her face against the sand. Sydney tries to stand and can't. There is no ocean floor.

With little breath left to hold, Sydney lets the wave take her. The water, indifferent, dumps her sideways onto the beach, rolling her

down the steep slope as it recedes. She is
a toy, a plaything.

Spent, Sydney cannot outrun the following
wave, and she is again submerged in water.
She digs her fingers into the sand. She
gasps for air and is hit from behind. She lets
the fourth wave push her forward on her
belly. She crawls out onto the sand, beyond
the reach of the worst of it. When she rubs
the stinging salt from her eyes, a man she
knows is standing with a towel.

Jeff wraps her in bubble-gum pink, gently
rocking her from side to side. He nestles his
chin at the side of her neck.
　"You're a goddess," he says.
　"I'm off my timing today. It's not working."
　"It's nerves," he says.
　"You think so?"
　He slips his hand into the hip band of her
bikini. The old tank suit is gone. Jeff insisted.

———〰———

Mr. Edwards, frantic at the disappearance
of his daughter, put up homemade posters
at the lobster pound and the general store.

Within an hour, a young woman with a French Canadian accent called. "I saw the girl on the poster," she said. "She was at a party with Hélène."

"Hélène who?" Mr. Edwards asked, his breath tight.

"She surfs. I think she lives in Montreal."

Mr. Edwards staged a sit-in at the Portsmouth police station, persuading the authorities to bring their considerable technological expertise to bear upon the suspected kidnapping—note notwithstanding. Hélène Lapierre, who had crossed the border on the night in question, was remembered by a border guard for her exceptional smile as well as her comment that she'd spent her vacation surfing on the coast of New Hampshire. She was tracked down and briefly questioned, the need for further interrogation unnecessary, as Julie Edwards, focused, intent, and clearly unharmed, was painting pears in a corner at the time of the unexpected arrival of the Canadian police. Julie, apparently surprised by the fuss, said readily, "Oh, I'll call," and went immediately to the telephone.

*   *   *

There were tears, the father's contagious. Within minutes, Julie was reduced to sobs. "Let me speak to Sydney," Julie said through ragged breath.

Sydney took the phone.

"They want to come, but I think it should be you," Julie said. "I want you to see Hélène's apartment. And meet Hélène."

How like Julie, Sydney thought, to re-arrange the priorities.

A short family meeting was held and a decision made.

"Sydney and Jeff will go to Montreal," Mr. Edwards said. "Julie will respond to Sydney best, but I don't want her to have to travel alone."

Jeff readily nodded his assent.

Ben was absent from the family meeting, having left for Boston within hours of the fight with his brother.

Sydney had to guess at Mr. Edwards's reasoning: were he or Jeff to go alone to Montreal, Julie's autonomy, not to mention Hélène's physical safety, might be in jeopardy.

Jeff and Sydney drove to White River Junction, just across the border from New Hampshire in Vermont. From there, they took the train to Montreal. The circumstances of the journey—the sense of mission, the rhythmic clacking of the rails, the fast receding lights in the distance—created an odd and wildly inappropriate sense of honeymoon.

So, too, did their physical proximity, Sydney unable to bear, even for insanely short periods of time (such as when Jeff stood in line at the café car to purchase boxed lunches) his absence. It was as though she had, since the night on the beach, entered an altered state, simple facts and a clear head entirely irrelevant.

Jeff seemed to share her physical need. They sat hip to hip, thigh to thigh, Jeff touching her constantly, dozing on her shoulder, running his fingers up and down her back and under her hair, a surprisingly intimate gesture that sent Sydney into a nearly hypnotic swoon.

"Your skin is delicious," Jeff whispered into her ear, causing a shiver all along her spine.

Each imagined Julie's Hélène, neither of them getting it right. Sydney pictured, having all too briefly seen the real thing, a wiry athletic woman with slick black hair. Jeff imagined—surely a male fantasy, Sydney thought—a lipstick lesbian with blond curls, an image in which he persisted in believing even when presented with Sydney's meager evidence to the contrary.

Jeff remained in their hotel room while Sydney took a taxi to the address given. Hélène, who met Sydney at the door of her fifth-floor walk-up in the old quarter of the city, was neither a lipstick lesbian nor dark-haired, but rather a petite woman with light brown hair and distinctly European features (the wet suit had elongated; the water darkened). Julie hopped off her stool in the corner and embraced Sydney with ferocity. Not the ferocity of the relieved, Sydney thought, but rather that of the newly liberated.

Hélène, mindful of the sensitivities, did not touch Julie during the visit—no caresses, no gestures of possessiveness—but did allow Julie, in her exuberance, to embrace her from time to time as she managed tea from a spartan kitchen, an indication of household discipline that held throughout the small apartment, even to the simple bathroom with the good accoutrements: the Frette towels, the marble pedestal sink, the cut-glass dispenser of remarkably effective hand cream.

The most extraordinary feature of the otherwise modest flat was an expanse of windows on the street side. They were set above dark-paneled wainscoting and had sixteen leaded-glass panes per window. In certain lights (Sydney visited often), she felt transported to seventeenth-century Holland, as if, turning her head, she might find Julie, with her Dutch-beauty face, in layered robes, embroidery hoop in hand.

"I'm sorry, Sydney. I'm so sorry. I should have told you. I just thought . . ." Julie stumbled through her apology, heartfelt and contrite.

"It's okay," Sydney said. "I understand. I do. It's just that the way you did it was frightening for your parents. For all of us."

"But you'd all have stopped me!" Julie protested, nailing her defense.

*   *   *

Sydney summoned Jeff from the hotel room. When he appeared in Hélène's apartment, Sydney had the unnerving sense of being on a double date.

While Sydney had been restrained but polite with Hélène (not wanting to precipitate a crisis that wasn't warranted), Jeff was harsh. He demanded to know how Hélène could have persuaded Julie to leave her home and family, and it was only after a lengthy discussion over tea and excellent pastries, Hélène's accented English and the Vermeer windows lending a distinctly foreign note to the occasion, that Jeff could be persuaded that Julie had begged to go to Montreal.

Jeff called home with the news. Though Mr. Edwards, understandably, could hardly be expected to view the bulletin as welcome (he missed his beautiful daughter and would be lonely, Sydney suspected, not to mention the fact that Julie would be dropping out of school), a compromise was agreed to.

Julie would return to the beach house the following weekend with Hélène and Jeff and

Sydney. A civilized detente would be the goal.

Julie's passport was mailed so that she could legally cross the border. (One could cross the border into Canada without a passport, Sydney learned, but one could not get back into the States.) Jeff and Sydney spent the week—Jeff's vacation week—not at the beach house, where all was suspended chaos, but rather in Montreal, in the small hotel room with its two exceptionally narrow iron beds.

Returning from that first visit to Julie, Sydney noticed that Jeff's hands were trembling.

"Do you think they're lovers yet?" he asked as they entered the early-twentieth-century hotel elevator.

"Yes, I do," Sydney answered, minding the slight dip with each stop. She didn't like elevators in which she was reminded of the possibility of cords snapping, pulleys malfunctioning.

"I just . . . It seems so . . ."

"I know," she said.

*   *   *

Jeff leaned against a padded bar at the back of the small compartment. He seemed spent. "Did she look happy to you?" he asked.

"Very."

"She's only eighteen."

"I'm happy for her," Sydney added.

"You don't think Hélène's just using her?"

"Using her for what?"

"For sex? As someone she can control?"

Sydney thought. "Both might be true. The sex is obvious. Julie is beautiful. She's also trusting. But I'm not sure that controlling Julie is as easy as you might think. I didn't do a very good job of it. I was with her essentially all day, and yet I never knew she was seeing Hélène."

"Should I worry?" he asked.

"We should worry *some*," Sydney said, including herself. "And keep an eye on them. I did manage to extract a promise from Hélène to let us know if they planned on traveling. I don't want your father to have to go through all that again."

"Did you . . . ," Jeff began, seemingly considering how exactly to phrase what might be a delicate question. "Did you notice anything that would have led you to believe that Julie was gay?"

"It was as surprising to me as to you."

"I just wondered if she'd ever . . ."

". . . made a pass? No."

The elevator dipped and stopped. "How old do you think Hélène is?" Jeff asked.

"She's twenty-five. I asked."

The door opened and Sydney stepped out into the dark corridor of the old hotel. Jeff led her through a warren of wallpapered hallways to their room. He unlocked the door and stepped aside to allow Sydney to enter. A maid had already drawn the curtains.

"Are you hungry?" Jeff asked. "Do you want to eat? I should have asked you before."

"I just want to lie down," Sydney said. She slipped off her sandals and lay on the narrow bed. Jeff, too, removed his shoes.

Sydney felt the relief of the bed. She watched as Jeff undid the first three buttons of his shirt, a gesture that pleased her. For a moment, he was a man lost in thought. She knew he was still worrying about Julie, running vast scenarios in his mind, trying out old formulae, hypothesizing, examining data. When finally he turned to Sydney, she made room for him on the bed. Barely a foot of space.

He laughed.

He studied the length of her, lingering on her bare legs. His face was changing, the alertness behind the eyes fading, the jaw losing its tension. There might be no more words.

He knelt on the rug and kissed her knees. He raised her skirt by inches.

Sitting on the bidet in the hotel bath, Sydney could not, even when she tried, remember the sexual details of former lovers and husbands. Tenderness she could recall, but not positions or single events. She thought this a female trait. She had no doubt that Jeff, if asked, could remember dozens of specific encounters.

When she returned to the room, Jeff was dressed. "Let's go out," he said. "I'm starved."

They walked through side streets to an inviting bistro. Sydney checked her watch.

It was nearly ten o'clock, and people—even families with children—were just sitting down to dinner.

Sydney ordered *moules frites.* When the mussels and french fries arrived, she ate without speaking for a good ten minutes. When she looked up, she said to Jeff, "I think this may be the best meal I ever had."

A few minutes later, elbows on the table, Sydney studied Jeff.

"You look like your father," she said.

"I do?" Jeff asked, taking a sip of the house red.

"Your eyes. Your build."

Jeff nodded slowly, taking it in.

"I think you're like him, too. A decent man."

Jeff, reaching for a *frite,* seemed surprised by the compliment.

"You think so?" he asked.

"Your mother struggles for position," Sydney said. "Your father has it effortlessly."

Jeff took from his pocket a pack of Gauloises, and, much to Sydney's astonishment, lit one.

"I didn't know you smoked," she said.

"I bought them at the hotel while you were gone. It seemed the thing to do. When in Rome . . ."

Sydney glanced around. He was certainly not the only one smoking in the small restaurant.

"Do you mind?" he asked.

"Not the odd one here or there," she said.

Jeff took a long drag, a bit too long, Sydney thought, for someone who smoked only occasionally. "I'm not sure anyone has ever put the family dynamic so succinctly," he said.

"I'm sorry," Sydney said. "I shouldn't . . ."

"Presume away."

"Well, I didn't mean . . ."

"Anyway," Jeff said. "You're not prying. Only observing. To hear Julie and Dad tell it, you're practically one of the family."

"I think your mother might see it a little differently," Sydney suggested lightly.

Victoria, from whose bed Jeff had so recently risen, intruded upon Sydney's thoughts, a spectral vision in a yellow sundress.

"Do you think about Victoria?" she asked. "Are you happy with your decision?"

"How can you even ask that?" Jeff asked, bringing a cup of espresso to his lips.

Sydney stared.

"I knew the moment you walked out of the ocean," he added.

Victoria, it would seem, was Sydney's ghost only.

They took the rest of their evening meals with Hélène and Julie, who were caught up in a sexual bliss of their own making. Sydney had a vague notion of what might be happening in the bed in the apartment with the seventeenth-century Dutch windows but did not dwell on the details. Though Julie was not a child and had every right to sexual fulfillment—indeed, she had never looked more luminous—it might take more than a week and a few indisputable facts for Jeff and Sydney to adjust to Julie's new life.

And indisputable facts did emerge. After Julie's foray into the water the day Sydney had taken her by the hand (and Julie's odd shout *I'M OKAY*, the repetition of which, in Julie's note, had jogged Sydney's memory), Julie had dressed and gone back out to the beach. There she had sat, arms wrapped around her knees, watching Hélène surf. As inarticulate as ever, Julie could only report, "It looked so beautiful," a reference either to Hélène in the wet suit or to the act of surfing.

When Hélène beached herself, the pair struck up a conversation. A party was discussed.

"Where?" Jeff asked, still smarting from his futile search.

"The cottage on the beach where all the surfers go," Hélène answered politely.

That Julie had gotten drunk had been unintentional and unfortunate. Hélène had extracted Julie's address from the girl (more information than Julie had given Sydney that night) and had driven Julie home. She'd walked her to the door, trusting in Julie's body to do the rest.

And there it might have ended had not Julie repeatedly sought out Hélène on her walks along the beach. (*What walks?* Sydney wanted to know. Had Julie left the house each day just minutes after Sydney had?) It wasn't clear if the sexual relationship had started that first drunken night or had developed over time, but neither Jeff nor Sydney felt inclined to ask.

When it was time for Hélène to return to Montreal after her vacation, Julie begged to go with her. Hélène had at first demurred but then finally had said yes. (Had happily said yes, Sydney imagined.)

Hélène had not known that Julie's suitcase contained canvases and paints until the smell of turpentine and linseed oil had made its way from the trunk of the old Peugeot to the front seat. By that time, the pair were in Burlington and in no mood to turn back.

Julie's happiness was palpable, tangible, destined to eclipse the happiness of anyone nearby. Though Sydney had no doubt that Hélène was truly fond of Julie, the French Canadienne's joy seemed subdued by comparison.

Jeff and Sydney's happiness, too, seemed muted in Julie's presence, a fact that bothered Sydney, as if in the realm of rapture, she and Jeff could never quite measure up.

*   *   *

Alone with Jeff, however, Sydney's life felt complete. The food, the wine, and the constant feeling of lassitude resulting from frequent and spontaneous sex contributed to a sense of pleasure and of ease. The week seemed but a happy passage of time that just below the surface dictated future expectations and fond reminiscences. Possibly, too, there were slight hints of incompatibility. Sydney noted, but did not then mention, the desire on Jeff's part to take long walks by himself while Sydney read in the hotel room, as well as the frequent lapses in attention, his mind elsewhere. Nor did Sydney point out, though she noticed, a subtle change in Jeff's personality, the city igniting in him a kind of wanderlust, an excessive fondness for things European, particularly its cigarettes and wines. She thought these small matters, hardly worth mentioning.

When the week was over, the four crossed the Canadian border by train and drove from White River Junction to the beach house. Sydney's status, instantly elevated, would never again return to that of employee, a circumstance that sometimes caused her to wonder if complex algorithms involving joy, disappointment, sexual tension, and barely concealed anti-Semitism could ever be resolved within the context of the family dynamic.

—~~~—

The first meeting with the parents struck Sydney as fortuitous. Because so much attention was focused on the clearly besotted Julie and the petite Canadienne, Jeff and Sydney escaped scrutiny. Indeed, the couple functioned as diplomats, seating themselves between the Edwardses on the one side and their daughter and her lover on the other. Occasionally, Sydney acted as interpreter.

"I think what Julie is saying is that she feels she is old enough to make her own decisions," Sydney found herself explaining.

The next day, Julie and Hélène headed north with assurances from Mr. Edwards that he and his wife would visit ("always wanted to see Montreal again"), while Sydney and Jeff drove south to Cambridge, the farewell remarkable for the singular occurrence of Mrs.

Edwards's—albeit without embrace—thank you to Sydney for fetching Julie. Not a word about the hours of tutelage or the happy accident of discovering Julie's talent, though almost certainly, Sydney thought, the talent would have burst forth on its own. The pears in Montreal had been exceptionally good.

Jeff's apartment resembled that of a bachelor who made a decent salary but had chosen to spend it in ways other than decor. Newly renovated, it had, through a break between two buildings directly on the Charles, a slim view of sparkling water. A leather couch and two good lamps had perhaps been purchased in an initial attempt to make something of the large front room with the bow window and the view. But this small stab at aesthetics had been eclipsed by either work or indifference, for the coffee table was of another era altogether and badly scarred as well (a hand-me-down from Needham?). The rest of the rooms struck Sydney as barren in a decidedly masculine way.

Clearly, Victoria had not lived in Jeff's apartment, though Sydney found in a front-hall closet a pair of alligator boots, size seven and a half, and rolled into the back of a drawer that was otherwise empty ("Vicki's drawer," it must have been) a pair of designer jeans that Sydney, in a moment of weakness, tried on. They fit in the hips, but bunched at the ankles. Sydney rolled them back up and stuck them in the drawer. When Sydney spent the night at Jeff's, she consciously avoided the dresser, using her suitcase as a kind of bureau.

Though Jeff's apartment was motley, it was spacious, dwarfing Sydney's stifling one-bedroom, which overlooked a RadioShack in Waltham. Upon entering her apartment for the first time in months, she could see at once why the offer of a summer at the beach had sounded appealing. The furniture was good (she and Daniel had together bought some fine pieces), but the apartment felt like a place in which no one had ever lived. When she had rented it, she'd had no interest in making it a home. She had simply wanted shelter.

In the fall, Sydney was accepted to graduate school at Boston University for the spring semester. She started in January in a program similar to the one she'd been in at Brandeis, though only a few of her credits and none of her research had been transferable. She crossed the Charles River often, sometimes arriving at the apartment before Jeff, who had regular office hours and teaching. At night, they drank wine (a lot of wine, it seemed to Sydney, a fact about which she was inclined to be apprehensive) and ate a meal she had cooked, or they met one or the other of Jeff's friends at a neighborhood restaurant. Ivers, a sportswriter at the *Boston Globe,* knew more about the inner workings of the Boston Red Sox than anyone Sydney had ever met. Frank, who had once been Jeff's restless colleague at MIT, was now unemployed and trying to make a go of it as a writer. Sahir, an old college roommate who worked for a bank downtown, sometimes received phone calls from exotic places. He spoke in Urdu, emphasizing, again and again, a single word that sounded like a sneeze: *Achaa!* Slight, Muslim, and looking like the Pakistani he was, Sahir had been detained by the Boston police twice since 9/11 and had once been chased out of a bar. Oddly, he seemed at peace with this harassment, as if this were simply his burden to bear. And then there was Peter, who could repeat verbatim the entire dialogue of *Office Space*. Nights with Peter, who ran the particle accelerator at MIT, were entertaining and full of laughter. None of Jeff's friends was married. None seemed particularly distraught over Sydney's replacement of Victoria.

Once a month, Sydney and Jeff flew to Montreal to visit Julie, who appeared to be thriving. In the late spring, she exhibited one painting in a group show at a crafts fair. It was clear that Julie had considerable talent and would go far, and Sydney believed the painting she was entering would sell in minutes. (Not true: it didn't sell, and Julie gave it to Sydney. Five pears lay in a blue Delft bowl, a sliced lemon on the table in the foreground. The juice of the lemon seemed real enough to lick.)

Ben had visited Julie twice, Julie freely announced, perhaps having no inkling of the rift between the brothers, though she might have wondered at Thanksgiving when Ben did not show for the meal, disappointing his parents. Sydney, too, was dismayed and had to let go of her imagined dialogue with Ben as well as the hoped-for reconciliation between the brothers. Sydney wondered if Ben would have come if she hadn't, but Jeff, who grew quiet whenever Ben's name was mentioned, thought not. It was Jeff with whom Ben was furious.

At Christmas, Ben went on a cruise.

Sydney could not get Jeff to say how much the rift hurt him, nor how angry it made him, anger fueling anger. But she could see on his face the slight moment of apprehension whenever he entered a restaurant in Boston and the way he quickly scanned the crowd, looking for his brother. Not once in the year since Sydney and Jeff had met had they visited Boston's waterfront or the North End or the financial district, areas where they might have encountered Ben.

―⚬⚬⚬―

Sydney had been fascinated, during her first visit to Needham, to see the family seat and to view some of Mr. Edwards's work. The man seemed pleased that Sydney took an interest. It had been some time since anyone had asked about the framed architectural drawings that hung here and there, most remaining modestly in Mr. Edwards's study.

The family homestead was a stucco colonial on a hill, a house with many rooms, the building too large for the yard, as were all the homes on the street. It had been erected in the 1930s and had lovely touches: a long butler's pantry with glass cupboards on both sides; arched entrances to each living room; an out-of-the-way niche in which one could read on a love seat; and spacious porches, both glassed-in and screened. Dinner was served on a highly polished Hepplewhite—a relic from Anna Edwards's family, from whom, Sydney deduced, most of the money had come. The meals were elaborate and formal, Mrs. Edwards cooking them herself. Sydney sometimes wished for a maid, however; the preparation of the meals made Mrs. Edwards tense and uncommunicative once the food was on the table.

In truth, the matriarch was looking more and

more windblown, as if having been wildly buffeted by the vicissitudes within the family.

Julie came always with Hélène, Jeff with Sydney, everyone working slightly too hard, Sydney thought, to make the evenings successful. From time to time, she would look up to find Mrs. Edwards staring at her as if searching for telltale signs of Jewishness, much like examining a room one had recently dusted for a place one had missed.

Mrs. Edwards never said Sydney's last name, introducing her only, when introductions were absolutely necessary, as "Jeff's friend Sydney."

One night, shortly after Sydney had moved into Jeff's apartment in Cambridge, Jeff stood on a chair to replace a lightbulb. He had on boxers and a T-shirt, and Sydney, remembering that first boat ride with Jeff and Ben, impulsively kissed his thigh. Jeff looked down at her.

"Marry me?" he asked.

"What?"

"Would you let me marry you?"

Startled, Sydney took a step backward

and sat on a kitchen chair. "I've been married twice," Sydney said.

"I know that."

"You've never asked me much about my husbands."

"I didn't want to have to imagine them," he said. "Besides, I can't compete with an air racer."

"Of course you can."

"Is he still racing?"

"No. He had an accident and broke his leg."

"How do you know that?"

"A friend told me."

"Oh." Jeff was silent a moment. "What's he doing now?"

"Teaching."

"My point exactly," Jeff said.

That night, as Sydney lay in bed listening to Jeff breathe beside her, she trembled, much the same way she had done the day Jeff had run his finger along her thigh. That gesture, like his asking her to marry him, seemed spur-of-the-moment, impetuous, perhaps even possessive. Yet she did not doubt Jeff's feelings for her. Hadn't he told her, again and again, how much he loved her?

Hadn't he declared, never wavering, that he had been certain about her since the first day they had met? Sydney had felt love before, and though she thought comparisons unfair and fickle (could anyone accurately remember love?), she was certain her feelings for Jeff were just as solid as they had been for either Andrew or Daniel.

Perhaps, then, it was the act of marrying itself that troubled her. Twice she had made plans, invited guests, participated in a ceremony and partied afterwards; both times, these ceremonies had produced marriages that had ended badly. It must be a kind of posttraumatic marriage syndrome, she thought, like having been sprayed with a toxic agent or having participated in a misguided mission in which there had been casualties. Would therapy be useful?

She rolled over to Jeff and woke him by kissing him on the shoulder. He half turned toward her, struggling for consciousness.

"Yes," Sydney said.

Jeff looked at her with one eye open. "Did I just ask a question?" he asked.

"Yes, I'll marry you."

He seemed confused. "You already said that."

"Yes, I did."

He nodded and then shook his head.

"I needed to say it again," she explained.

The following week, Sydney and Jeff drove to Needham to tell the Edwardses.

"This should be fun," Jeff said behind the wheel.

"Your mother will be thrilled." Sydney used the visor mirror to check her lipstick. "You could have called."

"Too cowardly," Jeff explained as he made the turn onto the steep driveway.

"At least your father will be happy," Sydney reminded him as she pulled on her gloves. Though Christmas was long over, a wreath hung from the front door.

Jeff yanked the parking brake. "I think he sees us as his last best hope."

There were greetings, warm on Mr. Edwards's part, distant on Mrs. Edwards's, as if they already knew what Jeff and Sydney had come to say. Not once had Jeff and Sydney initiated a visit to Needham, though they had gone willingly whenever invited. This time, however, Jeff had called and asked to come.

Coats were dispensed with, Mrs. Edwards letting Sydney's slide off its hanger onto the closet floor. Sydney was not surprised when Mrs. Edwards merely shut the door.

The four moved silently under an arch into one of the two living rooms, the one filled with chintz-covered, oversized sofas and chairs, the ottomans massive. Off-white side tables with faux nicks held antiques, all white. Stone birds. A filigree candelabra. A stack of books. Sydney wondered if anyone had ever read them.

No tea or drinks were offered. Jeff and Sydney sat together on one of the sofas, Sydney with her legs together, feet flat on the floor, her hands folded into her lap, a guest who'd never met Jeff's parents and wanted to make a good impression. It was the posture she had settled into, and to dismantle it would only call attention to herself.

Jeff sat with elbows on his thighs, fingers linked.

"Sydney and I are getting married," he said at once, getting it out of the way.

Mr. Edwards stood. Again, Sydney noticed the slight hitch in his back. He walked directly to Jeff, who stood as well.

"Congratulations," Mr. Edwards said, beaming. Jeff, suddenly moved, embraced his father as men do, patting each other hard on the back.

Mrs. Edwards crossed her arms over her stomach, warding off yet another blow.

Mr. Edwards leaned toward Sydney, who stood and welcomed his kiss on her cheek. He reached for her hand and squeezed it. "My dear," he said, but he was unable to continue.

Sydney quickly hugged the man, noting over her shoulder how small Mrs. Edwards looked in the oversized chair. As Sydney was released, she endured Mrs. Edwards's stare. Sydney imagined the woman calculating the percentage of Jewish blood in grandchildren.

"We're so pleased," Mrs. Edwards said.

She did not get up.

Sydney clinked glasses of champagne with Mr. Edwards, who kissed her again on the cheek. For a few hours, she reveled in his happiness and in Jeff's happiness at his father's happiness. But she noted as well a kind of falseness in the celebration, as if those who would be happy, even Jeff, were listening to a low vibrating note, such as one from a tuning fork, a note that at any minute might turn harsh and screeching.

Over dinner, a date was set. The beach house was decided upon. Julie, reached in Montreal, crowed into the phone, "I've never had a sister!" Julie mentioned wistfully a double wedding, a fact Sydney kept to herself, though she could see the moment when Julie proposed the same to her mother. Mrs. Edwards visibly shuddered and said, "Don't be silly." Her voice rang with finality.

The woman might well look windblown, Sydney thought. One child would marry a Jew. A second was a lesbian. A third, by all accounts heterosexual, had absented himself from the family indefinitely.

All this she blamed on Sydney.

Less fraught was the trip first to western Massachusetts to introduce Jeff to Sydney's mother and then to Troy to tell her father the happy news. Both parents had heard such bulletins from their daughter twice before, which took the edge off any sense of celebration. But if their own views of marriage were jaundiced, each wanted Sydney settled and happy after the trauma of Daniel.

Sydney's mother was much impressed with the fact of MIT.

"You must be very smart," she said to Jeff. "He looks smart, doesn't he?" she added to Sydney.

"Very," Sydney said, smiling in Jeff's direction.

The man for whom Sydney's mother had left her father was long gone—a salesman transferred to Minneapolis—but her mother's circumstances had improved considerably following an unexpected inheritance from her own mother. Sydney's mother now worked part-time as an administrative assistant in the admissions office at a community college.

"I can always spot them," she said knowingly.

Sydney's father, in New York, served them a spaghetti dinner he'd made himself. He seemed impressed by very little.

"My daughter is resilient," he said to Jeff after the meal.

Because it was late, Sydney and Jeff slept in her old attic room, the pink curtains and lavender shelves still intact, a fact that might have broken Sydney's heart had she not been so happy. She and Jeff spooned chastely in the narrow bed.

"I like your father," Jeff said into Sydney's ear, the two of them sharing a single pillow that promised a miserable night's sleep.

"I think we've been lucky in our fathers."

"Your mother seemed nice," he added.

"I'm not sure I've forgiven her yet for taking me away."

Jeff kissed her ear. His body was long and chilly behind her. In another bed, in other circumstances, she'd have felt him harden and press against her, but that night he was as soft as a boy.

Shortly after having delivered the news to all of the parents, Jeff and Sydney sat at a café near MIT, waiting for Ivers. The food was Indian and cheap, and the takeout lines were long. The Formica tables and pedestal chairs seemed mere receptacles for mountains of coats and scarves and backpacks. The glass window beside Sydney, lit by neon on the outside, steamed on the inside, producing a chartreuse fog.

"We'll have to tell Ben," Sydney said.

Jeff, sitting sideways to the table, rhythmically tapped the blunt end of a knife against the Formica as they waited for their food. He wore a navy sweater over an unironed dress shirt. He had let his hair grow out some, and it curled over his collar in the back, a look she liked. She wanted, right now in fact, to touch his hair at the nape of his neck.

She shifted her legs under the table, trying to cross them. She had on jeans and a black sweater, a kind of February uniform. Her hair, which had been pulled back into a ponytail, was filled with static from the cold. Her nose was running in the sudden warmth of the café. It was twenty degrees outside at best.

"I'm sure Dad's already told him," Jeff said.

"We should invite him, then," Sydney suggested, reaching into her backpack for a tissue.

"*Should we?*" Jeff asked, mocking her. "*Should we?*"

Sydney blew her nose and waited. She hated this habit of Jeff's when they were arguing.

"He wouldn't come anyway," Jeff said in a gentler tone.

"Does who started it really matter so much to you?" she asked.

Jeff planted his elbows on the table. "As I recall, you were there."

"He was drunk."

"He meant it."

"I disagree."

"Has he called?" Jeff asked. "Did he call and apologize when I wasn't home?"

Jeff sat back in his chair and allowed his chicken *tikka* to be set in front of him. A plate of roasted cauliflower was put in front of Sydney. Over her head, Jeff spotted Ivers in the doorway. "Ivers is here," Jeff announced.

"We'll talk about this when we get home?" Sydney suggested.

"*Will we?*" Jeff asked.

The following Wednesday, Jeff had a meeting at school that would run through the dinner hour. Sydney took a taxi to the financial district. She waited in the snow outside a building on State Street. When Ben exited, she approached him.

He stood still, as if he wasn't sure he recognized her. His mouth was rigid, his eyes unblinking.

"Sydney," he said finally.

"Hello, Ben."

"This isn't a coincidence."

"No."

"It's an ambush."

"Sort of."

Ben nodded slowly. He hiked the collar of his navy overcoat against the snow. "Come on, then," he said.

In silence, the pair tilted into the weather. They walked a block in the slush. Ben stopped and opened the door to a bar. He held it for her, allowing Sydney to step inside.

Already the room was half filled with men dressed in suits, woven scarves hanging from their necks. The men were drinking fast and hard. The snowstorm had lent a sense of abandon.

Ben and Sydney were led to a small table, wet underfoot. Ben, shedding his overcoat in the warmth of the room, ordered a complicated martini. Sydney asked for a glass of water, her sudden thirst overwhelming.

"You're not drinking. You want to keep your head. So you've come to tell me something," Ben guessed.

Despite his initial shock, Ben was looking remarkably fit. He had a tan.

"Ask you something," she amended.

Ben, loosening his tie, assessed her as if he were calculating the selling price of a new loft in the leather district. His scrutiny unnerved Sydney so much that she wished she'd ordered a drink after all. She tried to return the scrutiny but couldn't hold his gaze.

Though Ben looked fit, he seemed older about his eyes. Something hard in them that hadn't been there in the summer.

"I feel responsible," she began.

"Stop."

Sydney, daunted, paused. "Whatever happened, it can't be reason enough to break from your brother," she said.

"With all due respect," Ben said, watching

as the cocktail waitress set down his martini and Sydney's glass of water, "I don't think you have the slightest idea of what goes on between brothers."

This was true. She did not.

"You're getting married," he said after a time. "Congratulations." He raised his glass in a mock toast. Sydney did not join him.

"I hear you've already moved into his apartment," Ben added.

"I want you to come to the wedding," Sydney said, taking advantage of what she saw as an opening.

"So that's why you're here."

Sydney was silent. *Was* that why she had come?

"And Jeff?" he asked.

"Jeff?"

"What does Jeff want?"

Sydney took a drink of water. "I can't speak for Jeff."

"No, I didn't think so," Ben said, sipping his green martini. "Then I'm afraid you'll have to get hitched without me."

"What is it?" she asked, leaning toward him and flattening her palms on the table. "I don't understand this from any point of view—not yours, not Jeff's. Don't you care about your father? How much this is hurting him?"

"I care," Ben said, looking away.

"Then why not just forget the whole thing?"

Ben was silent. "I can't," he said.

"Why?" Sydney asked.

"I don't want to."

Ben drew away, rested against the back of his chair. They sat, neither moving, in the convivial noise. It was a mistake to have come, Sydney thought. Jeff would be furious if he knew. But Sydney would not tell Jeff. This had been her mission, and she need not tell him she had failed.

"We're going to Africa," she announced.

"Really," Ben said.

"Jeff has to go for his research."

"Where in Africa?"

"Nairobi. I've never been."

"Not even with your aviator?" Ben smiled over the rim of his glass.

He made a small motion with his hand to signal to the bartender that he wanted another drink. Sydney could see how Ben might be a regular, how he might, each night after work, stop by the bar for a pair of green martinis, perhaps sharing the second one with a woman who'd caught his eye. Sydney briefly pondered Ben's sex life. She was surprised to realize how little she knew about him.

"I guess I won't mind having you for a sister-in-law," he said.

Sydney wrapped her scarf around her neck and stood to leave. Ben leaned in quickly and trapped her hand.

"He'll never love you as much as you love him," Ben pronounced.

Sydney snatched her hand away from the malediction. She remembered the night they had gone surfing, that slithering touch.

—⁓—

"Your mom's here," Jeff says, laying the towel on the sand in response to Sydney's request that they sit a minute before going inside. "My mother has her well in hand, writing out place cards."

"She always did have beautiful handwriting. Has my dad arrived yet?"

"I don't think so. But I've been walking."

"Thinking it all over?" she asks with a gentle elbow.

"Went with Tullus," he says, which is no answer at all. He digs at the sand with a small stick, much like a boy would do. "Ivers is never going to let me forget this," Jeff says. "He's missing two Yankees games—tonight and tomorrow."

"And you don't even have a TV."

"He'll go crazy."

"We'll get him drunk," Sydney says.

"Good idea," he says, glancing up at her. His eyes linger a moment longer than they might.

"Jeff?"

"And Sahir," he says, looking away. "Sahir hates the beach." He chuckles and shakes his head.

"What is it?" Sydney asks.

"What is what?"

"You're thinking something."

"Tomorrow I'll be a husband."

Sydney lies back on her elbows. From somewhere inside the house, she can hear light feminine laughter.

Notably, there will be no best man at the wedding, though Julie, radiant, will stand up for both of them. Even Julie wears a wet suit now, astonishing Sydney the first time she saw her in it. Sydney, who, one night over cocktails, mistook simple rapture for artistic rapture.

"After the dinner, I thought we'd come out here and make a bonfire," Jeff says. "Do some serious drinking. Well, *we* won't drink too much. We'll bury Sahir's shoes."

Even without the sun, there is an unpleasant glare off the water. Sydney squints. "I couldn't have imagined this a year ago," she says. "I was tutoring Julie in math and English. I hadn't even met you and Ben yet."

Sometimes the name slips out when she least intends it. She would not have mentioned Ben today.

Jeff, as always, is silent at the name. They will not say any more about Jeff's brother.

"Lousy weather," Sydney says.

"There's a chance it might clear."

"Jeff, what is it? You seem . . . I don't know . . ."

He turns and kisses her bare shoulder. He trails his fingers along her inner thigh. "I'll be happy once we're on that plane."

Jeff had suggested East Africa for the

honeymoon, but Sydney pointed out that Africa would be too much like work. He'd be interviewing the whole time even if he didn't know it. No, they would go to Paris, to which she had never been, even with Andrew. Jeff could interview her to his heart's content at the small hotel in the Marais she had picked out.

"I love you," he says with some emphasis. He says the words often, sometimes for her, sometimes for himself—in astonished recognition or as a call to arms. Sydney can tell by the tone in his voice that today it is more of a call to arms.

She trails her fingers along the sandy hairs of his calf, as if in conversation with his fingers on her thigh. She has been amazed to realize, over the past year, how iconic the initial images are, talismans one returns to over and over again, even as new images are being created. For her it has always been the tanned legs, the faded bathing trunks, his eyes.

Jeff has cut his hair for the wedding. Sydney would have preferred it long. But he did not ask her.

"What time do we have to be at the airport tomorrow?"

"Eight," Sydney says. "It's a ten-o'clock flight."

In the year they have been together, a division of labor has been established. Sydney arranges the trips.

"So we'll leave here around when? Six-thirty?"

They will depart the reception in the early evening.

"A quick getaway," she says.

"Can't wait," he says.

———✠———

"Sydney!" her mother cries, opening her arms to her daughter, still wet with sea-water.

Sydney falters a step, not used to an exuberant welcome. Either her mother wants to annoy Sydney's father, who must have arrived early as well, or she intends to ingratiate herself with Anna Edwards, as WASP as they come. Sydney allows the embrace, folding herself into the white pantsuit and Talbots scarf, an outfit designed for the rehearsal dinner but not the three hours they all have to endure until then. Sydney notes the Coach pocketbook. The silk purses with women in purple convertibles expressing freedom have long since been abandoned. Her mother's hair is coming loose with the humidity, and the pantsuit feels damp in Sydney's embrace—sweat-damp all along its back. Her mother holds her at arm's length.

"To think . . . ," her mother says.

To think what? Sydney wonders. That her daughter is marrying yet again? That she will not die a childless spinster? That she is, in her mother's eyes, marrying up? Perhaps the beach house has spoken to her mother in a way the Feldmans' house in Newton did not.

"When did you get here?" Sydney asks as she draws away.

"About half an hour ago. Anna told me to come early. I've offered to help . . . ," she says, looking about helplessly.

"You look nice," Sydney says.

"Well, I thought it would be okay to wear white to the rehearsal dinner. You're not wearing white tonight, are you?"

"Nor tomorrow."

"Well, that's good, then," her mother says, smoothing the front of the jacket. "I didn't think it would be so hot, though."

"It'll cool off tonight," Sydney offers. "We'll have the dinner on the porch."

"Really?" her mother says, slightly taken aback. "I've heard the weather will be iffy."

Over her mother's shoulder, Sydney sees her father. He does not have a room in the house, but will be staying in a B&B further along the coast. He is sitting at the kitchen table (the very same kitchen table Jeff intended as a weapon against Ben; Sydney's sweater sometimes catches on the crack in the lip) with Mr. Edwards, each fingering a cup of coffee.

Her father has not had a good haircut in years. Irregular tufts of gray stick out from a bald tonsure, a contraband yarmulke after all. He is wearing an old seersucker suit, the white gone a faint yellow with the years. Any minute now, he will pull out his silver cigarette case, a gift from his wife on his wedding day, and light up an unfiltered Marlboro, bringing Mrs. Edwards screaming from the living room.

*   *   *

For a moment, Sydney lingers in the passageway. She will not interrupt her father's
conversation, not until she is dressed. But
something in the easy posture of the two
men—seemingly a matter-of-fact discussion with much nodding of heads—fills Sydney with an unhoped-for sense of good fortune.

Sydney, for the wedding, has her old room, a comfort. On the second twin bed is the black suitcase she will take to Europe. She has always prided herself on traveling light. Besides, she has modest plans to shop; she and Jeff are, after all, going to Paris. From the closet door hangs her wedding dress, a slip of salmon-pink. Hélène, who has demonstrated a remarkable talent for hair, has promised to arrange Sydney's in a loose bun Sydney once admired on Julie.

Across the hall, Jeff will dress in the boys' dorm, which he will share with Sahir and Ivers. (Peter and Frank will share one of the many guest rooms.) Sydney pictures the three grown men sleeping under the green plaid blankets, the childhood baseball caps slung over the bedposts. A year ago, Ben would have joined them on a cot rolled in for the occasion.

Ben, about whom no one ever speaks. His absence felt more keenly than anyone's presence.

A faint knock on the door causes Sydney to pull the sash of her terry cloth robe more tightly around herself. "Come in," she says.

Julie, with wrapped package in hand, sticks her head into the room.

"How are you?" Sydney asks.

"I'm good," Julie says.

Sydney particularly likes the way Julie's thin red scarf is knotted at the back of her neck. From her earlobes hang silver chains with large studded globes at the ends. All Hélène's doing. Sydney, once admiring the way Julie had arrived at a family gathering, said, in an aside to Hélène, that she'd be happy to have the woman teach her how to dress with as much panache. Hélène responded by removing Sydney's silver necklace and sliding it into Sydney's pocket. She then unbuttoned the top two buttons of Sydney's jacket and rolled the sleeves. Sydney, examining the results in a hallway mirror, was pleased to discover how well the editing had worked. The silver studs in her ears and the three inches of bare skin at the neckline were immensely more elegant than the two pieces of jewelry had been.

"I've brought you a present," Julie says, holding a small box aloft. The package has been wrapped in an artful manner—the bow arranged deliberately off-center, the ends of the moss-colored tulle ribbon uneven.

"Sit with me," Sydney says, gesturing to the bed. She hesitates before opening the box. "Is this going to make me cry?" she asks.

Julie shrugs and smiles.

Beneath the tissue paper lies a blue handkerchief, a patchwork of different materials. Sydney identifies a square of something that feels like oxford cloth, another of pale blue silk, a third of what appears to be a tie. Sydney touches a fourth patch and laughs. "Is this what I think it is?" she asks as she fingers a bit from Jeff's old, faded bathing trunks.

Julie nods. "I stole them. He's been looking for them for weeks."

"I know he has." Sydney smooths the

handkerchief flat over the lap of her robe. There are nine squares, three over three. Each square is approximately two inches on a side. "You made it," Sydney says with wonder.

"I did," Julie admits. "The blue lace here is from the sash of your grandmother's wedding gown. The oxford cloth is from my dad's shirt. The tie is from your dad."

"They all knew about this?"

"Everybody gave something." Julie pauses. "Well, almost everybody. This one," she says, pointing to the bit of pale blue silk, "is from me, from the tank top I wore all last summer. This flannel piece is from your mother's old nightgown."

Sydney brings the handkerchief to her face and inhales the flannel square, imagining herself transported back to the nights when she would lay her head on her mother's lap while her mother read to her, a scenario that, in fact, may never have happened.

"And this one, with the tie-dye, is from your friend Emily . . ."

"I remember that shirt," Sydney says.

"This piece here is from my grandmother, who you never met, but I know she would want you to have it. It's from a Belgian tablecloth she always used when we had Sunday dinners at her house."

"Your mother's mother?"

"My father's.

"And this one," Julie says, pointing to the ninth and final square, "is from a baby blanket your mother said you had when you were born."

Sydney fingers the scrap of waffle weave. Each square is a different shade of blue— cornflower and lavender and indigo—all carefully stitched together with a wisteria-colored border, just as a patchwork quilt might be.

"Julie, thank you!" Sydney says, embracing the girl. "I will always treasure this." For a minute, Sydney is unable to speak. "I didn't know you could sew," she says finally, reaching for a tissue and blowing her nose.

Julie shrugs again, as if sewing were a skill anyone might pick up.

"Where did you get the idea?"

"I just did," Julie answers, unable, as always, to explain the source of her creativity.

Sydney again studies the squares. She

notes that there is no contribution from Mrs. Edwards or Ben.

Julie sits back against the headboard and surveys the room. "Is that your dress?"

"For tomorrow, yes."

"It's pretty."

"Thank you."

"It's the right color for your skin. Is that why you picked it?"

"I just liked the color."

"I wish Hélène and I could get married," the girl says wistfully, drawing up her knees.

Sydney turns, surprised. "You're too young."

"I don't know if it's legal in Canada," Julie muses.

Julie is nineteen—old enough to marry in any country, Sydney guesses. But Julie doesn't mean that. "Have you discussed this with Hélène?" she asks.

"We could have a ceremony," Julie says brightly, "and invite our friends."

Sydney touches the handkerchief.

"Would you come?" Julie asks.

"Of course I would come." Sydney turns her body so that she is facing Julie. She lays the handkerchief between them. "Julie, you have a lot of years ahead of you."

"I'm happy nearly all the time," Julie says in expert defense. "I'm only a little sad now because of Ben."

Sydney nods. "I tried to get him to come."

"Did you? And what did he say?"

"Not much. I think the invitation has to come from Jeff."

"I don't understand what happened," Julie says.

"I don't either."

"But you were there. Dad says there was a fight."

"Not a physical fight exactly. But, yes, it felt like a fight."

"They used to fight a lot when they were little. Dad talked to me about it."

When Julie was born, Sydney calculates, the brothers would have been seventeen and thirteen.

"And then Ben went away to college and it just stopped. But Dad thinks they didn't really, you know, work it out."

Sydney imagines Mr. Edwards trying to explain Ben's baffling absences at family gatherings to Julie. He would have hated the rift for her sake as much as for his.

"What are you wearing tonight?" Julie asks.

"A blue sundress. With a sweater if it's cold on the porch. How about you?"

"I have a dress Hélène picked out. It's black. Black's okay, right?"

"Of course."

"It's kind of, I don't know. It has a low back."

Sydney smooths the hair on Julie's forehead. "This is the best present I ever got," she says.

Sydney showers in the bathroom she shares with the minister, trying to avoid a water-stained copy of *Hemmings Motor News* on the floor. Hanging from a hook is a much-worn toiletries kit with items inside that Sydney does not want to have to think about. Without even trying, she can see a small glass bottle of golden corn remover.

For a time, in her room, Sydney attempts a wave over her forehead to which she can then affix an onyx-and-rhinestone barrette she bought for the occasion. She is aiming for a 1940s look to go with the vintage sundress she bought in a thrift store in Cambridge. But after several attempts, she abandons the effort and draws her hair straight back into a knot made from a pony-tail.

Guessing what Hélène would do, Sydney tries on but then discards several pairs of earrings, finally opting for small buds of cut glass with screw backs, another find from the thrift shop. She examines herself in the small mirror at the back of the closet door. Her face has color from the rare bits of sun they've had over the last several days, but her hair, still wet, looks too severe. She un-pins it, letting it fall and not touching it. The fake jewels at her ears are a perfect choice.

The dress fits well through the waist and hips. Below that, Sydney cannot see in the mirror and has to guess at where the hem lies.

In the space of a year, she has gone from someone who might or might not have been introduced to visitors to being the center of attention. She senses there is something in-herently unstable in such a rapid rise, a gov-erness elevated to the status of wife. A sus-pect promotion.

It occurs to Sydney that she hasn't seen or heard Jeff come up from the beach. She walks to the window and spots him sitting on a kayak, watching two boys skim-board in a small lagoon made by the receding tide. He looks as though he wishes he could join them.

Sydney carefully folds her new handkerchief and tucks it into the pocket of the blue sundress. She will show it to Jeff and to her mother, but not to Mrs. Edwards, who may or may not have been asked for a piece of cloth. Who may have refused to give one. She takes a long breath. Apart from worrying about her mother and father and a possible killing frost that may occur if the two are inadvertently paired for any length of time, as well as not wishing to upset the delicate truce she has managed with Mrs. Edwards, not to mention trying to ignore the clanging gong of Ben's absence, she thinks the evening should be fun.

When she steps into the upstairs hallway, she can hear a man singing in the shower—doubtless the happy minister with vehicular interests. From below, there is chatter, a female voice with which she is not familiar. The caterer perhaps. She hears then a distinct exclamation of surprise and joy from Mrs. Edwards, though the latter sound has become so rare of late, Sydney isn't at all certain she is correct. If Jeff is still on the beach, Sydney will go out to him and tell him to hurry and dress. Ivers will arrive soon, doubtless cranky about his missed Yankees games. Sydney rounds the newel post and descends the stairs.

She sees him in the mirror, a round mirror with gold braid that sits over the telephone table. He has on a dress shirt; he has come from work. Over his shoulder is a garment bag, and in his hand a small duffel.

She stops on the stairs. In the mirror, he spots her, but there is no change in his expression. Sydney now understands Anna Edwards's exclamation of joy. In seconds, there will be other cries of surprise.

Sydney tries to smile, but his rigidity is inhibiting. She descends another step, and he moves in her direction. He looks drawn and slightly pale, bluish where his five-o'clock shadow would be. Not as robust as when she spoke to him in the bar. He seems a man not in command.

"Did you really think I'd skip your wedding?" he asks when she reaches the bottom step.
   Not Jeff's wedding, but hers.
   "I'm glad you're here," she says.
   "Wouldn't have missed it for the world."

He brushes past her, the duffel briefly touching her hip. She listens to ascending footsteps behind her. She puts her hand into the pocket of her dress and touches the blue patchwork handkerchief.

———〰———

Mark Edwards generously insisted on providing the roses for the wedding. A week earlier, he took Sydney on a formal tour of the garden to pick out specific species for her bouquet. It would have to be a simple arrangement, he said; he could grow the flowers, but he had no skill at arranging them. Simple would be fine, Sydney responded, and together they settled on a series of colors that ranged from tinted ivory to a red-orange, all picked to coordinate

with Sydney's salmon silk. Mr. Edwards will
wrap them so that she won't prick her fingers. Sydney will carry them loosely, as if
someone had just laid a bouquet in her
arms.

Predictably, Mr. Edwards is on his knees.
She notes that he wears pads now, something that wasn't necessary the year before.
He has on a sun visor and is working a pair
of clippers, pruning stray shoots. It is early
July, peak season for roses in New Hampshire. That he has been able to cultivate so
many species so close to the ocean is something of a marvel, and those who know about
gardening often stop to see the flowers. It is
not unusual to notice a strange car parked
on the street, a man or a woman wander-
ing—with Mr. Edwards's permission—the
rows of blossoms.

For a time, Sydney stands at the edge of
the garden. The plot is laid out in the shape
of an arched rectangle and is wonderfully
tended, the roses set in mounded hillocks
and evenly spaced. Sydney knows the wind
off the water is a constant menace; often,
when she glances out the kitchen window in

the mornings, so many petals have been blown off during the night that the plot resembles the aftermath of a party at which a great deal of confetti was tossed into the air.

Mr. Edwards notices her then, an expression of pleasure on his face.

"Don't get up," she calls, but she is too late. She watches with some concern as he stands.

"I'm filthy," he says as she approaches. He takes off his gloves and bends and kisses her cheek. "How is the bride on the day before her wedding?"

"Very well. I just saw Ben."

"Isn't it terrific? I spoke to him when he pulled in. He's up now having a shower. Quite a surprise. Anna is thrilled. Did he say much to you? How do you think he looked?"

"He didn't say much," Sydney answers. "He looked a bit, I don't know, tired maybe."

"I thought so, too. Works too hard. Has, um . . . ?" Mr. Edwards claps his gardening gloves together hard. "Does Jeff . . . ?"

Sydney shakes her head. "I don't think so."

"It will be good for them both," Mr. Edwards says firmly. "A reconciliation. Not speaking is never a good thing. Never. Tears families apart for years. Usually, it's money that does it. Not sure what did it in this case. But there's a kind of loyalty there, don't you think? Perhaps you know more."

Sydney shakes her head. "I don't," she says.

Mr. Edwards waves an arm to take in the entire garden. "I've selected all your blossoms. Won't pick them till morning, of course."

"We should be having the wedding here. It's incredibly beautiful."

"Never have a wedding in a rose garden. Wind picks up, you're left with empty stalks."

"I just came to thank you," Sydney says.

"Gives me a chance to show off," Mr. Edwards says. "Don't you know that every gardener is at heart a braggart?"

She smiles.

"I'm glad you're marrying here," he says, making a gesture to take in the entire house. "Lots of history. Want to sit?"

It is clear to Sydney that Mr. Edwards needs to sit. "Yes, I do," she says.

With a small whisk broom propped up by the side of the stone bench, he carefully brushes off its surface.

"You interested in history?" the man asks. He knocks the loose dirt from his trousers.

"Some," Sydney answers.

"There's tremendous history to this house. I've been to the library and the local historical society and so forth. I've made it quite a hobby. Of course, a house with any age is bound to have history, but this has more than most, I think. Six, seven, eight families have lived here. Did you know that it was originally built as a convent?"

Sydney is surprised and casts her eyes over the aging house, focusing on the dormers. Bedrooms for nuns?

"A French Canadian order down from Quebec. Twenty sisters. A contemplative order."

"It's an ideal place for it."

"There was a scandal involving a priest and a young novitiate." He pauses and shakes his head. "Sometimes I think nothing changes but the date."

Sydney feels a cool, damp breeze along the backs of her arms. The rose leaves, dark and glossy, seem to vibrate in the moving air.

"After the scandal, and we can only guess at what it was," Mr. Edwards continues, "the house was sold to a man who was the editor of a literary magazine in Boston. Don't know much about him, but I do know that his daughter started a home for unwed mothers here, which apparently precipitated another scandal. Can't imagine the unwed mothers would have been any trouble to anyone, but the villagers tried to evict them. They were thought to be corrupting the morals of the local young women."

Sydney looks again at the upstairs dormers. First the sisters and then the unwed mothers. Children, probably many of them, born in those rooms.

"What happened to the babies?" she asks.

"I don't know. I imagine they were put up for adoption. It's a dreadful thing to contemplate, isn't it? Taking a woman's baby from her. Still, though, I guess in those days it was better than the alternative—being cast out onto the street."

Sydney nods.

"The townsfolk may have been successful in ousting these unwed mothers, because in 1929, there's mention of an abandoned property sold to a man named Beecher, who, I *believe*, was involved with a Marxist printing press dedicated to unionist involvement. Textile workers at the mills over in Ely Falls. I have a copy of the newsletter they put out—*Lucky Strike*—that I found in a rare-books store. Quite interesting. Both rabid and witty, an odd combination, like reading *The Daily Worker* combined with *The New Yorker.*" Mr. Edwards sets the gloves he has been holding on the bench. "And, again, I *think* this happened here, there was an attack by the Ku Klux Klan on this group of radical unionists, and one of their members was killed."

"A murder here?"

"You wouldn't think the KKK operated so far north, would you? Shortly after that, Beecher fled. The house was foreclosed on—this would have been in 1930—and was bought by a woman who became something of a minor playwright. She lived in New York but summered here. Did you ever hear the name Vivian Burton?"

Sydney shakes her head. Mr. Edwards bends forward and snatches a rose hip from a cane.

"She had plays on Broadway. She owned the house until her death in 1939. Then it passed to a family named Richmond. The house seems to have inspired not only scandal but also talent, because this Richmond fellow, Albert, was a trompe l'oeil painter. A fine-art painter, not the decorative kind."

" 'Fool the eye,' " Sydney says, considerably more knowledgeable about still-life painting than she was a year ago.

"Precisely. Totally out of fashion, but very good in the manner of Harnett and Peto. There's one hanging in the Museum of Fine Arts in Boston. I keep meaning to go see it, but I never seem to find the time."

"We'll go together one day," Sydney suggests. "And have lunch."

"Wonderful idea," Mr. Edwards says with enthusiasm.

There is a pause, during which each imagines the future. A future that might contain several lunches, the occasional walk together, many conversations, grandchildren.

"Now this painter, Richmond," Mr. Edwards continues, "he sent three sons to World War Two. He was too old for the war himself, but he had sons. Possibly one daughter. You hear so much about the sacrifices mothers had to make, but one seldom thinks about the fathers."

Sydney is silent, imagining a father driving first one son and then another and then another to the train station, sending them off to Europe or the Pacific, not knowing if they would return or not.

"Did the sons make it back?" Sydney asks.

"I don't know," Mr. Edwards says. "The house wasn't passed on to any of them, but that doesn't necessarily mean they didn't survive. It would be very bad luck to lose three sons, wouldn't it?"

"Unimaginable."

"After that, ownership passes to a family named Simmons, who used the property exclusively as a summer cottage. They let the place go, I'm afraid to say. Then it was bought in the nineteen eighties by the Vision pilot and his wife. You know about the crash."

"I do."

"And I—well, we, Anna and I—bought it from the widow. I don't like to profit from someone else's tragedy, but the house was going to go to somebody. I like to think we've kept it up as best as can be."

"It's lovely," Sydney says. "I've always liked it. I'm not sure I'll ever be able to think of it the same way again."

"And now you'll be a part of the house's history," Mr. Edwards says with what appears to be great satisfaction.

"Well, you, too," Sydney points out.

"Sydney, are you happy?" he asks suddenly.

Sydney is taken aback by the question. "Yes," she answers, putting a hand to her chest. "I was hoping that it showed."

"I'm glad, then. I was afraid that the Ben and Jeff situation would have put a damper on your happiness. And I've wondered at times if you wouldn't be a bit gun-shy about marrying again. I hope you don't mind my mentioning it."

"No," she says. "It's a fact. I don't feel gun-shy. Maybe I should, but I don't."

"My son is a good man," Mr. Edwards says, a strange declaration under the circumstances.

"I know he is," Sydney responds, moved by this father's endorsement.

The vibration of the glossy rose leaves has turned to a flutter. The sky, gray and dull be-

fore, has become dramatic, both threaten-
ing and promising: dark clouds to the west,
slashes of blue to the east.

Sydney gazes up at the house. The nuns
and the priest. The unwed mothers. The
Marxists and the murder victim. The playwright and the artist. Did the man eat alone,
looking at maps each evening, placing
markers where he thought his sons had
been sent? And then the pilot's widow,
dealing with the crush of press. Sydney remembers the faces of the pilots on television. How ordinary they looked.

She follows the roofline of the house with
her eyes and then settles on the front porch.
She wonders if there have been other weddings in the house. There must have been,
she guesses, multiple weddings and births
and deaths. She hopes on balance there
has been more joy than pain in the building.

"They came here for the beauty," Mr. Edwards says.

—–〰—–

Sydney moves through the house, admiring
its fancy dress. Julie and Hélène are engaged in decorating the stairway with rib-

bons and white bows. Bowls of white roses have been set upon the dining room table and the coffee table in the living room. In the kitchen, there is bustle, Mrs. Edwards animated and directing traffic. Sydney walks to one of the long floor-to-ceiling windows and looks out over the beach. No sign of Jeff. Perhaps he is even now up in the boys' dorm dressing for the rehearsal dinner. She hopes that he and Ben have met and spoken. Jeff, despite everything, will be moved that Ben has finally come. If nothing else, his brother has capitulated. No man could refuse that gesture.

Sydney glances about for Ivers. She thinks her father may have gone for a walk. Her mother, she knows, is lying down in her room. Periodically, the porch is aglow with sudden sun and then is cast in shadow.

Jeff, who has moved all of his belongings into Sydney's room, is sitting on the spare bed next to her suitcase. Piles of clothing have been dropped onto the chair and the floor. Jeff still has on his bathing suit and his T-shirt. He seems oblivious to his sandy feet. "You might have warned me," he says.

There is no answer to this. Sydney shuts

the door. Yes, she might have warned her fiancé that his estranged brother was in the house. Instead, she sought refuge in the garden with the patriarch.

"This is your doing, isn't it?" he asks. "He as much as said so."

Sydney notes that Jeff does not say Ben's name.

"I thought it would make you happy," she answers.

Jeff raises his eyebrows.

"Have you spoken to each other?" she asks.

"Of course we've spoken to each other."

Sydney doesn't ask what was said. Right now, she isn't certain she wants to know.

"It cast a pall," she argues in her defense. "I could feel it. Everyone could feel it. It was something that we would never forget. That could never be made right again."

"You should have asked me first."

She leans against the closet. "Jeff," she says.

"What?" he asks, barely looking at her.

"I think you're being unreasonable."

More than that, she thinks privately: *petulant* is a word that comes to mind.

"Ben and I have our differences," Jeff says. "I don't think they'll ever be made right. I'm sorry you don't like it. I don't really like it either, but there it is. And believe me, he hasn't come here out of love for me."

"Then, what is it?" Sydney asks.

But Jeff is silent, either unwilling or unable to answer her.

"Jeff, listen."

"What?"

"There's a story my grandfather used to tell me about himself and his brother," Sydney says. "One day when he was a boy, his brother came into his room and destroyed a dozen model airplanes he'd painstakingly built out of balsa wood. I don't know why; they'd had a fight. They didn't speak for six years."

Jeff sits on the bed, arms crossed. She senses that he is barely listening.

"Then World War Two came," Sydney says, "and my grandfather's brother was being shipped off to Europe with the Army Air Corps. His parents walked the brother to the train station, but my grandfather wouldn't go."

Sydney wonders what has made her remember a story she hasn't thought about in years. Mr. Edwards's mention of World War II? The painter waiting for his sons to come home?

"At the last minute, my grandfather thought about how he might never see his brother again, about how the man might die in Europe. He sprinted all the way to the train and got there just as it was pulling out. He shook his brother's hand and said good-bye."

Jeff looks up from the bed. "And the brother died."

"No, nothing that dramatic."

"So your point is?"

"Well, I think Ben has come to the train station," Sydney says.

Ivers, as always, delivers baseball trivia at a gunner's pace.

"Happens every year. Sox-Yankees, July Fourth. Wells on the mound for New York. Lowe for Boston. You'd be thinking to concede this one, but with Jackson's hitters hot—forty-two homers in June, twenty in the last five games, eleven in the last two—anything can happen. Put your money on the Sox. Sydney, have I mentioned that I'm going to kill you for getting married tomorrow afternoon?"

"We'll set up a TV on the porch," she says.

"Really?" Ivers asks, a note of hope in his voice.

"Ivers, no," Sydney says, smiling.

Sahir, across from Sydney, is in earnest political discussion with Mr. Edwards. The topic is gay marriage, which Sahir seems passionately in favor of. Anna Edwards darts nervous glances in Julie's direction. In a complex series of eye movements and hand signals that make her appear tic-plagued, she seems to be trying to tell her husband to button it; but he is either oblivious to his wife's facial twitches or forgetful of his own daughter's sexual orientation. Julie is not asked for her opinion on the subject.

Jeff, mindful of his responsibilities as a host, is engrossed in conversation with Sydney's mother about the best route by car to Portsmouth from western Massachusetts, though the real reason for Jeff's intense attention, Sydney knows, is so that when Ben finally comes down to dinner, Jeff can pretend not to notice.

The table, lovely with white linen, is awash in roses, the guests in finery a notch up from the norm. Dress shirts, sleeves rolled, no ties. Sydney notes that Jeff has on flip-flops, which might or might not be due to the fact that he left his good shoes in the boys' dorm. He will not now enter that room.

Sydney cannot help but notice Sahir's shoes—dark, highly polished brogues with thick soles. They remind her of men in the 1950s, when expensive shoes were a sign of good breeding.

Ben shuffles down the steps as if he'd been on an important business call and were now just minutes late for a lesser event. He has showered and dressed and is rolling his sleeves as he enters the dining room. He missed the rehearsal itself, a strangely life-less playlet in which the principals faced a white sofa and repeated brief lines. The production lacked choreography, lights, any sense of drama. Jeff especially seemed wooden, as if none of this was his idea. Sydney, annoyed, let it go and tried to com-pensate with nervous laughter, Ivers helping her along. What precisely they were laugh-ing about Sydney could not have said. From the opposite sofa, Anna Edwards sighed frequently, as though at children who were misbehaving.

Sydney's vision splits—one camera on Ben, the other on Jeff, still deep in conversation with Sydney's mother, still strenuously ignoring the newcomer's presence. Julie leaps up in her smart backless dress and hugs Ben. Mr. Edwards introduces him to the minister and to Sydney's parents, who smile and nod their greetings to the wayward brother. Anna Edwards frantically waves Ben over to sit in the chair next to her. If one didn't know better, one might think it was Ben and not Jeff who was the bridegroom.

Jeff can no longer pretend to be otherwise engaged. When he turns to Sydney, his eyes are glassy and opaque.

The dinner is served by a woman in black pants and a white shirt. A lobster stew is presented in sturdy crocks that Sydney doesn't think came from Emporia. The roses on the table mix with the humidity from the sea air to produce an intoxicating ether that seems pumped in for the occasion.

Sydney is acutely aware of Ben to one side of her, Jeff to the other. She hardly dares to breathe lest her body escape the rigid space allotted her. To touch Jeff, which ought to be ordinary and even called for, seems, now, a gratuitous gesture that would remind Ben of the reason for the gathering, which, in turn, might remind him of the fraternal rift, of a year of injured feelings.

Touching Ben is out of the question.

Occasionally, Sydney feels that she is losing her bearings, that she is not as sharp or as observant as she used to be, that somehow in the previous year, she has substituted, in incremental degrees, emotion for intelligence. In cooler moments, she wonders if this is an altogether profitable trade.

Mr. Edwards stands and proposes a toast. "Tonight," he begins, "we add another chapter to the history of this wonderful house—a joyous chapter, for it brings into our family the lovely and lovable Sydney Sklar. Good fortune has smiled upon our son. There is a Yiddish word that means, roughly translated, 'fated to be together.' I hope I can pronounce it correctly. *Beshert.*" Mr. Edwards raises his glass. *"Beshert,"* he says again.

The guests, Mrs. Edwards wanly, raise their glasses and repeat the word. Sydney wonders if she will be the first Jew to take partial possession of the house, however inlawed and tenuous that possession might be. She also wonders something else: Are she and Jeff really fated to be together? And by what or whom? Brought together by a complex set of circumstances to put Jeff on the porch at the precise moment Sydney emerged from the water? Who could believe in such an unseen hand? Did Daniel have to die to allow fate to have its way? What a cruel, indifferent, and whimsical god to have done such a wanton thing. And for what purpose?

Jeff does not rise to thank his father. A strained silence lengthens.

Ivers stands and skewers the groom, listing, for the bride's benefit and before it is too late to cancel the wedding, a few little-known facts about Jeff Edwards. The groom, Ivers reveals, once urinated on a statue of John Harvard after losing to his competitors in Cambridge a breathtakingly close debate regarding the validity of NATO. After he was caught, he was brought before a disciplinary committee at his own college (Brown), the members of which stood and applauded when he walked in. Ivers also wishes Sydney to know that her fiancé once sank into a state of mesmerized reverence bordering on the spiritual when watching synchronized swimming at the last televised summer Olympics. Jeff declared the sport to be "really difficult." And, finally, does Sydney know that her husband-to-be is a secret gambler, once betting on the Yankees to win over the Sox by a margin of four runs in a play-off game? Because of these unforgivable and grievous flaws, Ivers is more than a little happy to bequeath the man to Sydney in less than twenty hours. And, in case anyone wants to know, the score is Boston 3, Yankees 0.

Cheers go up, and Ivers sits down.

A second course, Thai shrimp, is served. Jeff seems wholly concentrated on his meal, as if he were a restaurant critic. Beside her, Ben reaches often for his water glass and surveys the gathering. Sydney is reminded of the day Victoria first came to the house, the way Ben stood on the landing taking in the entire scene.

Because of her earlier conversation with Mr. Edwards, Sydney cannot help but think of the people who might or might not have eaten dozens of meals in this very room. The sisters in their dark habits (did they not freeze in winter?). The man of letters (would he have had distinguished guests with triple-barreled names to his dinner table—Edward Everett Hale and John Greenleaf Whittier?). The unwed mothers with their infants (or were the infants gone before the mothers rose from their beds?). The Marxists (would they have had formal meals or would that have seemed too bourgeois for them?). And what of the playwright? Or of the artist with three sons gone to war? Sydney sees him alone at a large table, the seats empty, a wide expanse of cherry or mahogany covered with maps of the Rhine and of Belgium. And then, of course, there was the widow with her daughter. No, they would not have eaten in the dining room, Sydney decides. Meals, if there were any, would have been had at a table in the kitchen, the press shouting at them from the street.

Sydney takes a sip of wine. It seems to her, as she surveys the current occupants of the walnut table with the uneven bevel, as though the personal history of the house has thinned out, that it is now less dramatic, less consequential, than it used to be. So little seems to matter when stacked up against plane crashes, a murder, unwed mothers, a war. Sydney's time in the house will not be spoken of in years to come, will not make for a single impressive anecdote.

And yet, she wonders, setting her glass on the table, are there not stories at this table, each with its own dramatic arc, the ends of the tales not yet known? She thinks of the young daughter who ran away from home for love. Will her unlikely happiness last? Of the feud, seemingly ancient, between the two benign brothers. Will one forgive the other? Of the matriarch who can barely conceal her jealousy and disdain for the young woman who will enter her family, the mother who even now is touching her eldest son as if he might vanish at any moment. And Sydney thinks, too, of her own parents, who once made a family, who presumably loved each other, and who now separately watch a daughter, their only child, marry for the third time.

And what of the minister swooning over the Thai shrimp? Is he a secret cross-dresser?

A pool shark? Or is he merely what he seems, a modestly pious man not immune to the pleasures of a good bedroom on the sea and a remarkably fine meal?

"Checked the weather just before I came down. Supposed to be beautiful tomorrow afternoon," Ben says, consciously making a positive contribution to the gathering. Or has the comment been offered as proof that he is now taking the higher ground?

Dessert and coffee will be served on the porch, Mrs. Edwards announces. Sydney rises and waits for Jeff, who, in turn, waits for Sydney's mother, who is having a hell of a time extricating herself from her chair. Arthritic knees, she explains, an ailment about which she complains often, though she seems disinclined to do anything about them. It is understood that the "young people," as Mr. Edwards has lightly dubbed them, will stay for a time on the porch with the "old folks" before changing their clothes and descending to the beach, where there is to be a bonfire and, one assumes, considerably more fun.

Jeff excuses himself to go out to greet Peter and Frank, who have been stuck in traffic. Purely by circumstance, Ben seats himself next to Sydney in a hard teak chair. Not to have chosen the empty seat would have called even more attention to the fraternal tension than there is already, not Ben's style. For a time, Sydney and Ben listen to the banter, none of it important, a sense of real life being lived elsewhere. In tandem, they raise their cups and drink, Sydney embarrassed by the gesture.

In a moment of noisy laughter, Sydney asks Ben if he has spoken to Jeff.

"We talked."

"What did you say?"

"We called each other assholes and then shook hands."

"That was it?"

"That was it."

In her room, Sydney exchanges the blue sundress for a pair of linen shorts and a sleeveless white shirt. She ties a navy sweater around her shoulders. Already, she can hear laughter on the beach, can see the fire from her second-story bedroom. Replacing the dress in one of the two shallow closets, Sydney thinks again of the French Canadian sisters. Were the closets built for them? Shallow because they had so little to wear?

As promised, Jeff and Ivers and Peter and Frank throw Sahir onto the sand and divest him of his shoes. He protests, but helplessly. Julie makes s'mores and hands them out one by one, the sticky concoctions devoured rapidly, as if everyone hadn't consumed a heavy meal an hour earlier. Most have changed into shorts and T-shirts, distinguishing themselves from the old folks, who can still be heard on the porch, even though they are fewer in number, and their laughter is dwindling. Sydney half expects Anna Edwards in culottes and halter top to descend the stairs, refusing to be left out of an event that includes her sons.

Sparks spray the air. Occasionally, the wood emits sharp reports. Sydney feels warm in front, cool at her back. Ben, arms behind his head, one knee raised, has commandeered the only chaise and thus has achieved his usual position of comfort. Jeff and Sydney share a log. Periodically, friends of the brothers stop by, having emerged from the gloom surrounding the fire, to congratulate the couple. Word of the impending marriage has traveled down the beach. Other young men and women, regulars on the summer circuit, arrive with beers in hand, arms linked, repositories of childhood memories repeated now and hooted at. Sydney, apart from greeting these strangers, is required to say little, having not been present during the precious events being recounted. Instead, she eats marshmallows and watches the sparks write messages she cannot read on the dark air above.

Sydney buries her feet in the cool sand. Near her, Julie and Hélène sit cross-legged. Earlier, Julie fed Hélène a s'more, the older woman laughing like a bridegroom at a wedding. Perhaps, Sydney thinks, this is the closest they will ever come to a ceremony of their own.

Sydney feels a finger trailing along her shoulder.

"I'm going up," Jeff says.

"Now?" Sydney asks, surprised. "So soon?"

"Ivers will take care of the fire," he says.

When Sydney rises, Ben looks away, as if something out at sea had suddenly snagged his complete attention.

"Good night, all," Sydney calls, raising both hands and waving. It would be unseemly for her to stay on the beach if her husband-to-be is going up. "Thank you for coming. The groom needs his beauty sleep."

Sydney smiles at the boos.

"Don't forget, you can't sleep with Jeff the night before your wedding," Ivers says. "Bad luck forever. The score is ten-two, by the way."

Sydney raises a fist in victory. She bends and kisses both Julie and Hélène. "You'll come in at ten tomorrow?"

"Is that too soon?" Julie asks.

"No, it's perfect," Sydney says.

The porch is abandoned, the old folks having achieved their beds. In silence, she and Jeff pass through the house and climb the stairs. In the bedroom, Sydney sits and brushes the sand from her feet.

"I'm going to sleep here if that's okay," Jeff says.

"I assumed that," Sydney says, though it is hard to ignore the vestigial sense of bad luck that Ivers mentioned.

"I can't do the Ben thing," he adds.

"What's the Ben thing?"

"Pretend."

Through her window, Sydney can see a shower of sparks, as if someone had poked a log. "What about Ivers and Sahir and the others?" she asks. "We invited them here. I think we're being rude."

"They're all set."

"They know about you and Ben?"

"Of course they know."

"You're a little sharp with me tonight."

"I'm sorry, Sydney. I'm spoiling this for you, aren't I?"

"A bit."

Jeff moves to the other twin bed and sits once again beside her suitcase.

"I'll get that," Sydney says, rising to fetch her luggage, surprised when Jeff allows her to do so.

Jeff, seemingly poleaxed, lies down fully clothed.

Sydney stands beside his bed and for a

moment is consumed by tenderness. She kneels, her forehead pressed against the side of his chest. Idly, Jeff plays with her hair.

"I'm sorry," she says. "I asked him to come, and now I wish I hadn't. It's ruining the whole thing for you, too, isn't it?"

"It's not your fault," he says.

From the opened window, Sydney can hear laughter. Shouldn't she and Jeff be where the laughter is?

"Do you really hate him so?" she asks.

"Sometimes I do. Actually, I think it might be more the other way around."

"That can't be true."

Jeff is silent.

"Your father was telling me about the history of the house," Sydney says, propping her chin on the edge of the bed. "About the nuns and the Marxists and the unwed mothers. I was thinking that tomorrow you and I will become a part of that history."

"To hear my mother tell it," Jeff says, "she practically knew the nuns."

Sydney lifts herself up and kisses his arm. "I love you," she says, conscious of the fact that she doesn't say it as often as he does. She sometimes wonders if this is because she doesn't need to, that Jeff knows all too well how she feels.

"Come here," he says.

Sydney raises herself even further and straddles the man who is now her lover. Tomorrow, with a few words and the merest of gestures, he will become her husband.

"I love you, too," Jeff says. The words seem weightless, airborne.

Tempting fate, Sydney unbuttons her sleeveless white shirt.

—⁓—

"I'm going kayaking," Jeff announces in the morning. He slips on his bathing trunks.

Sydney rises up on one elbow. After they made love, she retreated to her own bed, both agreeing a good night's sleep could not be had together in such a narrow twin. "On your wedding day?" she asks.

Jeff parts the curtains to check the weather, which, from where Sydney lies, still appears to be "iffy."

"The wedding isn't until three."

"Yes, but . . . ," Sydney begins. She sits

up in bed, the sheets just covering her breasts. She has never had a successful discussion while naked.

"It'll probably be the last time we'll be up here until, I don't know, late August, September."

The wedding trip will consume three weeks. After that, they have another wedding to go to, in North Carolina, and following that, a conference at Johns Hopkins.

Still, it feels wrong for Jeff to go off on his wedding morning. Sydney cannot say why and doesn't.

"I can't stay here," Jeff says.

Jeff will not remain in a house in which he might inadvertently find himself alone in a room with Ben.

"Enough of this," Sydney says. "You're behaving like two schoolboys," she adds, when actually she means that Jeff is behaving like a schoolboy. Ben has seemed agreeable enough.

"Won't be gone long," Jeff says, bending and kissing her. "I'll come back, get my things, and dress in my parents' room. Stay out of your hair."

"Be careful," Sydney says.

Jeff shrugs her off. "Love you," he says as he opens the door.

Sydney cannot help but notice his quick glance into the hallway before stepping outside. Under normal circumstances, she might interpret his darting glance as one of not wanting to be caught leaving his lover's room—a charming, if anachronistic, gesture. But Sydney knows its true intent: to make sure Ben is nowhere in sight.

Sydney lies back on the pillow. She wished for sunshine when she woke. There is, she supposes, always the hope of some sun later, sublimely timed. "Just for the ceremony," she says aloud, bargaining with whoever will man the lights for that particular bit of theater.

She stands and looks for her robe. Her mother might even now be in the kitchen, searching for the silverware, not knowing where the cereal is kept.

—∼∞∼—

The morning seems intolerably long. Ivers sits in the dining room and listens to sports talk on the radio, the volume low, intermittently gesturing or speaking to unseen voices. Sahir reads the *New York Times,* the *Boston Globe,* and *Barron's,* which he drove into Portsmouth to buy. Sydney's mother, unoccupied, is invited to join Sydney and Julie and Hélène in Sydney's room while the latter fixes Sydney's hair.

Sydney enjoys Hélène's delicate hands and is lulled by the voices behind her. When she is asked by Hélène to turn, she glances out at her ocean-liner view for a glimpse of Jeff—neon orange life vest atop a neon yellow kayak, a bright signal on a gray day— but he has not returned. It is, she tells herself, still early. He has hours yet to remain free, if indeed that is what he wanted, a last breath of freedom. The thought depresses her, for she prefers to think of marrying as a freeing-up, a passport to a country she once visited and now wishes to return to.

"So I said to him, 'Did you *not* get my e-mail? Did you *not* open it?' "

Emily, Sydney's friend, recently arrived, has joined the assembled in Sydney's cramped room. "And he said, get this, 'I don't consider e-mail to be a valid mode of correspondence.' I said, 'You don't?' and he said, 'No, I don't,' and I said, 'Well, how about this? *Fuck off.* Does that work for you?'

"You should have seen his face, the pompous prick."

Women complaining to women about men, some of it heartfelt, most of it not, some anecdotes amended as soon as the words have been uttered. Julie and Hélène cannot, of course, complain about men, and Sydney cannot really complain about the man she is about to marry, so that leaves mostly Emily and Sydney's mother, who tells stories that might embarrass Sydney in another venue.

"Oh," Sydney says, getting a look at herself in the mirror as Hélène has her sit facing it. Her hair is done up, as promised, but the knot is so artful as to appear to be coming loose, though any number of pins and a prodigious amount of hair spray have been necessary to accomplish it.

"Put these on," Hélène says.

Sydney unwraps a box in which lies a pair of pearl earrings. "These are for me?"

"They're your wedding present," Hélène says.

"But I assumed the hair was the wedding present," Sydney says, fingering the tear-drop-shaped pearls.

Hélène kisses her cheek. "Put them on," she repeats.

And, of course, Hélène might have known the effect of the earrings with the loose bun. Sydney's face is flatteringly framed, her jaw-line and throat prominent, the pearl earrings two lights at her ears. The earrings will be all the jewelry she will need.

"Thank you," Sydney says, standing and embracing the Canadian woman.

"I envy you," Hélène says.

Sydney will not put on the dress that still hangs from the closet door until the last minute. Her sandals and shawl have been set upon a chair. The other women have left to tend to themselves, and from the hallway, Sydney can hear showers running. She imagines steamed mirrors, dresses hanging from bathroom hooks, makeup arranged on the lip of a sink.

Downstairs, men are pacing. They remain convivial, though Sydney can hear questions asked twice, three times, worry apparent only in the repetition. Sydney looks again at the clock on her bureau, a glance that incorporates a view through which no neon yellow kayak has yet passed. In minutes, Sydney thinks, the questions might become more pressing, the tone more urgent, worry laced with anger.

When the showers stop, the voices downstairs raise themselves a notch, not enough to worry the bride upstairs, whom they might imagine blissfully oblivious, but enough to gather the men together. A search party must be formed, Mr. Edwards says.

Oh god, Sydney whispers in her room.

Mr. Edwards addresses the guests. Sydney, in her robe, listens from her open doorway. She has tucked Julie's handmade handkerchief into her bra. She wants to have it on her for the ceremony.

"I'm sure he's all right," she hears Mr. Edwards say. "Maybe he beached himself and is looking for a way to get back here. He wouldn't have taken his cell phone because he'd have known he could easily flip the kayak. My guess is that he went for the islands. It's his usual destination. What in god's name possessed the man, today of all days? Ben, you go with Ivers and Peter in the Whaler, check out the islands. The three of you." And here Mr. Edwards addresses Sahir and Frank and Sydney's father. "You come with me. We'll drive into the village. We may have to split up. I'm not sure how to go about this. Good god, what was the boy thinking?"

Jeff, Sydney notes, instantly demoted.

The men, in tuxes, white boutonnieres in place, leave the house. Sydney is embarrassed for the fuss. At the very least, all the village will know of the groom who was so careless and so casual as to go kayaking on his wedding day. Of the flock of man-birds who descended upon the town to scour it for traces of the wayward fiancé. The embarrassment, however, is nothing compared to her fear. Sydney imagines. And then she imagines again. She cannot censor her thoughts.

Feeling a nearly unbearable urge to lie down, Sydney does so, propping her head up on the pillows so as not to destroy Hélène's work. The news will be good, she decides. Jeff has simply forgotten the time. Or Mr. Edwards was correct—Jeff had to beach himself and is even now frantically looking for a way back. Any minute, everyone will come home, Jeff good-naturedly taking a ribbing, mounting the stairs two at a time, looking for his tux and his shoes, blowing a kiss at Sydney and telling her he will explain all after the ceremony.

From time to time, Sydney hears the doorbell ring. Guests have begun to arrive, Julie and Hélène charged with occupying them without revealing the fact that the groom is missing. In time, however, the guests are bound to suspect that something is wrong. Sydney bites down on her lip.

A prisoner in her room, Sydney puts on her dress and shoes so that she can go to the landing and wait. She will not, however, mingle with the guests.

"There you are," Emily says, running up the stairs and giving Sydney a hug.

"This is insane," Sydney says.

"It's going to be all right."

Emily has on a gunmetal-green silk sheath. Her glasses frame and enhance her dark eyes. "In a few minutes, we'll all be laughing about the son of a bitch and how he got lost."

"Will we?" Sydney asks.

"You bet."

Sydney, slightly light-headed, puts a hand on the railing. "Your dress is stunning," she says to her friend.

"I was just about to say the same to you."

"Is everybody here?"

"Becky was stuck in traffic, but she's here now. Everyone is eating and drinking and, frankly, could care less when the ceremony starts. You know a wedding is only an excuse for a great party."

Sydney is silent.

"But when Jeff walks through that door," Emily says evenly, "I'm going to wring his fucking neck."

Sydney retreats to her room and sits on the bed. She reviews her marital history. *Twice married: once divorced, once widowed.* She hoped to make another entry today, but who can say what that entry will read?

Sydney hears car doors slamming, raised voices from below. An energy seems to tumble up the stairs and spill into her room. Sydney runs to the railing and watches as the front door opens. Mr. Edwards walks in, his face rigid.

"Is Jeff back?" Sydney, breathless, calls.

But Mr. Edwards appears not to have heard her.

Sahir and Ivers immediately follow Mr. Edwards through the door. "Is Jeff all right?" Sydney asks from above.

Ivers glances up, his face unnaturally pale. "We've got him," he says. Ivers stops and turns toward the door.

Jeff enters the hallway, a burst of garish color, the orange life vest unclasped but hanging from one shoulder. He stands barefoot. His hair and body are still wet, his bathing trunks clinging to his body. His feet are nearly blue.

Sydney laughs and weeps together. "Thank god," she cries. "Thank god you're all right." She holds on to the railing, relief weakening her legs.

"I'm fine," Jeff says in a quiet voice. Not the quiet of the chastised, Sydney suddenly notes, but the quiet of someone who has already removed himself, has set himself apart.

His voice chills her. She does not understand.

She looks at the stony face of the father, the wet trousers of the brother.

"Asshole," Ben says.

Guests begin to spill into the hallway.

It is as if they are in costume for different plays: Jeff in clinging bathing trunks, the life vest tossed to the bedroom floor; Sydney, who has shut the door behind them, in salmon-colored silk and pearl earrings.

"Where did you go?" she asks, a hand to her chest.

"One of the islands."

"You made it that far? Who found you?"

"Sydney, I can't do this. I'm sorry."

"What?"

Jeff is silent.

Sydney shakes her head, bewildered. "You don't love me anymore?"

"I love you," he says.

She opens her palms. "You don't want to marry me?"

"No, I don't."

And Sydney knows right then that it is all over.

From downstairs, she can hear exclamations of surprise, the front door opening and shutting. The sun comes out, which strikes her as unnecessarily cruel.

"Did you think I was happy?" Jeff asks.

"I thought you were"—Sydney searches for the word—"anxious."

"I was. I am."

Sydney cannot move.

"I'll go back to the apartment," Jeff says. "Clear my things out. It would be best if you could stay here for the night. I'll be out by tomorrow afternoon."

That already he can think about clearing out the apartment stuns Sydney. But then again, Jeff has always been so far ahead of her.

He turns toward the window. He puts his hands flat against the glass. Sydney gazes at his long back, his tanned legs. Is he crying?

"Would you have done this to Victoria?" Sydney asks.

Jeff is a long time in answering. "No," he says finally.

Something lurches inside Sydney's chest. "Why not?"

"It would have been a bigger deal," he says.

Sydney is amazed that Jeff has no intention of softening the blow.

Jeff puts his hands on his hips. "I suppose you could say I did this to Ben."

Once again, Sydney doesn't understand. "To Ben?" she asks.

"To spite Ben."

Her head spins. She hasn't eaten since early in the morning. She thinks suddenly of all the catered food that will now go to waste. All those lovely flowers. Mr. Edwards. Julie. Who even now might be waiting, hopeful, downstairs for the bride and groom to emerge—a little tattered, perhaps even a bit bludgeoned, but ready nevertheless for a ceremony in the sunshine.

"I can't marry you," Jeff says. "You see how it would be false."

Sydney shakes her head.

"He wanted you," Jeff explains simply.

Sydney turns her face away, as if to throw off a misheard remark.

"I could see it that first day when we arrived at the house and you were body surfing," Jeff says. "He couldn't take his eyes off you. And then later, after that first boat ride, he said he thought you were different from other women—smart and unpretentious. It was clear to me that he was interested in you."

"But you had Victoria."

"Yes, I did."

She searches her room for some sign of normalcy. There is a can of hair spray on her bureau. The white box the earrings came in is beside it. A book has fallen from the bedside table. When did that happen?

"These things . . ." Jeff gestures to the door, the window. "These things, they're not as coldly thought out as you might imagine. Sometimes it's only in retrospect that you realize what you've done."

Sydney pulls a pin from her hair and holds it in her lap.

Jeff takes a long breath, a prelude to the

final confession. "Victoria was once Ben's girlfriend."

Sydney is silent.

"I'm amazed he didn't tell you."

"He didn't tell me."

"Well, that's one for Ben, then."

"This is a game?" Sydney asks.

The blood leaves Sydney's head, her face, her shoulders, and pools somewhere in the middle of her chest. Her hands tremble from shock or from anger. All that she has imagined—her life with Jeff, their marriage, children she might one day take to visit their grandfather—will never happen. None of it was real.

Jeff walks toward her as if to embrace her. She shakes him off, denying herself his sympathy, now fraudulent and treacherous. Already she sees herself walking alone on city streets, pausing to sit on benches or lean against railings, a speechless dread inside her. She thinks of all that will have to be done to dismantle a life.

"Sydney," he says.

"Go away," she says.

Behind her, she hears him shut the door.

—⁓—

Sydney locks the door and lies on her bed. She waits. Occasionally, she can hear a raised voice, a woman crying. From time to time, people come and knock and call her name, but she does not respond. She waits an hour, two hours. She waits long enough that she thinks everyone will have gone home. Certainly, the guests will have dispersed. She hopes that Ivers and Sahir and the others have gone back to Boston. She prays that her parents have had the sense to return to their respective homes. In a minute, she will collect her purse, descend the stairs, and walk out of the house. She will walk in the direction of Portsmouth and from there she will take a bus. To where, she has not yet decided.

She reviews her marital history. *Nearly thrice married. Once divorced. Once widowed. Once left at the altar.*

When she guesses it's safe, Sydney opens the door. From the landing, she can hear nothing. As she descends the stairs with her black suitcase, she listens for any sounds of life in the rooms adjacent to the hallway. She wonders if they all know she is there, if they are allowing her to leave. Her raincoat hangs from a coat-rack by the front door. It is not raining, but Sydney takes it from the hook anyway. She puts it over her salmon-colored dress.

"Sydney," Mr. Edwards says from the doorway that leads to the kitchen. He still has on his dark suit, but the tie has been undone or ripped off in anger. "I can't begin . . ."

Sydney holds up a hand to silence him.

"I'll call you a taxi," he says. "Do you have money? You're welcome to stay here as long as you like. I am ashamed of my son."

Mr. Edwards takes a step into the hallway. "I want to disown him . . . Julie is inconsolable."

Sydney moves toward the door.

"I bought this house for the family, for the *idea* of family," Mr. Edwards says. "I imagined it would be a place where the family would gather. It would attract the boys and Julie, make them come to see us more often. Who can resist the seaside? And then later there would be grandchildren, and they would love it here." His lower lip trembles. "The beach. The water . . ."

Mr. Edwards shakes his head. His face collapses. He pulls a white handkerchief from his pocket.

Sydney puts a hand on the man's arm.

"You'll let us know . . . ," he says, bringing the handkerchief to his face.

"I loved him," Sydney says.

Mr. Edwards nods.

"I'll let you know," she says.

On the train to the city, Sydney passes abandoned mills, asbestos-shingled houses, a shop called Tom's Autobody. She imagines the atoms of her own body disintegrating into a kind of chaos, an emptying-out of her center.

The trip is meant to last an hour. Or two hours. She has no sense of time.

A young man in a white shirt approaches her. Will he speak to her?

"I'm sorry," he says. "I was sitting there."

Sydney looks up and notes a small duffel bag in the luggage rack overhead. She smells bacon on the young man's breath. Not trusting her legs, she simply shifts to the window seat.

Slightly abashed, the young man joins her. "Where are you going?" he asks.

Sydney opens her mouth.

"Boston?" he prompts.

She nods.

"Shopping?" he asks. "Theater?"

At the best of times, Sydney might have found these questions intrusive. Now they are a torment.

"The city" is all that she can manage.

The word itself an oasis.

The train passes houses and farms and haystacks. Sydney tries to persuade herself that she is in England. She wonders if all of her life now will be an attempt to convince herself that she is somewhere other than where she actually is.

When the train arrives in Boston, Sydney follows signs for the subway to Park Street. Heading toward the exit to the street, she discovers that the escalator is out of order. She has to bump her black suitcase up the stairs. By the time she gets to the top, the handle has broken.

Sydney leaves Park Street station and walks in the direction of the State House, drawn by the gleaming gold dome. She has the idea that if she reaches the top of the hill, something practical will occur to her.

At the summit, she sits on a stone step. She ought to have taken a taxi from the train station and asked the cabbie for advice. She glances down the hill. A doorman is helping a man unload a car. Sydney stands and walks toward him. When she reaches him, she discovers an entrance to a hotel so discreet that it appears to have no name, merely Roman numerals. Sydney pushes through a revolving door into a lobby.

It might be a club. The wood paneling and marble floor are masculine in feel. Black-and-taupe chairs flank a gold sunburst clock on a wall. A glass screen trimmed in wood hides a concierge. Small metal tables like sculptures are arranged about the room. Sydney wants only to sit down, which she does. Nothing in the lobby reminds her of any place she has ever been before, already an asset.

Behind Sydney is a marble staircase with a gold banister. She wonders where it goes. She glances at the clock. It reads 6:20.

Would she and Jeff have been on their way to the airport by now?

"Can I help you?" asks a young man behind the desk. He has on a black uniform and seems foreign. Eastern European? Romanian?

Sydney stands with effort, as if she were decades older than she is. She drags the suitcase with the broken handle behind her. She realizes for the first time since she left the Edwardses' house that under her raincoat she has on her salmon-colored wedding dress.

"Have you been with us before?" the young man asks.

Sydney shakes her head.

He enters information into a computer, though she has given him none. She wonders what he is writing. *Woman in distress? Shabby suitcase with broken handle? Hasn't been with us before?*

"Will it be one adult?" he asks.

The question seems unnecessary. "Yes," she answers.

He slides a paper across the desk. The room rate is more than she anticipated, but moving on is simply unthinkable.

"Room nine-oh-six is available," he says. "It's quite nice," he confides.

The elevator has a glass front. Sydney has a sensation of vertigo as she passes from floor to floor. On each is a table with a bowl of apples, suggesting that the floors are identical. But they are not. As she rises, Sydney tries to discern a difference. By the eighth floor, she has the answer: the art on each is original.

The key is gold-colored and tricky, and she has considerable trouble inserting it into the lock. Sydney imagines this to be a hotel where powerful men have trysts. She pictures well-dressed women with scarlet lipstick and matching shoes.

Sydney might have anticipated the room from the lobby. The walls have been painted a rich coffee color. Mounted on them are black-and-white photographs of gargoyles. Sydney has a corner room with six large windows. Beyond the windows, there is much protruding scrollwork, as if she were being housed on an upper story of an ornate cathedral. She might be in Italy or Prague, though there is something essentially American, even Federalist, about the room's masculinity and solidity. Against one wall is a four-poster bed with a dark canopy.

Sydney wanders about the room, touching objects. She discovers stationery in a wooden box. She pulls out the TV from inside the entertainment console. When she turns it on, the words are harsh and garish. What they are saying is clearly false.

She calls down to the desk clerk. "No newspapers," she instructs.

She has a fireplace, a sofa, a bronze-colored ottoman. There is a chair in black and taupe similar to the one in the lobby. Large hardware is affixed to the doors. She sits on the ottoman and stares. Too much has to be absorbed.

From a room-service menu, Sydney orders a plate of cheese. She hasn't eaten since the sliced apple she had at breakfast. She hadn't wanted her stomach to protrude from the silk dress. What a quaint notion, she thinks now.

She exchanges her wedding dress, which she lets fall to the bathroom floor, for a hotel bathrobe. When she takes off her bra, she discovers the blue handkerchief tucked inside. For the first time since Jeff walked into the house in his bathing suit and life jacket, Sydney begins to cry.

All that effort on Julie's part, she thinks as she fingers the different squares. All that love.

Sydney doesn't pick up the wedding dress from the bathroom floor. She will leave it for the maid. Perhaps she will give it to the maid.

She draws a bath and slides into it. She discovers that if she doesn't move, the water remains completely still and flat. She is becalmed.

No body surfing here.

Later in the evening, after Sydney has had the bath and a plate of cheese, she calls her mother.

"I'm here," Sydney says.

"Where?" her mother asks, relief immediately apparent.

Sydney names the hotel. "It's very swank," she adds.

"Don't worry if it's expensive," her mother says, an atypical response. "What happened?"

"I don't know," Sydney says. She cannot just now explain Jeff's actions to her mother.

"I'm just stunned," her mother says. "He always seemed like such a nice man. I never thought he would be capable of something like this."

"I didn't either," Sydney says.

"What will you do now?"

"I don't know," Sydney answers.

"You'll walk," her mother suggests.

Sydney nods. She thinks this might be the most useful piece of advice her mother has ever given her.

"Maybe some shopping?" her mother adds, immediately ruining the good advice.

"What would I shop for?" Sydney asks.

Sydney hangs up. The conversation has exhausted her. She hates the telephone.

She lies back on the bed, her feet on the floor. For a while, she stares at the canopy over the bed and thinks about what Jeff might be doing at this very second. Is he still at the beach house? Did he go back to the apartment in Cambridge? Or did he take the flight to Paris? Might he have called Victoria?

Sydney slips off the plush hotel robe and crawls under the silky taupe sheets. She pulls the duvet over her head.

The telephone rings, and Sydney thinks about not answering it. At the last minute, she tosses off the duvet and picks up the receiver.

"I'm so sorry this had to happen to you," her father says.

Sydney remembers the Jewish word. *Beshert.*

"But you know what I always say," her father continues.

"That I'm resilient?" Sydney offers.

—— ⟋⟍⟍ ——

For several days, Sydney comes and goes from the hotel. The doormen nod. The clerks behind the desk say good morning or good evening, but little else. Sydney thinks this a perfect arrangement.

She neglects to charge her cell phone.

She calculates how much money she has
left in her personal savings account. She
takes the elevator downstairs and negoti-
ates a reduced rate with a nice young manager named Rick. Together, they decide that
she can stay at the hotel for twenty-two
days, which is one day longer than her intended honeymoon would have been. Sydney decides to think of her time in Boston
as a kind of anti-honeymoon.

Sydney discovers that if she is careful and
not reckless and leaves her room only periodically, she is not unduly reminded of Jeff
or of the Edwardses. Though, in truth, they
never leave her.

The feeling is similar to that she had when
Daniel died suddenly. But then she had not
wanted to forget Daniel.

Across the street is a residential building.
For hours, Sydney sits on a silk-upholstered
chair and gazes out a window in her room
and tries to divine, through movements in
the windows opposite, the lives within. The
infrequent comings and goings require some
imagination on her part, so she invents stories that occupy her for hours.

*   *   *

Sometimes, when Sydney is sitting in the hotel dining room or is walking the streets of Beacon Hill, she contemplates a version of herself who knew what the future held. Had she been told when she was eighteen and just graduating from high school that she would have a husband and then another and that she would be left at the altar by a third— all by the age of thirty—would she have needed to reach out a hand and grope for a chair so that she could sit down? Would she have been excited? Alarmed? Sad? Wouldn't she have wanted to know *why?*

One day, when Sydney is in the room, a maid comes to clean. She points out to Sydney a switch on the wall that Sydney has noted but ignored, not knowing what it was for. "It's a privacy switch," the maid tells Sydney. "When you turn it on, a red light appears outside your door, and no one will bother you."

Sydney shakes her head in amazement. "A privacy switch," she repeats with awe.

Sydney wonders if Jeff understands what he did to her. Perhaps he does, for he does not call her or make any further attempt to explain. When Sydney thinks of the Jeff she never knew entirely well—the man whose thoughts were often elsewhere—such a treacherous move seems just possible. Who could know what he had on his mind all those times she saw him looking off into the distance? And yet when she thinks of the Jeff who fixed the lightbulb, the man who asked her to marry him, such a betrayal is nearly impossible to imagine. And when Sydney can stand it and thinks about the man with whom she made love, his actions are truly inexplicable.

Sydney sometimes wakes to the memory of Jeff standing in her bedroom on her wedding afternoon, explaining to her why he couldn't marry her, that it had all been an elaborate game. She remembers her shock. It wasn't so different, she sometimes thinks, from hearing that Daniel had died on the floor of one of the best teaching hospitals in the world. The news had stunned her; she could not comprehend it. Her mind had simply refused to accept the facts. Yet she knows now that with time—for didn't this happen with Daniel?—a kind of necessary acceptance will form around her, like a lobster making its new shell, one that will be soft and easily breakable in the beginning but so hard that only lobster crackers can shatter it in the end.

She can hardly wait.

Leaving the hotel one morning, Sydney sees a middle-aged couple sitting on the striped sofa in the lobby. They are holding hands. They look alike. Sydney thinks about how it is that couples who have been together for a long time begin to resemble each other. She wonders if she and Jeff looked at all alike, if they would have come to do so over time. She wonders if the couple on the sofa have just renewed their vows.

Sydney is aware that there are matters more important than love and the loss of it. A child's incapacities. A climate of terror. Suicide bombers. As she walks the city streets, she repeats this fact to herself again and again.

She tries to read, first magazines and then a book. She is successful at neither. She cannot bear the television, and so she walks.

Having brought little with her, she purchases sensible clothes. After a week, she buys a bottle of her favorite bath oil and considers this a victory.

Sydney counts out the days. First there are twenty-two. Then there are fifteen. Then there are ten. When she has nine days remaining, she leaves the hotel in her sensible shoes, prepared to walk a mile for her breakfast. If ever she lives on Beacon Hill, she will know all the best eateries.

The desk clerk says good morning. The doorman nods and smiles. Sydney passes through two parked cars on her way to cross the street.

A calamity at the bottom of the hill—a car accident—catches her attention. She steps into the street and hears the screech of brakes shortly before she feels the impact.

There is a moment of pure wonder and then a bolt of pain. Sydney is catapulted down the street.

The doorman, a cabbie, and a man who looks European hover over her. Sydney tries to sit up. The pain in her wrist is a serious matter, though she notes a slight shift in consciousness, as if she had woken up from a nap.

The European—Sydney notes that he is marvelously dressed in a dark suit with snowy cuffs—has his cell phone out even as he is cradling her head. A policeman, out of breath, bends over her as well. For a moment, Sydney sees only faces.

"It's just my arm," she says.

"You stepped between the cars," the European explains with perhaps a British accent. "I was watching you as I waited for my car to be delivered. The taxi couldn't stop."

"I should have looked," Sydney says.

"Yes, yes," the cabbie says.

Sydney gives her name, the hotel as her address.

As she is being lifted into the ambulance, Sydney notices the taxi stopped at an odd angle on the street in front of the hotel. Behind it stretches a line of cars as far as she can see.

Rick, the manager, accompanies Sydney to the hospital. A man used to making things happen, he arranges for her to see a doctor straightaway. The broken bone is pointed out on the X-ray. While the doctor sets her wrist, Rick squeezes her other hand.

When Sydney, her wrist in a cast, returns to the hotel later that evening, personnel come out from a side door to greet her. She is not allowed to get in the elevator by herself. A desk clerk and a doorman accompany her up to her room. She hopes she hasn't left anything embarrassing draped over a chair.

Already, there are bouquets. She knows the hotel flowers at once because they are ivory. The staff would not have ruined its own decor.

The card set before a second, smaller vase of pink snapdragons is signed *Mr. Cavalli.*

Italian, Sydney thinks.

A table has been set up with a cold meal—good cheese, flat bread, grapes, strawberries, olives, nuts—in front of the ottoman. Sydney notes that it is a meal that can be eaten easily with one hand.

She notices something else as well—something quite strange and wonderful. For the first time since the wedding-that-didn't-happen, she feels alert.

On the fourth-to-last day, Sydney receives a handwritten note brought straight up to her room by a doorman named Donald. Mr. Cavalli is having coffee in the restaurant and wonders if she might like to join him. He hopes that her wrist is feeling better.

Sydney examines herself in the mirror. She is not dressed well, but that is perhaps better than appearing to have cared. Because of her wrist, her hair has been left to its own devices, never felicitous. She sighs. It is not that she specifically does not want to meet Mr. Cavalli, or that she thinks he will pursue her. It is that in eighteen days she hasn't had a conversation lasting longer than a few sentences with any person.

He stands as soon as she enters the hotel restaurant. His suit is very fine, unlike any she is used to seeing in her universe of academia or summer folk, his shirt so white and crisp she thinks it must have been purchased that morning.

"I am so pleased," he begins in perfect, if formal, English, learned not in America but in London perhaps, the accent a mix of Italian and British. The man—she could not have seen this at the time of the accident—is quite tall. This disparity in their heights unnerves her for a moment, but he gestures for her to sit down.

Mr. Cavalli must already have spoken to a member of the staff, because there is a pot of coffee and a plate of pastries on the table. Sydney sees that Mr. Cavalli is a man who orchestrates his own future, who does not wait to be waited upon. She wishes, under the circumstances, that she had dressed in something less dreary, had at least put a comb through her hair.

"If there is anything I can do," he says as a waiter pours their coffees. She thinks, What if I had wanted tea? And then she has another thought: Did he, in advance of her arrival, ask the staff what Sydney Sklar customarily drinks in the morning?

"I would have called you earlier," he adds, "but I thought you would be resting. Are you in much pain?"

"Not much, no."

"That is good, then."

*   *   *

"Where are you from?" she asks.

"I grew up in London and Naples," he answers.

Outside the dark-paneled restaurant, traffic flows freely down the hill. Not thirty feet away, a taxicab came in contact with her right wrist. By the bar, a female staff member is polishing wineglasses with a white cloth. She might be listening, or perhaps she is daydreaming. Might she mind the occasional arrogant guest who demanded a restaurant be opened especially for him? Would money have changed hands?

In an hour, two hours, the room will be filled with businesspeople of both genders paying large sums of money for Chilean sea bass and salads of *fruits de mer.* Sydney knows the menu well, but always times her appearances in the room so that she arrives early or at the tail end of the dining hour. The salads are, of course, exceptional. Sydney has learned over the past several days how to eat even complex meals using only one hand.

"What do you do?" she asks the Italian man.

"If I might be permitted to ask a question," he says without answering hers. He brings his coffee cup to his lips. She noted earlier that he took a great deal of sugar with his coffee—so much that she imagines the sugar like silt, undissolved at the bottom of his cup. "Do you live here? In this hotel?"

Sydney has not wanted to discuss her presence in the discreet hotel. She has not told anyone why she is here, though she imagines the staff speculate. Twenty-two days is an odd number, too many for sight-seeing or for a business trip. In any event, it must be perfectly clear that Sydney Sklar is not conducting business of any sort.

"I was supposed to be married," she says. "But my"—and here she hesitates over nomenclature, always revealing—"my fiancé changed his mind on the morning of the wedding. I came here as a kind of anti-honeymoon."

"I am so sorry," the man says, and she sees, in his eyes, that he truly is. "This man did not deserve you," he adds.

"You can't know that," Sydney replies somewhat defensively.

Defending what? she wonders. Jeff? Her judgment? She takes a sip of coffee. "It might have been the other way around," she says.

"That you would say that means it is not true. I was correct the first time. He did not deserve you. Did he explain himself?"

"He simply didn't show up. His father and his brother had to go find him. I don't know what he hoped to accomplish by staying away. It only made his appearance more public, more shameful, though I was the one who felt the shame."

Mr. Cavalli merely nods. Of course a woman would feel the shame of abandonment. It is, he might think, her responsibility. "It seems an act of pure cowardice on his part," he says.

"He told me he had asked me to marry him for the wrong reasons. That he had done it to hurt his brother."

"His brother loved you?"

"It was more complicated than that, I think. His brother showed no signs of loving me. Quite the opposite, in fact."

"I'm sorry if this is painful for you," he says.

"It's the first time I've talked about it." Sydney folds her hands in her lap. She feels inside herself a great, and welcome, capitulation.

"I do not wish to pry."

"It's something of a relief."

"Yes, I can see that."

"It was just . . . just so . . ." She stumbles. "I was part of a family, and now I'm not. They meant something to me, that family."

"Has it been helpful being here?" Mr. Cavalli asks, indicating the hotel.

"I think so. Yes, it has. I can't imagine what I would have done otherwise."

Mr. Cavalli sits back on the leather banquette, one hand still touching his coffee cup. He inhabits his clothes with gestures as elegant as the cut of the cloth.

Sydney senses the abnormality of the meeting. The young woman polishing the glasses will think them merely one more illicit couple, though nothing has been done or said to indicate that. Still, there is an agenda that isn't entirely clear to Sydney. She could stand and leave now and not know the subtext, which might be curiosity, or simply attraction.

But the man seems, on balance, too sophisticated to make the usual pass. He would know her to be skittish now on the subject of love, a bad bet all around. Either too eager or unwilling.

"I was in love once," Mr. Cavalli says, perhaps wishing to share a confidence similar to hers to balance the equation. He has perfect manners. Anticipating Sydney's question, he offers, "She was British. I met her at university. Her parents objected."

"She must have been very young, then," Sydney says, "to allow her parents such sway."

"I think some part of her was afraid of me," he says, "afraid that I would want to live in Naples."

"Would you have done that?" she asks.

"Not if she didn't want to. I don't think she ever understood the power she had over me."

"Does she still? Have that power?"

"Oh, yes," he answers, smiling.

He has, Sydney thinks, a lovely smile. His eyes are large and heavy-lidded, his hairline high on his forehead. He might be any age between thirty and forty-five.

*   *   *

"What happened to her?" Sydney asks.

"She has risen quite high up at her bank."

Sydney takes a sip of coffee. "Maybe she's more secure now and would defy her parents."

"This was years ago," Mr. Cavalli says. "She has been married and divorced since then."

"I'll bet the parents are sorry now," Sydney says.

The man smiles. "I doubt they give it a single thought. They are not in the least the sort of people who ever look back."

Sydney sighs. "I wish I could be like that," she says.

"No, you do not," he says. "To never think about your actions, your past, what might have been? All the rich tapestry that was your life until this moment?"

"I've been hoping for amnesia," Sydney says.

"Are you in pain right now?" he asks, touching the cast on her wrist with the tips of his fingers.

"Hardly ever," Sydney says. She cannot feel the touch. If she can't feel it, it doesn't

count as a touch in the usual sense. "Sometimes at night it aches."

"When does it come off?" he asks, removing his fingers.

"In five weeks."

"So you will stay here until then?"

"Oh, no," Sydney says. "I'm going to run
out of money in four days."

Immediately, she is embarrassed. "I can't
stay," she adds. "I have a lot to do. I have to
move out of the apartment I shared with . . .
with Jeff," she says, naming the treacherous
fiancé. "I have to find a new place."

"In Boston?"

"Possibly."

A waiter comes to ask if he can fill their
cups with hot coffee. Both decline. Neither
has touched any of the pastries, though
Sydney thinks the meringues appealing. "I
didn't know him very well," she says suddenly, surprising even herself. "Jeff, I mean.
In retrospect, and I've been thinking about
this, there was a great deal I didn't know
about him. He was often daydreaming.
About what, I never knew."

"You didn't ask?"

"I thought I would have years to discover
where he went in his mind."

*   *   *

"You have had a bad time of it, both emotionally and physically," Mr. Cavalli says.

Sydney shifts her wrist in her lap. "The odd thing is," she says, "I was almost grateful for the accident. I felt that it woke me up from a deep sleep. It was a relief to feel real pain, physical pain. I don't know if I'm making myself clear."

"Absolutely clear. May I ask you what your fiancé does?"

"He's a professor at MIT," she says. She thinks a moment. "You're not at MIT, are you?"

"No, no," he says. "I'm in the import-export business."

That might mean anything, Sydney thinks. "Do you live here?" she asks. "In Boston?"

"I am back and forth, London and Boston."

She thinks him evasive. To ask any more questions, however, would be rude, and there is no need for that. Beyond a certain point, she doesn't care what he does.

"I knew that something was missing," Sydney says after a time. "There was a slightly unreal quality to all of it."

"You're speaking of your fiancé."

"It was a very fast courtship." She remembers the day Jeff sat down with her on the porch and announced that he'd left Victoria for her. And how she thought he was so far ahead of her already. "It's as though we skipped several steps that now, in retrospect, seem necessary."

"What steps?" he asks, pouring himself a second cup of coffee.

"A mutual recognition that you're both moving closer to something. The relationship seemed to have happened before I even realized it."

"This was your first love?" he asks.

"I'd been married twice before," she says. Sydney waits for a flicker of surprise to cross Mr. Cavalli's face, but he has perfect poise. "One of my husbands died," she explains. "The other one I divorced."

"I am very sorry," Mr. Cavalli says.

Sydney tells him about Andrew and Daniel. She tells him, too, about how she and her mother left her father one day in New York and moved to western Massachusetts, and about how she's never quite forgiven herself for allowing that to happen. She tells him about Mr. and Mrs. Edwards, about Ben and Julie. In turn, he tells her about his extended family, his annual visits to Naples. Once he reaches over and touches the wrist of her free arm, and she inadvertently flinches. Immediately, she is sorry but can think of no way of conveying her regret without mentioning the incident, which she knows will embarrass them both, or without touching him in return, which might give him the wrong message entirely. She sits for a moment in an agony of confusion.

"I have an appointment," he says almost apologetically. Sydney didn't see him glance at his watch. Perhaps he has learned how to do so without alerting his guest—a neat trick. "I wonder, would you be insulted if I asked you to dine with me tomorrow night?"

Sydney is surprised by the invitation, which she knows to be partly a product of good manners.

"I'm terrible company right now," she says.

"I have not found that to be true."

"Thank you for the coffee. This has been pleasant . . . Well, more than pleasant."

"Very pleasant for me as well," he says.

"You're like the stranger on the plane," she says.

When Sydney returns to her room, she sits on the bed, wondering if she regrets having accepted Mr. Cavalli's invitation. She cannot deny to herself that she finds the man attractive, and she wonders what it means that she can so soon feel attraction of any sort for another man. When she thinks about entering into a relationship with such a man, however, she feels only fear—a fear similar to, yet not as intense as, the fear of living her life alone.

The next night, Mr. Cavalli meets her in the lobby. He has made reservations at an Italian restaurant just off Trinity Square. The dining room is two stories high with voluptuous quilted draperies and comfortable banquettes. They are seated in an intimate corner near a lighted mural of cypress trees that Mr. Cavalli says reminds him of Italy. The menu is replete with dishes that can be ordered in whatever quantity or sequence one wishes. At her request, Mr. Cavalli orders for both of them. The appetizers are langoustines, prepared with their heads still intact, another reminder of his childhood, he points out.

Sydney stares at the spiny lobster, already broken for her.

Sydney and Mr. Cavalli stay in the restaurant for hours. They drink Prosecco and red wine and talk about near misses and marital mishaps. When she leaves the table, she thinks she might be drunk.

On the way back to the hotel, her wrist aches only a little. She knows that in two days she will have to leave the hotel with her broken suitcase (perhaps tomorrow she will do something about that) and go out into the world in which she once lived. There she will have to begin all over again: find a place to live, get a job, make friends, perhaps even stumble into another relationship. She doubts the latter will happen for quite some time. The hotel has been her private halfway house, a buffer between the woman she was and the woman she must now become. It has cost her all of her savings (indeed, she will now need to borrow money from her father for a security deposit on an apartment), but she does not regret a penny spent.

Mr. Cavalli parks the car just shy of the hotel. Sydney wonders if he will expect her to invite him up to her room, but then she thinks not—he would not embarrass her in that way.

He bends in her direction, and she offers him her cheek. Deftly, he turns the kiss into a European one—a peck on both cheeks.

"I have to go to London tomorrow," he says.

"I have to go out into the rest of my life," she says and laughs.

He gives her his card. "Will you call to tell me that your wrist has healed?" he asks.

Sydney smiles and nods, but already she knows that she will not do that. That this has been an interlude in their lives is perfectly clear, and already she is assailed by mild nostalgia.

"Thank you," she says.

"For what?"

"For making everything just a little bit easier."

There is a moment, recognizable to each of them, when she might linger and change everything entirely. But she lets herself out of the car. She doesn't look back as she walks toward the hotel door.

When Sydney checks out on the twenty-second day, personnel come from a side room to say good-bye. A great to-do is made about putting her small but brand-new suitcase into the back of a taxi. She is not allowed to give the doormen tips. Rick steps from around the counter and tells her to take care. Sydney thinks that she might cry. She is made to promise that she will come back, but she guesses that she will not, that she will never again be able to justify spending that much money for a single night, never mind twenty-two of them.

As the taxi draws away, she blows the staff a kiss.

When they reach the intersection, the cabbie swings his arm over the back of the front seat. "Where to?" he asks.

2005

Floods of biblical proportion have destroyed a southern city. Gas prices are soaring. Sydney notes that the Hampton tolls now have E-ZPass. In high season, the wait was sometimes a half hour, occasionally an hour. Now there are no lines, as if the north has been evacuated.

So much change. London bombed. Iraq shelled daily. It is an act of will, she sometimes thinks, simply to turn on CNN each evening and take in the day's news—hardly believable, all too believable.

Sydney enters the public parking lot, her car rolling over the loose gravel. There is a bathhouse, a badly weathered fence, a boardwalk. She lets her window down and inhales the air. It smells of dark sand and fish, signaling a low tide. The breeze is warm on her arm, poised on the sill. Warmer still will be the water, as it often is in September. Sydney knows that there will be few people on the beach.

The family never stays after Labor Day. Never.

She removes her shoes and rolls the cuffs of her black dress pants. She locks her car and slips the key into her pocket. The boardwalk is covered with thin drifts of sand. A last gasp of beach roses, most already turned to hips, crowd the wooden planks. She will cross the boardwalk, take in the beach, and then walk to the house. When she has accomplished this small but necessary task, she will return to her car and continue her drive north to Durham.

But when she reaches the beach, the view cuts unexpectedly to the quick, her body armor shoddy and out-of-date. She stands with her hand to her chest, as if that gesture might protect her. It is not only that she had lost the memory of what this particular beach looked like. It is, too, that she had forgotten that this air is the same that was once alive with sounds and smells and words. Sydney is suddenly fearful of those aural and tactile sensations.

The view, though. The view. It is undeniably exhilarating.

Sydney sits where she has planted herself. She closes her eyes against the naked sun and listens to the waves. She can detect their height just by listening—can tell the large smashers from the slow rollers. Has there recently been a storm? In the city, she is sometimes unaware of the weather alto-gether, or only mildly reminded of it as she walks from apartment to office and back again. Most of her days are spent in the psy-chology building, in a room with no windows. Sometimes, emerging in the early evening, Sydney is surprised to discover a heavy down-pour, or its opposite, an evening so beautiful she can hardly believe she almost missed it.

Sydney has not been north of Boston since the day she said good-bye to Mr. Edwards at his doorstep. She could not pretend, though, that when she and her colleagues received the invitation to the conference at the University of New Hampshire, she didn't begin to be obsessed with thoughts of driving to the house and looking at it. She can't articulate to herself exactly why this particular undertaking loomed so large; it seemed to occupy her mind much like the notion of calling an old boyfriend might have done. Whenever she pondered the drive north, the beach flickered like a beacon on an imaginary map.

The sun is a pleasure, and her heartbeat begins to slow. She has seldom been outside this summer, except to sit on a bench and eat her lunch or to take a quick walk, and already she has the pale face of February. She lies back in the sand. She thinks it is probably unwise to lie in the dunes so close to the water without any sunblock, even in September, but she had forgotten how forgiving sand can be, how it seems to accept the body and even to swallow it up. In the distance, she can hear a dog chasing gulls.

———~~~———

Sydney sometimes wondered if Jeff had used the tickets and gone off to Paris by himself. By the time she worked up the courage to enter the Cambridge apartment, it looked just as it had when they'd left it together to drive north to the wedding-that-hadn't-happened: a suitcase lay discarded on the bed, the ironing board was still out in the kitchen. Not willing to bother a friend, though it was perfectly clear from the number of messages on the answering machine that friends had been trying to contact her, she hired a local moving van to put her belongings in storage until she found a place of her own.

Jeff had left an emptiness, shameful for its timing and its public nature. More astonishing in retrospect was not the fact that Jeff had abandoned her but rather that he had pursued her at all. It seemed a remarkable act of will, a performance running many days, the notices all raves. When she thought he was contemplating algorithms and terrorists, was he, instead, pondering his own treachery? Did he understand each day what he was doing? Or was he operating at a subconscious level that became clear to him only as the wedding drew near? Sydney found it hard to believe in all that dissembling. Scenarios in Montreal and Cambridge had to be played and replayed to watch his face for clues of his subterfuge. And wouldn't Jeff have to have been desperately unhappy, either for himself or for Sydney, assuming that he had cared for her at all? Was she to believe in a single moment of the nearly eleven months she had been with him? Would she have to second-guess all her decisions now?

It was Emily who convinced Sydney to return to school, though she had been leaning in that direction for some weeks. She remembered the research, the classes, the sense of deadline—it seemed to be what was needed. She looked for an apartment near the psychology building where she would be spending most of her time. Rents were high, and she had little money, refusing on principle to tap into a joint account she and Jeff had built together for their future, there being no joint future now. She imagined that in time he would send her some of the money, which he did. No note accompanied the check.

*   *   *

Sydney tried never to think of Jeff or Julie or Mr. Edwards, whose crumpled face she had the most difficulty erasing from her mind. After several weeks of searching, she found a dismal studio apartment just a few blocks from the building in which she would soon immerse herself in work. Unlike most of the returning graduate students, Sydney was so eager for the new term to begin that she arrived an hour early for her first lecture. She was made to understand by her adviser that even more in the way of teaching and research would be expected of her now, which was, she thought, undeserved yet perfect timing. By then, most of the need for solitude had exhausted itself—so much so that she found she could occasionally go out to dinner or to a baseball game with some of her colleagues after work. She had not, however, dated any man since she had had dinner with Mr. Cavalli, which, she thought, did not count as a real date in any universe with which she was familiar. She had gone to a few parties at which there had been men, and some of these men had made initial overtures, but it had been reassuring, if slightly alarming, to learn how quickly these men could be made to turn away. A ducking of the head. A refusal to meet the eyes. A patently weak smile. With Daniel's death, avoiding men had had a different tenor to it: around Sydney, there had been a wall of respect. If men approached her, they were careful, wary, always sympathetic. After Jeff, however, Emily joked that it was as if Sydney gave off negative vibes, and Sydney thought this completely true: vibrations, emanating outward, might prove an effective buffer.

Sydney liked her work, could even occasionally talk herself into thinking of her research as timely and necessary, though she had the normal panicky sense of needing answers more quickly than the scientific method allowed. It was, she thought, a diluted sense of what cancer researchers must feel: an intense need to find a cure before thousands more died. Though her own research was less pressing, she seldom failed to notice at-risk girls on the streets of Boston. They were often overdeveloped, underdressed, very young, and accompanied by older men. In grant proposals, Sydney's goal was to decrease the negative life outcomes for such adolescent girls. Privately,

Sydney hoped simply to help save the girls from themselves.

After Jeff had sent the check, having called Sydney's mother for her new address, he had forwarded a bundle of letters from Julie and Mr. Edwards. Sydney had the sense that Jeff was out of the country often, though she resisted calling his department at MIT simply to see if he was listed as an active teaching professor there.

In time, even Julie had stopped writing, discouraged at last by the lack of any reply from her friend, her almost sister-in-law. Sydney had suffered, reading the heartfelt, if artless, missives, yet not as much as she would have had she entered into that correspondence, or, earlier, one with Mr. Edwards, whose brief letters had always ended with an apology, never his to make.

From Jeff, she had heard nothing. From Ben, she had heard nothing. From Mrs. Edwards, Sydney sometimes picked up, like a sudden word amid a sea of static, a distinct if muted sigh of relief.

———ᗰ———

Sydney wakes to a dog nosing at her foot, and instinctively she snatches her leg away. She sits up, barely conscious. She shields her eyes from the sun and squints in the dog's direction.

"I let him off the leash," a man says.

Sydney feels her body stiffen even before she is fully alert. She can't see the man towering over her, his face backlit by the sun, but she knows well enough who it is.

"Hello," Ben says. "What are you doing here?"

The family never stays after Labor Day. Never.

"What time is it?" Sydney asks, trying to disguise her confusion.

"Eleven-thirty."

"I'm late," she says, standing. Tullus, moving like an agitated horse, bobs around her legs.

"What are you late for?" Ben asks.

"A conference. At UNH. The first presentation is at noon."

"Offhand, I'd say you won't make it."

Sydney bends and scratches Tullus's ears, buying time. Her heart is hammering.

The dog seems satisfied and lopes away. When Sydney straightens, she sees that

Ben's white T-shirt is stained with sweat. He appears to have been running. His body is much the same, fully muscled and therefore covered.

"What are *you* doing here?" she asks, a not entirely illogical question. It is, after all, mid-September. The beach, apart from a few souls out for a walk, is empty.

But Ben seems reluctant to answer her.

"Sydney," he says finally and pauses.

Sydney tilts her head. Why the deliberate use of her name, the unnatural pause, suggesting a pronouncement? "What?" she asks, already beginning to be afraid of his reply.

"My father died."

The news hits her at the back of her knees. Her hands float in front of her, unoccupied. "Oh, Ben," she says.

Ben glances at her and then away. "He had a series of strokes. A meteor shower of strokes really. They left him largely incapacitated. The decline was very fast."

"When?" Sydney asks.

"June."

As if in slow motion, her arms like kites collapsing, Sydney sits in the sand. She draws up her knees and presses her forehead against them. She wraps her arms around her head. Of all people, this should not have happened to the man she will always think of as Mr. Edwards. The man whose letters she did not even bother to answer. The man who was never anything but unfailingly kind to her.

"We're here to clean up the house," Ben explains above her. "My mother sold it. The closing is next week."

"I'm so sorry," Sydney says, a sentence more true than he knows. Or perhaps he does. Ben always had her number.

—⚋—

Sydney cannot keep the cuffs of her black pants from filling up with sand. She stops from time to time to adjust them, rolling them as tightly as she can all the way to her knees. Ben carries her briefcase. In it, she has her computer, her files, her cell phone—inanimate proof that she has made a life elsewhere. Sydney holds her shoes, black pumps with small heels, her trouser socks balled inside. Absurd clothing for a beach.

"Your mother," Sydney says.

"She won't care. Well, she might care, but

only for a minute." Ben pauses. "It would make Julie so happy to see you."

When Ben asked Sydney to walk back to the house with him, she considered saying no only briefly. She had asked one question.

"Kenya," Ben had replied. "Except for the funeral, Jeff's been there for a year."

Sydney thinks about the time she suggested in the garden that Mr. Edwards and she one day go to the museum to see the painting he was curious about—the one by the man who had sent three sons to war. She imagined she would be Mr. Edwards's daughter-in-law by then. Why did she not simply call him and do it anyway?

"It happened over several weeks, really," Ben is saying beside her. "At first, we didn't notice. Last Easter, when we were all in Needham, we saw that he seemed to have trouble getting up from a chair. I guessed arthritis, but then I noticed that he also had difficulty walking, as though something were wrong with his mechanics. After that, it was all there for anyone to see: he had trouble eating, he made involuntary gestures with his arm, he couldn't see properly. But you knew my father, Sydney. He would never have let on if he could have helped it. He was always trying to make us feel better."

"And your mother?"

Ben shakes his head. "She's had a rough time of it," he says. "After my father got out of the hospital, we came up here. My mother cooked and cleaned. She had to keep in motion. Sometimes I wanted to yell at her to sit with him, but I learned that each of us has to get through it in his or her own way. There's no rehearsal for any of this."

Sydney thinks about how there was no rehearsal for Daniel's death, how shocking that was. She thinks, too, about the irony of having had a rehearsal for a wedding, but no rehearsal for the pageant that actually unfolded that July morning.

"He died at the house?" Sydney asks.

Ben wipes his forehead with the bottom of his T-shirt. "It's where he wanted to be," he says. "They couldn't stop the strokes. He was surprisingly calm, though sometimes he grew agitated at the loss of his abilities. One day he would be lucid, the next day he seemed to float in a blessed fog. We had my father's hospital bed facing the long windows out to the water. He kept turning his head toward the kitchen, thinking that Jeff was back. The last thing he said before he died was, 'Is that him?' "

"Jeff didn't make it?"

"He made it in time for the funeral."

Sydney briefly closes her eyes. She wants to sit again in the sand. It is too much to take in. Weeks of a man's dying compressed into a few seconds of telling.

"Julie was wonderful," Ben is saying. "I think she couldn't imagine death and so had no fear of it. She saw my father weakening, but she didn't allow herself to take it in. It was a sort of blindness. The actual event was terrible for her."

"Julie's still with Hélène?"

"They rented a cottage not far from us." Ben turns and looks for Tullus. "You know, it's hard to clear the life out of a house."

When they reach the house, Ben sets her briefcase on the bottom step. "I'll go in and prepare them, tell them you're here. Then I'll come out and get you. I think it's better that way."

"Ben," Sydney says. "I have questions."

"About my father?"

"Yes, that, too. But . . ."

"I imagine you do. We'll talk."

"And listen," Sydney adds, "if your mother doesn't want me here . . ."

"I know."

"Your father wrote to me, and I didn't answer his letters!" Sydney cries out suddenly. "It's awful when I think about that now. What would it have cost me to answer the man's letters? None of what happened between me and Jeff was his fault."

"He knew that."

"I've missed him."

"I think your wedding day was brutal for him. Not only to watch his son do that to you, but in doing so, to take you away from the family."

Sydney waits on the bottom step, her briefcase on her lap. If she is not welcome at the house, Ben will drive her to her car, and she will return to Boston. She can't imagine sitting through a lecture now, paying attention to a single word.

She waits for nearly twenty minutes, a time that embarrasses her. She hopes Ben has had the sense not to push the notion of Sydney's visit, to let the idea go if his mother is adamantly opposed. But what else can it mean, taking all this time?

She watches a couple in blue windbreakers walking along the wet part of the beach, exposed when the tide is at its lowest. The breeze flattens the thin material to their bodies and blows their hair off their faces. She and Ben walked with the wind, and she didn't feel it as much. Now, sitting on the step, she is chilled. She didn't think to stick a sweater into her briefcase.

Each time Sydney tries to imagine Mr. Edwards's death, her mind veers. She sets the briefcase down and puts her head in her hands. Would it have been so terrible to have called Mr. Edwards and invited him to meet her at the museum, a building so close to her own apartment she could have walked to it? What must he have thought of her refusal to reply to his letters? Her silence would have hurt him; Ben had as much as said so. How could she have been so callous?

*   *   *

She can feel Ben in the vibration of the wooden steps even before he appears on the deck.

"I'm sorry that took so long," he says. "It wasn't that there was any disagreement, I just couldn't find my mother. The house is a mess. Well, obviously."

Julie runs along the boardwalk shouting Sydney's name. The strong girl lifts Sydney up and twirls her around. Sydney cannot help but laugh.

"Where have you been?" Julie scolds as she sets Sydney down. "Why didn't you answer my letters?"

Sydney has no answer for the exuberant girl who would have been a magical tonic for a dying father.

Julie keeps her arm wrapped tightly around Sydney as they walk toward the house. Sydney would like to pause on the steps and collect her thoughts, but there is no time for that. Julie, dressed in jeans and a pink sweater, pulls her up the stairs. The girl is twenty-one now.

But once inside the door, as if understanding that Sydney might now need a moment to herself, Julie lets her go.

*   *   *

The white sofas are covered with large black trash bags. A note has been pinned to one of the bags: *Salvation Army.* On the floor are piles of household items—appliances, paintings, books. Sydney tries to discern an order to the piles. Perhaps each is meant for a member of the family. Which is Julie's pile? Sydney wonders. Or Ben's?

The sense of emptiness is palpable. Discolored oblongs dot the wall where paintings and maps once hung. Lamps have been disconnected, stacks of magazines tied with string. Slipcovers have been removed, rugs rolled up. A broom is propped up against a wall. A bottle of Windex sits on a sill, and, beneath it, a roll of paper towel has unraveled nearly to the center of the room. The last time Sydney was in this house, ribbons and bows decorated a stairway, and bowls of roses sent up a celebratory perfume. The last time Sydney was in the house, champagne and people waited for a wedding.

In the periphery of her vision, Sydney can see Mrs. Edwards standing by the counter in the kitchen. Sydney says hello, and Mrs. Edwards says hello back to her. The woman is astonishingly gaunt. She has cut her hair short and has lost all the weight any woman could ever wish to lose—worry and grief an immensely more effective diet than counting carbs. Sydney guesses there are few normal meals now. She walks to the counter. "I'm so sorry," she says.

"Why should you be sorry?" Mrs. Edwards asks, taking up a sponge and wiping the granite.

Over Mrs. Edwards's shoulder, Sydney can see through the window to the rose garden, or what is left of it. Single blooms bend from mostly leafless stalks. Where there are leaves, there are black spots. An entire garden of rose hips and rotted blossoms moves in the breeze. Part of the decay is due to the time of year, but most, Sydney can see, is simply from neglect.

The contents of a kitchen drawer have been laid out upon the counter above it. On a table in the dining room are cartons marked *Dishes.* Tablecloths, not yet put away, sit in a neat stack. Sydney recognizes the oilcloth used for lobster dinners, the damask nap-

kins—old Emporia finds. Ben opens the refrigerator and takes out two bottles of water.
He hands one to Sydney.

"We were just about to eat lunch," Julie
says. "Are you hungry?"

"I'll just take a quick shower," Ben says.

Bread, ham, mayonnaise, tomatoes, and
lettuce have all been arranged on the granite counter. The spread reminds Sydney of
the sublime confections Mr. Edwards once
put together in the panini maker. Sydney
fixes herself a plain sandwich and is glad for
it. She hasn't eaten anything since an early
breakfast.

She sits with Julie at the kitchen table. Instinctively, Sydney looks for the crack in the
wood on which she used to catch her
sweaters.

"How are you?" Sydney asks. "How are
you really?"

Julie's face and nose immediately turn
red. "It's so hard!" she blurts out.

"I know," Sydney says, though, of course,
she does not. Not entirely. Both of her own
parents are still alive and apparently healthy,
still speaking to each other, though not particularly friendly. Daniel happened, but that

was different, over before Sydney even knew about it.

Julie takes a paper napkin from a loose pile and blows her nose. "I'm okay," she says. "Most of the time. Hélène's been coming on weekends. Oh, I'm having a show."

"That's great," Sydney says. "In Montreal?"

"In a suburb near the city. It's a group show. I'll have three paintings in it. I should have brought slides."

"I'd love to see the show. When is it?"

"In January."

"Then I'll come."

"Would you?" Julie asks, her face alight. "There'll be a party. Hélène's sure there will be a party."

"I'll definitely come," Sydney says, only just then realizing how hard it might be to visit Montreal again.

Beside her, Julie folds and refolds a new napkin. Sydney is reminded of the blue handkerchief now in a drawer in her apartment. "I can't believe he's gone," Sydney says. She can see so clearly the package of Gummy Lobsters in Mr. Edwards's hand; the spots of lobster juice on his pale green polo shirt; Mr. Edwards holding his stomach and bemoaning the doughnut he had at breakfast.

"He'd be glad you're here," Julie says.

"I wish I had known," Sydney says. "I would have come sooner."

"I knew you would have!" Julie cries. "Ben said no, but I was sure you would have wanted to come."

"You thought of calling me?" Sydney asks.

"God, Sydney," Julie says. "I only wrote you a hundred letters."

At the counter, Mrs. Edwards is wrapping up the ham and the lettuce. She puts them in the refrigerator. Sydney senses a slight reproof for not having done so herself. She stands with her dish and glass and walks them to the sink.

"You won't want your old room," Mrs. Edwards announces.

Sydney, startled, turns. "Oh, I can't stay," she explains.

Though an invitation has hardly been delivered, Mrs. Edwards appears miffed. "I thought you were staying," she says.

"Oh, stay!" Julie pleads from the table.

Sydney shakes her head. "I can't," she repeats.

"But surely you can stay for dinner," Mrs. Edwards says.

And Sydney decides, glancing at Mrs. Edwards and then at the young woman who has so recently lost her father, *Yes, I can stay for dinner.*

Sydney, loading the dishwasher, feels as if she has unintentionally fallen into her expected role—something between a guest and a servant. Julie has gone upstairs to pack her room. Behind Sydney, Mrs. Edwards wipes the granite counter. Sydney thinks by now it must be nearly sterile.

"I've never liked you," Mrs. Edwards says in a low voice. "I can't pretend I ever did."

Sydney holds a glass, someone's glass, in her hand. Despite the truth of the statement, and the fact that it is hardly news, she cannot believe what she has just heard. She slowly turns toward the woman.

"I suppose I should be sorry about that," Mrs. Edwards continues, not looking at Sydney, "but I can't pretend to be someone I'm not." The woman's sleeves are rolled to the elbows; the veins on her forearms are raised. "I can't pretend that I wasn't glad when Jeff . . . when Jeff did what he did.

Well, I wasn't glad exactly," she says, folding the rag she is using and wiping the same spot she's been polishing. "It was embarrassing, and it was a tremendous hassle. Of course it was. But there was relief, too. I won't say there wasn't."

Sydney can think of no way to respond.

"I watched you leave the house," Mrs. Edwards continues, "and I said to myself, *That's that.*"

Sydney sets down the glass and wipes her hands on a sheet of paper towel. "I think I should go," she says quietly.

"Oh, for heaven's sake, don't go," Mrs. Edwards says, as if Sydney has missed the point entirely. And only now does the woman look up at her. Perhaps she has been practicing this confession for months. "No, don't go now that you've just got here. Ben and Julie are glad that you've come. It's been hard on them. Especially with Jeff away . . ." Mrs. Edwards looks quickly up at the ceiling. "No, you're welcome now," she says. "That's not what I meant at all. I just wanted to say that I know I was rude to you all that time, and I'm, you know . . . It's too bad, that's all."

It is, Sydney thinks, an appalling confession. She searches for a reply, which Mrs. Edwards appears to expect. The silence draws itself out.

"Well, you wouldn't know what to say, would you?" Mrs. Edwards says. "I expect this is all a shock to you. It is to us, too, even though we've had months to get used to it. But it doesn't matter, does it? Time? There's never enough time."

Mrs. Edwards pauses in her cleaning, hand on the granite, and closes her eyes, like a woman trying to rid herself of hiccups. "I just miss him so much," she says. She covers her eyes with her arm, the cloth dangling from her hand.

Sydney, not knowing what else to do, moves toward the woman. She lightly touches her elbow.

Mrs. Edwards flinches, as if she had been singed.

Sydney seeks refuge in an upstairs bathroom. She walks to the window, draws back the curtains, and looks out at the marsh, moss-green and russet in the afternoon light. The water has left deep trenches in the mud. A flock of birds soars, an air show over the grasses. The birds change from gray-winged to white and back again, making crazy eights in perfect formation. They do it for the fun of it, she thinks.

To the north is a house on a hill, its white facade gleaming. Sydney spots a fox. Occasionally, she can hear, but not see, a car. All along the road, thickets of beach rose and something else make a nearly impenetrable wall. From where she stands, Sydney can peer into the backyard of the house next door. A slim boat waits in its blue plastic sleeve for summer. The windows of the cottage have been shuttered.

Across the marsh, the grocery store and lobster pound are closed. A few fishermen are coming in for the day, but they will have unloaded their catch elsewhere, perhaps in Portsmouth. The low-tide waters are reflective in parts, corrugated in others.

Sydney fingers the white curtain. The Reverend *"Hemmings Motor News"* used this bathroom. So did Art and Wendy. Sydney flashes on the image of a lamp in the shape of an antique car horn. Over the years, the house has sheltered perhaps hundreds of guests. Did the nuns have visitors? Did the unwed mothers? Would parents have come and scolded their young daughters and then wept at their bedsides? Would the political agitators have ignored the beauty of the marsh entirely, interested only in signs of smoke from the mills beyond?

Sydney thinks about Mrs. Edwards's confession. A death, her grief, has given Mrs. Edwards license. There will be no more dinner parties now. Sydney is reminded of the small double bed in the parental bedroom, of the photo on Mr. Edwards's desk. Sydney can never know how much love, physical or otherwise, there was between husband and wife.

Mrs. Edwards is now a widow. At last, Sydney thinks with some irony, the two women have something in common.

Sydney hears a knock on the door.

"Yes?" she calls.

"You okay?" The voice is Ben's. "You've been in there forever."

"I'm fine," she answers. "I'm just coming out."

She washes her hands, dries them, and opens the door. Ben is standing in the hallway, holding two sweatshirts.

"Want to go for a ride?" he asks.

Sydney, asked to hold the faded navy sweatshirts, wonders what they are for. They walk to a Jetta parked at the back of the house.

"Where's the Land Rover?" she asks.

"Sold it," Ben answers.

She takes the passenger seat and shuts the door. Ought she to be apprehensive about being alone with Ben, a man with whom she has never felt comfortable? But then the moment passes. The man has just lost his father, Sydney reasons. Isn't everything a little different now?

They drive in companionable silence the length of the beach road and into town, each place infused with both new life and abandonment: the new life in the girders and rafters of construction on the beach; the abandonment in the shuttered windows of the houses in the village. Only the post office has a vehicle parked in front of it.

Ben says, "You may have to get the cuffs of your pants wet. Is that all right?"

Sydney answers, yes, that is fine. It seems to her, as Ben turns on the engine of the Whaler, that she has hours ago stopped caring about her clothes or her appearance.

She zips up the sweatshirt and sits on the bait box.

The blue above the ocean is determinedly cleansed and rinsed after a long hot summer. The salt wind seems full of pure oxygen. The engine strains against the tide. It is impossible to speak to Ben, who is standing at the wheel behind her. Perhaps he means to round the point and have one last look at the summerhouse before it no longer belongs to his family. She understands that impulse but wonders why he wanted to bring her along. Possibly, having overheard his mother, he is only being kind.

But when they clear the gut, Ben heads west rather than east, his destination unclear to Sydney. The wind whips her hair straight back. The Whaler picks up its pace, slapping against the chop. She notes that the white cushions have turned a faint pink in spots, that the abraded deck is stained. A sense of disorder pervades the boat: a balled T-shirt in the bow; uncoiled rope on the console; a fishing rod, unsheathed, its hook dangling.

They round a promontory she has never seen before. They travel what seems a good distance, and Sydney begins to doubt the wisdom of having accepted Ben's invitation. She wonders, too, if she ought to have called one of her colleagues: Will they worry about her?

The Whaler heads along a shoreline she is not familiar with. Sydney is aware of islands, lobster buoys, a fishing boat coming into port. She feels, too, an odd sense of freedom, of having escaped the village as they run fast along the shore. Perhaps there is an agenda after all.

Ben slows the engine. Ahead of them is an island on which stand three or four shacks.

He cuts the engine even further, and the Whaler drifts. He examines the water depth closely. She, too, peers over the side, and sees below them an unending bed of shells, dark shells with pearl-like spirals in between. She wishes she could reach down and touch them.

They drift on until there is only sand under the boat, rippled sand like that at the bottom of a river. Sydney runs her hand through the water and is surprised at its warmth. Between the boat and the island are several sandbars.

"We'll have maybe twenty minutes," Ben says.

He anchors the boat and lets the line play out in shallow water. Sydney heaves herself over the side of the Whaler. She has rolled the cuffs of her black pants, but instantly they unravel. She wades through the seawater to where Ben is standing.

"Sorry about that," he says, looking down at her soaked legs.

But Sydney is gazing at the island in front of her. "This is amazing," she says.

*   *   *

The sand on the bars is rippled as well, and the ridges massage her feet. Sydney is struck by the number of shells, some in piles, some at the edge of the bar, all begging to be collected. Sydney and Ben cross one sandbar and then another and then begin to climb up a steep slope. Ben leads the way.

The cottages are clustered at the top of the hill. All but one have been boarded up for the winter—or perhaps they have been that way for years. There are four, each one facing out to sea. The island is the size of a baseball field, and in its center is a well. Someone has mown the grass, suggesting recent habitation.

She follows Ben to a modest brown-and-yellow cottage with a porch. The shingled roof has four dormers in it—each one a point of the compass. Sydney can see the shoreline of the mainland half a mile away.

"Where are we?" she asks.

"Frederick's Island," Ben says. "The locals call it Freddie's."

"Is this the one . . . ?" Sydney asks, thinking of her wedding day.

"No," Ben answers quickly.

*   *   *

The brown stain is badly weathered, the yellow trim nearly cream-colored. Lobster buoys hang from an outside wall. Beside a door that Ben unlocks, two plastic rain buckets hold what looks to be discolored water. He steps inside the house and waits for her to enter.

It takes a minute for her eyes to adjust. She discovers she is standing in a small kitchen, all the walls and rafters whitewashed. Sydney notes a rudimentary stove and a tiny refrigerator with rusted hinges. On a shelf by the front door is a spotted mirror, a plastic glass full of toothbrushes, a pair of scissors, a can of Off. Below the shelf is a soapstone sink filled with plastic water jugs. To its right is a glass pitcher with red and yellow stripes, reminiscent of pitchers her mother might have used in Troy for iced tea. On the wall next to a counter is a kerosene lantern.

"There's no water or electricity," Ben explains. "The stove and fridge run on propane. Let me show you the other rooms."

They step inside a charmless living room with thin white curtains at the windows. A gas lantern hangs from the ceiling as do brass chimes meant to move in the wind when the front door is open. The bare wood floor is covered with furniture: a maple sofa with a blue quilt, a chrome chair from the 1970s, four green molded-plastic chairs of the sort one might keep on a porch, two lovely old wicker chaises, unpainted, and to one side a round table covered with an oil-cloth printed with red lobsters. A worn braided rug that matches nothing sits in the center of the room.

There is a bedroom, too small to hold much more than a bed and a bureau, a bathroom that looks as though it has been recently used by fishermen. Sydney likes the dining room, with its slanted ceiling and the exposed azure boards of the walls. Flower-patterned oilcloth covers a dark table. A matching sideboard and chairs seem oddly formal. In the center of the table is a green-glass kerosene lantern, and Sydney imagines dinners in the lantern light. She notes a vinegar cruet on the sill, a rolled flag, a whisk broom.

"Is this yours?" she asks Ben, who is standing in the doorway with his hands in the pockets of his jeans.

"I just closed on it. It needs a lot of work."

"The people who owned it left all this stuff?"

"You have to with an island house. It's too much trouble to haul it back to the mainland."

"Why did you buy it?"

"I did it when I learned that my mother was selling the beach house."

"It's funky," Sydney says, "but it's kind of wonderful—like stepping back in time."

Ben leads the way up a narrow staircase. "There are three tiny bedrooms on this second floor," he explains, "but I'm going to knock the walls down and make one big room. Here, let me show you this."

At the landing, Ben opens a window and steps outside onto the slightly pitched roof of the porch. "Come on," he says to her. "It's pretty flat."

Sydney crawls out onto the roof, the asphalt rough on her knees. When she has settled herself, she looks out to a startling view of islands to the north and, beyond them, the Atlantic. There are no sounds except for the faint slapping of the water against rocks. "The view is fabulous," Sydney says. "Do people really live here?"

"You can't live here year-round. None of the houses is winterized. But people do come out in the summer. I've met one or two of them."

"How do you get on and off?" she asks.

"At low tide, you can walk. There's a sandbar on the other side. You can drive, too, but you really want a four-wheel-drive to do that. I shouldn't have sold the Land Rover. Usually, I come over in the boat. I'll do a little work this fall. I'll probably get a second-hand truck for the job."

"I'm confused," Sydney says. "What about your other job?"

"I guess you could say I'm on sabbatical. Indefinite sabbatical would be more accurate."

"Did you get fired?"

He laughs. "No. I've quit. For now anyway."

Ben leans back against the frame of the window. "At one time, most of the New England coastline was like this," he explains. "Small cottages without running water or electricity. There were one or two on the beach when my parents bought the big house, but they're gone now. Torn down to make way for newer construction."

Sydney is impressed by the simplicity of the view. "It's disturbing in a way," she says, "all this beauty, isn't it? You want it forever, but you can't have it. Your father once said that he thought all the people who had owned the beach house had come for the beauty."

"My father said that?" Ben ponders the thought. "It's not true, though, is it?"

"How do you mean?"

"The beauty is there, certainly, but the beach has its ugly side as well. Even this view can be harsh if you look closely enough. Those flies all over that seaweed there? The rocks there covered with gull shit? And can you smell the diesel fumes from that lobster boat?"

"I've always wondered if beauty is simply trying to capture something you never had," Sydney says, "or if it's something you once had in childhood that you want back. The wonder of it, say, or the magnificence."

"It's the light," Ben says. "The same scene on a cloudy day is depressing as hell."

Ben adjusts his position. "Sometimes I think it's a kind of pornography, this lusting after beauty," he says. "I used to see a lot of it in my job. The great rooms with the granite and the Sub-Zero, the triple-paned windows and the French doors, the walk-in closets as big as their grandmothers' living rooms used to be. Everything I wear all summer could fit into two drawers in a bureau. That's why I loved this place when I saw it," he adds, gesturing to take in the house they are sitting on. "You were too well mannered to say so, but it's pretty grim."

Sydney laughs. "It's *authentic,*" she says.

Her pants dry in odd shapes. The roof is hot. She wonders what it would be like to be here in a storm. "Ben, what happened?" she asks. "Why did he do it?"

Ben turns to look at her. "Are we talking about Jeff?"

"Yes."

Ben sets his jaw, and there is a kind of hardening of the lower part of his face. "I can't answer for him," he says, "but I do know that we had a remarkable conversation at the airport waiting for his flight."

"Jeff took the flight to Paris?" Sydney asks.

"He felt he had to get away."

Though Sydney had imagined Jeff going

off to Paris, the reality of it rattles her. "What did he say?"

"He said he'd just done the worst thing in his life."

A vestige of hurt moves through Sydney's body like a cloud. In seconds, it is gone.

"I agreed with him," Ben says.

"That afternoon," she says and hesitates— now on the verge of assuming more than might be true—"he said he did it to you."

Ben is silent for a long time. "I suppose he did."

"He'd done it with Victoria, too, he said."

"He had."

"What happened?"

Ben, head bent, picks at a loose shingle. "Vicki and I had just started going out. We'd been together maybe ten days, two weeks. I think we'd gone out to dinner and we'd been to a party. Then Jeff met us at a benefit, and next thing I know, they're a couple."

"You weren't mad?"

"I was *surprised,* let's put it that way." Ben pauses. "I thought, you know, may the best man win, water under the bridge. What was I going to do? Ask for her back?" Ben looks up. "But when he did it again . . . I realized that even Jeff's taking Victoria had been deliberate. I could forgive him the first time, but not the second, and he knew it."

"But why did he do it?"

Ben is hesitant. "He saw I noticed you, so he wanted you," he says after a beat. "End of story."

"That was it?" Sydney asks.

"That was it."

"And I let him have me."

"So you did."

Sydney closes her eyes. A sense of shame, of foolishness, engulfs her.

"Jeff was always competitive," Ben says, perhaps sensing her embarrassment. "Some of it was just the natural order, some of it was pure Jeff. When I was twelve, Jeff was eight. When I was eighteen, he was fourteen. By definition, I was better at most things than he was. Athletics, for example; he could never compete in that arena. He used to try, and then he just gave up, decided to find other ways to beat me. School was one. Women was another. He got very, very good at getting women." Ben glances sideways at Sydney. "Are you sure you want to hear this?"

"I think so."

"Jeff was brilliant at it. He would seem to do it without really trying. I'm not quite sure how he pulled it off. You would know better than I."

Sydney remembers the day Jeff came out onto the porch and traced his finger from her knee to the hem of her shorts, a shockingly intimate gesture given how little had gone before. She can see that such gestures might make for an effective technique—throwing a woman off balance, taking possession of her before she understood that she had been possessed.

Sydney straightens out her legs on the rooftop.

"I'm going to build a small deck right where we're sitting," Ben says. "I'll put in a door where the window is, and then have a space big enough for a couple of chairs and a small table."

Sydney is amazed at the absence of sound. No children running on a beach, no cars, no whine from a boat engine. "You know, I had a sense, that first day on the porch, that I was upsetting the family equilibrium. That I was intruding."

"People were intruding all the time."

"Not like I was."

"No, probably not."

"I was seduced."

"By Jeff?"

"Well, yes, but also by the beauty of the place, I think, and the sense of family."

Ben studies her. "I can see that. A double whammy: beauty and family. Though, truthfully, I think you fell a little in love with my father."

Sydney is taken aback by the suggestion. "But not in the way—"

"No, I didn't mean that. Everybody was always falling a little in love with him."

"He was a great man," Sydney says.

"Yes, he was."

"I thought Jeff would be like him," she says.

"Fatal mistake."

"Ben, why didn't you tell me? About Jeff. Before the wedding."

Ben takes a long breath and lets it out. "At first I was reluctant because I didn't want to see you get hurt, and then the longer it went on, the more I thought maybe Jeff really cared about you, that this was it for him."

"So you stayed away."

"If he was doing it to spite me, I didn't want any part of it. And if he loved you, I had to stay away." Ben pauses. "Listen, that night in the snowstorm, at the bar, if I'd told you about Jeff, would you have believed me?"

Sydney remembers the slush underfoot, the green martinis, the way Ben captured her hand on the table.

"Probably not," she says.

Sydney unzips her sweatshirt. Her blouse is wrinkled. "What will happen to your mother?" she asks.

"She got a good price for the beach house. And she'll get a good one for the Needham house as well. I'm trying to find her a condo in Boston."

"Where is your dad buried?"

"In Needham."

"Maybe I'll go there one day."

Ben, beside her, pats down the loose shingle.

Yes, she will go to Mr. Edwards's grave, and she will bring roses. Not hothouse roses, but real ones from someone's garden.

But first she will go to see the painting at the Museum of Fine Arts.

"Did you love Jeff very much?" Ben asks in a tight voice, as if he has been saving up this one question all afternoon. Sydney can hear, in his tone, how much the answer might mean to him.

"I did," Sydney answers honestly. "But when something like that happens, it puts into question everything you once felt. What comes after taints it." She turns to see if Ben is satisfied with her answer or not, but he is standing, looking at the tide coming in.

"Christ," he says.

They swim back to the boat. The tide has risen faster than Ben anticipated. He stays near Sydney, and when the weight of her clothes drags her down and her mouth fills with seawater, he clutches her arm and holds on to her until they reach the Whaler.

At the boat, Sydney crawls up the stern and tumbles inside. She helps Ben lift the anchor. "I'm really sorry about this," he says repeatedly, but she waves him away. She tells him she is glad for the sense of adventure, for the time they had on the rooftop. If she had to do it again, even with the risky swim, she would. She hunkers down inside the cockpit. The sweatshirts are of no use now.

"We'll be there soon," he says.

*   *   *

Sydney shivers, and when she glances up, she can see that Ben, too, is shaking inside his jeans and his soaked sweatshirt. He is running the boat as fast as he dares, the tide blessedly with them this time. As they pass through the gut, he cuts the engine at the dock. "I'll let you off here," he says, "and go out to the mooring. I'll row in in the dinghy. Find someone and ask for a blanket. I'll be back as soon as I can."

Sydney does as she is told and waits for Ben in a small room meant to suggest a yacht club. Sepia photographs of sailing teams hang over the mantel. Elaborate silver trophies sit on wooden shelves. In a corner is a children's library, a stack of board games on the floor. A young man has given Sydney a green flannel blanket in which she has wrapped herself. Still, she shivers—from the memory of the conversation on the rooftop or the cold, she doesn't know.

When Ben comes, she sheds the blanket, folds it, and thanks the young man. She and Ben jog to the car. Once inside, he turns on the heat full throttle. Again, he apologizes.
"Ben, stop," Sydney says. "It was fun."

"You're still shivering," he says.

"I'm fine," she insists. "I'm absolutely fine."

"You use the guest bathroom," Ben decides as they step from the Jetta. "I'll use the one at the end of the hall." He calls to Julie as Sydney and he enter the house. Julie, emerging from her room, pokes her head over the upstairs railing. Ben takes the steps two at a time, and Sydney follows. "What?" Julie asks, a look of alarm on her face.

"Sydney's going to need some warm clothes," he says.

"Did you fall in?" Julie asks.

"Not exactly," Ben says.

Sydney thinks it may be the best shower she has ever had. She runs the hot water for as long as it takes to warm her body, which seems to have chilled itself to its core. After a time, her shoulders begin to relax, the nearly scalding water on the back of her neck doing its job. She finds a quarter inch of shampoo in a bottle and washes her hair. Earlier, she heard Julie open the door and lay a pile of clothes on the sink. "They'll be

way too big," the girl called from the doorway.

"They'll be great," Sydney said.

"There's towels here, too."

Sydney feels as though she has just completed a long sail, as if she'd been in a race
and won. A bowl of hot chowder would be
perfect.

She wraps her hair in a knot, using an elastic band she finds on the shelf of a nearly
empty medicine cabinet. She dresses herself in Julie's clothes—a navy velour running
suit at least two sizes too big. Sydney ap-
preciates the roominess and feels as she
did as a child after a bath: cleansed all over,
wrapped in the warmth of a towel nearly as
large as she. She has to wipe the steam off
the mirror even to see her face, pink now
from the hot water. She wonders briefly if
she will be the last person ever to use this
shower, if the new owners will feel com-
pelled to renovate the house or, worse, tear
it down for new construction. She examines
fondly the features of the bathroom she
once shared with houseguests and a minister: the toilet with the handle one has to jig-
gle to get it to flush right; the slightly rusted

chrome towel bar; the medicine cabinet with its metal shelves; the two globular lights at either side of the mirror, suggesting lanterns. When she opens the door to the hallway, steam travels with her.

Ben is waiting downstairs. "Can I get you that beer you wouldn't let me get you three years ago?" he asks.

Sydney laughs.

Sydney and Julie and Ben, bottles in hand, find seats in the rearranged living room. In the kitchen, Mrs. Edwards is making dinner. Sydney can smell pork chops.

Ben said, earlier in the day, *It's hard to clear the life out of a house.* It goes in black trash bags and boxes, Sydney thinks, surveying the room that once was familiar. It goes to the Salvation Army and to the dump. It goes to new walls and to new rooms, perhaps to a condo in Boston or to an apartment in Montreal. Will a painting or a small piece of furniture make the boat trip to the brown-and-yellow cottage on Frederick's Island? Where will the white couches go? Or the long dining room table around which the family had so many dinners? Will Mrs. Edwards keep her flea-market finds?

"After dinner, I'll finish with the windows," Ben says to Julie, "though I don't know what good it will do. By Thursday, they'll be salted up again."

"I'm almost done with my room."

"I'll begin the cellar, too," he adds.

"Good luck with that," Julie says. "I hate cellars," she explains to Sydney. "I almost never go down there."

Sydney would like to help, but to offer is to suggest that she might be spending the night. It bothers her to remain idle, however. It seems to her that the time she once spent in the house demands some effort on her part in its dismantling.

She will do the dishes, she thinks. At the very least.

Ben has dressed in a black sweater over a white T-shirt. His face is coarse and reddened, his hair finger-combed over his ears. Perhaps he forgot his hairbrush. He is wearing a pair of khaki shorts he might have found in a drawer in the boys' dorm. Sydney wonders if her old room has been cleared out, if the blue cobalt vase is now gone. Who'd have wanted that? Is it in one of the trash bags marked *Goodwill?*

"Sydney's going to come to Montreal to see my show," Julie announces to Ben, who has drained his beer and is thinking, Sydney can see, of getting up to get another one. If he offers a second to her, she will accept. It may be hours yet before she has to drive back to Boston. Surviving the swim to the boat has made her reckless.

"Good," he says. "That's when?"

"January," Julie says.

"Well, I'll come, too," he says. Sydney notes that Ben assiduously avoids looking in her direction.

"You will?" Julie asks excitedly. "Hélène says there will be a party."

The dinner consists of the pork chops, rice from a box, and a bag of salad with bottled dressing. It's a meal not unlike the ones Sydney used to have in Troy: simple, rudimentary, tasteless. The chops are so well done Sydney can barely cut through them with a serrated knife. The four eat at the kitchen table, plastic mats under their plates.

Sydney cannot escape the odd feeling that they are an ordinary family sitting down to its evening meal after a routine workday. Mother, son, daughter. What would Sydney's role now be? Old family friend? Distant family friend? Former employee who almost married the second son?

Mrs. Edwards chews slowly, as if she has no desire for the meal she has just made. Perhaps all of life to her is now tasteless. Sydney remembers similar sensations after Daniel died and after Jeff left her on her wedding day: the notion that the world had lost its sensory properties, or she had lost the ability to perceive them. She would like to be able to share this thought with the woman but can only imagine Mrs. Edwards's dismissive look were she to do so. The woman's skin is red and blotchy. Grief has heightened her color.

Across from her, Julie seems subdued. This might be the last dinner she will ever have in the house. She has not said yet when she is returning to Montreal. The death of Mr. Edwards would have been hard on Julie, too young to have a father taken from her. And mightn't Mr. Edwards's grief have been equally keen? To leave the child he clearly loved most at such a tender age? Would he have felt relief that Julie had Hélène? Did the dying have such thoughts? Or did one become more and more detached, ready to enter a different universe?

Ben finishes his meal quickly. Sydney notes that he is on his third beer and is polishing that one off at a good clip.

The man has lost his father and his brother, his mother to her mourning. His sister will continue to live in a different country. He pushes his chair back and turns his body so that he is gazing into the living room. He rests an elbow on the kitchen table.

Sydney once again glances around the table: Mrs. Edwards, still fussing with her pork chop; Julie finishing her bottle of beer; Ben, tired, taking a long swallow. It is, she thinks, as if the family has been caught in a riptide and carried out to sea, each of them swimming sideways, parallel to shore.

—⁓—

When Sydney has finished washing the last of the pots, she cleans the stove. She wipes down the surface, removes the burners, soaks them in the sink, and digs out the debris stuck in the seams between the stove and the granite countertop. She opens the oven door and briefly ponders tackling that as well. To do so, however, would require asking for oven cleaner, to which Ben or Julie would certainly reply, *No, don't do that; that's too messy a job.* Mrs. Edwards might not reply at all.

Sydney decides to clean out the refrigerator instead. She wipes down the interior, washes the shelves and the bins in lukewarm water. She throws out food she is absolutely certain no one would want: rotten onions in a net bag; liquefying lettuce; a jar of olive tapenade with a layer of flourishing green plant life. The other items, even the marginal ones, she replaces exactly as she found them. Mrs. Edwards might think the refrigerator is not Sydney's province, that she has overstepped her bounds.

The freezer is filled with unidentifiable items in plastic bags, most with a fur of frost on them. Sydney shuts the door.

*   *   *

When she has done as much as she can with the refrigerator, Sydney begins to clear out the cabinets. Definitely not her province, but she doesn't feel, despite the impending drive back to Boston, that she can quit working until everyone else does. Perhaps there will be a small celebration at the end of the evening, with slices of the triple-berry pie Sydney spotted earlier in the cake tin.

She removes every item from the first cabinet: second-string dishes one might use for cereal, aqua bowls that can only have been a house gift, small juice glasses with bright red cherries on them, plastic dishes in the event one didn't want to use real ones on the porch. Never once, the entire time Sydney lived in the house, did anyone ever use a plastic dish.

Mrs. Edwards passes through the kitchen without comment. Sydney is mildly surprised that the woman doesn't even stop to stare. She glides silently through twice more while Sydney is on her knees on the counter, reaching into the back crevices of a cabinet with the sponge. It is as though the woman has forgotten how to talk.

When Mrs. Edwards enters the room for

the fourth time, Sydney hops down from the counter. The woman sighs and climbs the stairs to the second floor. Sydney listens for footsteps overhead. Mrs. Edwards is on her way to her bedroom.

Sydney can hear Ben in the rough drag of heavy objects against the cellar floor. She thinks Julie may have gone up to bed. She sits at the kitchen table with a glass of water from the tap. Her presence here is superfluous and suspect; it is time she was on her way. She wonders briefly where she put her briefcase with the key she earlier removed from her pocket. Maybe her clothes will be dry. In a minute she will go to fetch them, dress quickly, and then find Ben so that he can drive her to her car at the public parking lot. That accomplished, she will head south.

But first, she must do one more thing.

Sydney enters her old room and closes the door. The beds have been stripped, the bureau and the nightstand cleared of all debris. Even the bedside table lamp is gone.

Sydney sits on the bare mattress and lets her eyes adjust to the ambient light.

There is no cobalt vase with a feather on a sill, no red-enameled chair against the wall. She wonders who slept here after she left the room two years ago, and when it was finally emptied in preparation for the closing. She remembers Jeff standing by the window, Sydney thinking he might be crying.

She knew her decision to divorce Andrew was simply a painful choice she had to make. Daniel's death was evidence of a cruel and capricious universe at work. But Jeff's actions might always puzzle her. Were they a missive from the dark underbelly of human existence, indicating a fatal narcissism and a stunning lack of empathy? Had he done it for the sport, the kill? Or could he not help himself, caught up in a rivalry that had begun before he'd even realized it? Jeff was selfish, certainly, and perhaps hardwired to be competitive in spite of his own best interests. But did that make him evil? Or merely a flawed and all-too-real human being?

It was impetuous what I did, she remembers Jeff saying to her in Julie's bedroom the night the girl went missing. *Even careless.*

Sydney stands and glances once more around the room, trying to remember herself before there was a Jeff or a Ben or a Mr. Edwards or a Julie. She can see only the faintest of images, barely substantial: a young woman, twenty-nine, living from day to day, suspended between a life she was trying to recover from and a life she could not then have imagined. The images fade even as Sydney watches. The room falls very dark, and she shuts the door behind her.

When she turns, she sees Mrs. Edwards standing in the upstairs hallway. The woman has a cardboard carton in her arms. "Are you lost?" she asks.

Interesting question, Sydney thinks.

"Mark wanted you to have this," the woman says. She holds her arms out, indicating Sydney should take the box from her. Sydney is surprised by its weight. On the top of the box, in black marker, are written instructions: *This box to Sydney Sklar.*

"I was going to have it shipped to your address," Mrs. Edwards says, "but since you're here . . ." She pauses. "Before he died, while he was still able, Mark packed up a few things and made notes as to where they should go. I don't know what's in here," she adds, her tone implying *and I don't want to, either.*

"Thank you," Sydney says to the woman, who is even now brushing her scant hair off her forehead.

"I don't suppose you'll be here long," Mrs. Edwards says.

"No. I was just going."

"Well . . . ," Mrs. Edwards says, seemingly at a loss for words. She gives an odd wave of her hand. "Safe trip!" she adds—a woman seeing off an acquaintance about to head to distant lands.

Sydney carries the box into the dining room, where there is not much light but less likelihood of someone walking in on her. With a breath for courage, she opens the carton.

There are dozens of upright manila files. Sydney sees the name *Beecher* on one and knows immediately what the box contains. Mr. Edwards has given her the history of the house.

She closes the flap of the box, as if protecting it. That the man, knowing he would die soon, put his files into this carton and wrote her name on it is almost more than she can bear. Did he understand that his wife would sell the house? Did he think that someone might come in and tear it down, destroying all that history? Did he believe that, of all of them, Sydney would be its most appreciative trustee?

She cries until it is all out of her: the longing for the family, her grief for Mr. Edwards, her anger at Jeff. She cries until she gets the hiccups, and then a headache.

Sydney fetches her clothes from the drying rack and puts them on where she is standing. She folds the navy velour sweat suit into a neat package. Through the front windows, she spots Ben sitting on the porch. With the box under her arm, she opens the door.

"Hey," he says. "I wondered where you were."

"I'm leaving now. Would you mind giving me a ride back to my car?"

"What's that?" he asks, pointing to the box.

"It's . . ." Sydney opens her mouth, but

cannot answer him. Wisely, Ben doesn't press her. Perhaps he can see that she is in some distress.

"Sit here a minute," he says.

Sydney sets the box on a teak chair and joins Ben on the top step. The air is warm, suggesting a tropical climate. Sydney has to remind herself that it's mid-September in New Hampshire.

"Your clothes are dry?" he asks.

"A little damp."

"You want a beer?"

"I have a two-hour drive."

"A cup of coffee?"

"No, I'm okay."

Actually, she would like to lie down. She wishes she had an excuse to sleep in the house tonight, to slip out early tomorrow morning. But she will not do that. "It smells like the sea tonight," she says.

"East wind."

"It's nice," she says. "What will you do now?"

"I'll work on the cottage until it gets too cold. There's a fireplace there, but the house isn't insulated. Then I'll return to the city, commute back and forth when there's a stretch of good days in the forecast. By November, the cottage will be uninhabitable. And then I guess I'll have to think about the rest of my life."

An insouciant statement, suggesting risk and bravado. Knowing Ben, however, Sydney guesses he'll have a scheme or two up his sleeve. She doubts Ben would cut himself off completely. Doesn't he have to make a living?

"You'll go to Julie's show?" he asks.

"Yes, definitely."

A gull, brazen, lands on the boardwalk. As if rebuffed, it turns and faces away from them.

"You've never liked me," Ben says suddenly. "Right from the get-go, there was an almost visceral dislike. I've never understood why."

Stunned by the boldness of his statement, Sydney can feel the color rising in her face. How can she answer the man? Does he not remember?

"Ben," she says, wishing he hadn't done this. The day, while sometimes sad, has been relatively free of tension between them.

"There *was* something, wasn't there?" he asks. "I could feel it."

"This is . . ."

"Is it just me? Just who I am?"

"I wish you wouldn't bring this up."

"There *was* something."

"Oh, Ben," she says, "it was that night."

Ben narrows his eyes and frowns. "What night?"

"The night we went surfing."

In the light that spills from the front room of the house, she can see that he is trying to remember. She searches his face for some sign of dissembling. He shakes his head, still staring at her. His eyes have not shifted from hers, as if he wanted to read the answer in them. "I'm sorry," he says. "The night we went surfing?"

"Yes."

"Did I say something rude to you? If I did—"

"No."

He seems baffled. Maybe he truly doesn't know, she thinks. Maybe he is not pretending. "The hand?" she suggests.

Ben tilts his head—a question.

"In the water?"

In her embarrassment, she is inarticulate. She must get this over with. "When you slid under me and touched me?" she adds quickly.

Ben studies her. "Honest to god, Sydney, I have no idea what you're talking about."

"It wasn't you?" Sydney asks, sitting forward. "Ben, seriously, listen to me. Did you or did you not touch me all along my body while we were in the water that night?" She tries to make the question businesslike, without accusation.

"I wondered why you seemed so frosty," Ben says. "It started that night, didn't it?"

"It wasn't you?" she asks again.

"Let me get this straight," he says. "Someone—a person—messed with you in the water?"

Sydney nods. She waits.

Ben puts his hands on his knees and then stands. He lets out a breath. He stares at the water for what seems like a long time. He glances down at Sydney.

"That son of a bitch," he says.

Sydney bends her head and closes her eyes. The porch pitches beneath her, as if there had been a tectonic shift in geological plates. She replays the scene that night three years ago, trying to recall every detail. She remembers that the water was a vise around her ankles. Simple tasks seemed impossible, like learning to walk after a long illness. She sees the white edges of a wave, the sense of not wanting to be the first to quit. The roar of the water in her ears, the utter blackness. She had no power, none at all. The surge was a living thing. She staggered. She crawled onto dry land. She went back into the ocean. And all that time, Ben was beside her, was he not?

She felt a shape beneath her. The flesh slithered the length of her body, touching her, feeling her. She flailed and tried to force herself out of the surge, but couldn't. She had water in her mouth.

The slither along her breast, her stomach, her pubic bone, her thigh.

Fleeting and yet deliberate.

Difficult to accomplish and therefore intentional.

Ben, a shape in the dark, announcing himself. But Jeff. Where was Jeff?

Ben called for his brother, and there was no answer. Ben waited an interval and called again. How long was that interval? The timing now seems critical. A minute, two minutes? Only half a minute? Was there enough time to swim away and answer from a distance?

Ben, a man whose touch has always re-
pulsed her, who from that night on has
seemed to her something subterranean.
Who always seemed to have her number.

"Ben," she says, looking up.

But Ben is already at the end of the deck,
looking down over the water. Above them, a
moon, a distant light, illuminates the man.

"Ben," she calls again, but the surf is too
loud. He can't hear her. She watches him
jog down the stairs to the beach.

The reel begins a fast rewind. Sydney sees
Ben drinking from a juice carton. Was it a
deliberately boorish gesture, as she once
thought, or merely a holdover from exuberant teenage behavior? And the offer of a
beer during that first dinner party—not
predatory, but simply good manners from a
genial host? Ben's closed-lipped demeanor
in the bar—not the agenda of an angry man,
but merely a warning? Ben refusing to attend family gatherings—not with an air of
superiority and fury as Sydney had once
surmised, but simply stepping aside?

Sydney thinks suddenly of the way Jeff
drew his finger along her thigh. Of the shape
that claimed her in the water.

*   *   *

She sits for a time on the steps, waiting for
Ben to come back. Perhaps he is taking a
walk, burning off his anger. More likely, she
guesses, he wants nothing to do with her.

She cranes her neck to look back at the
house, and in doing so sees the box on the
teak chair. The new owners will enter the
house in three, four days and have no idea
at all of the life once lived within. Nothing
of the Edwards family or the Beechers or
the Richmonds. Nothing of the births and
deaths, the promises kept, the promises
broken. The fear, the terror, the joy, the love.
The realization, a simple one, disturbs Sydney. How is it possible that years of a family
life can be erased in the minutes between a
closing and the retaking of a building? There
ought to be a history written, she thinks, a
small journal passed from one owner to the
next. *A big fight was had on this day,* the
journal might read, *but we made it up before bed.* Or, *There was to be a wedding this
afternoon, but the groom didn't show.* Or,
*My father died peacefully in the front room.
We are all crying.*

If the new owners decide to tear down the
old house to make way for a new one, a

bulldozer will come in and dig up Mr. Edwards's rose garden. All those blossoms, all those species, all that care—gone in an instant. The shallow closets on the upper floor will buckle and tumble. The long front windows will shatter, and the porch will splinter into bits. This could happen in days. Two weeks from now, if she were to return to the place where she once loved Jeff and Julie and Mr. Edwards, would there be nothing but a landscape of smooth, flat dirt? Would a new foundation have been dug already?

"Sydney?"

She turns to see Ben at the foot of the steps. His feet are covered with sand. "Ben," she says at once. "I'm sorry."

He puts up a hand to stop her.

"When I think of all that time . . ."

"Don't."

"We were had," she says. "Both of us."

Ben nods. Sydney senses that he doesn't want to talk about the past, that he might not ever speak again about what his brother did or did not do to each of them.

"Are you okay?" she asks.

He shrugs. "Are you?"

She tilts her head as if to say, *Maybe.*

There is a long silence between them.

"So," he says.

"So," she says.

He puts his hands on his hips and nods toward the ocean. "How about it?"

Sydney stares. "How about what?"

"One last time?"

Ben can't possibly mean what she thinks he means.

"I just went down to test the water," he says. "It's warm."

"I don't . . . ," she protests. "I don't have my suit."

Ben shrugs again.

Sydney gazes out toward the sea. She can barely make out the waterline. "I'll walk out onto the sand with you," she says. "But that's all."

Ben heads along the boardwalk before she can change her mind. He is already on the beach as she begins her descent. She leaves her shoes on the bottom step. She digs her toes into the cool sand. The water might be freezing despite the luxurious air.

She wraps her arms around her chest and runs toward the shoreline. Once, she turns and looks back at the house. Some of the rooms are lit; others are dark. She thinks briefly of nuns and young mothers, men who had sons, men who died. When she finds Ben again, he is a dark shape near the water's edge. He lifts his shirt over his head, unbuckles the belt of his shorts.

She stops where she is, not wanting to intrude upon his nakedness. She will have to stay on the beach now, to look out for him.

Ben high-steps over the low surf and then dives into what looks to be a monstrous wave.

He stands, wiping his face and sputtering. "Come in," he shouts. "The water's a bathtub."

"No!" she calls back to him.

"What's the matter? Don't you trust me?"

"Trust you?" she calls, laughing.

Ben turns and makes an expert dive into an oncoming wave.

She leaves her clothes in a pile. She raises her arms. The air is soft and luscious on her skin. She runs toward the ocean, gathering tremendous speed as she goes.

Acknowledgments

A novel almost never belongs solely to the author. I have had several editors for this one—some of them professionals, all of them friends. I list them here in the order in which they looked at the manuscript. John Osborn. Rick Russo. Katherine Clemans. Jennifer Rudolph Walsh. Michael Pietsch. Asya Muchnick. Celeste Cooper. Elinor Lipman. Pamela Marshall.

About the Author

Anita Shreve is the critically acclaimed author of twelve previous novels, including *A Wedding in December, The Pilot's Wife,* which was a selection of Oprah's Book Club, and *The Weight of Water,* which was a finalist for England's Orange Prize. She lives in Massachusetts.